# Monsieur René

Also by Peter Ustinov

*The Loser*

*Krumnagel*

*hessian =*
*parlous*
*opposite*

# Monsieur René

### PETER USTINOV

POCKET
BOOKS

LONDON · SYDNEY · NEW YORK · TOKYO · SINGAPORE · TORONTO

First published by Verlag Kiepenheuer & Witsch Köln, 1998
First published in Great Britain by Simon & Schuster UK Ltd, 1999
This edition first published by Pocket Books, 2000
An imprint of Simon & Schuster UK Ltd
A Viacom company

1 3 5 7 9 10 8 6 4 2

Simon & Schuster UK Ltd
Africa House
64–78 Kingsway
London WC2B 6AH

Simon & Schuster Australia
Sydney

A CIP catalogue record for this book is available from the British Library

ISBN 0–671–03321–2

Typeset by Palimpsest Book Production Limited,
Polmont, Stirlingshire
Printed and bound in Great Britain by
Caledonian International Book Manufacturing, Glasgow

Peter Ustinov is one of the world's most versatile and talented contributors to the Arts. As an actor, producer, director, novelist, playwright, ranconteur and ambassador-at-large for UNICEF he has accumulated a considerable list of credits and won numerous awards. He now lives in Switzerland with his wife.

# I

MONSIEUR RENÉ drummed his fingers with impatience on the shiny tabletop. It was the habit of a lifetime. Behind him, in the early sunshine of a beautiful summer morning, his several trophies sparkled, and seemed to have lives of their own as they reflected the gentle animation on the surface of Lake Geneva.

A wasp entered the parlour and performed a quick inventory of the contents of the room before flying away again through the window, leaving silence in its wake. M. René hardly noticed the wasp, since he had weightier matters on his mind. His guests were late, which was unlike them. He quickly surveyed the bottles of liquor lined up like a regiment on the bar. Everything was in place, which was not surprising, since he had not touched them for a week, other than dusting them. He had no taste for alcohol, nothing which clouded the vision, or affected the iron control which every man must exercise over his faculties. Especially after the age of seventy, when crystal clarity was more difficult to maintain with infallible consistency.

M. René was a widower, who took his solitude as a matter of course. He had never expected anything else. As a man who had spent all of his adult life and much of his youth in and around hotels, the death of his wife had meant, among other things, the vacating of a room. His marriage could hardly have been dignified by describing it as one of convenience; rather it had been a marriage of efficient administration, of overlapping responsibilities. The couple had met when she, born Elfie Schlütter, was in charge of housekeeping at the Hotel Alpetta Palace in St Moritz and he, René, was the Chief Concierge. Neither had ever felt totally at ease unless formally dressed, and, as a consequence, they had never had a family. Not even a pet. Oh, occasionally in the summer he had put on a short sleeved sports shirt and she a floral print, but only to emphasize that they were off duty.

Now, life had changed. He had given her a funeral worthy of her status as his wife, many flowers and a pompous tomb in doubtful taste, with weeping angels, badly sculpted by a hack specializing in such aberrations. He did not indulge in this moderate extravagance because it was to his liking, but because he thought she might have appreciated it. Now, on a purely practical level (and finally, what other level was there?), things were not as different as all that. True, he made his own coffee of a morning, but it was rather better than the one she used to make. He now aired the bed and changed the sheets, but even that was not so unusual, since, if truth were told, she had become lazy and self-indulged in her dotage, in the habit of speaking to herself in order to justify her indolence, usually striking a querulous and aggrieved note, which even out of coherent earshot succeeded in making its mournful point. M. René had developed his own counter-offensive by uttering isolated but disconnected phrases which made no sense but left a disturbing afterglow. He never rose to any of the occasions so profusely offered because he guessed that these discreet outbursts were something to do with her final illness, and that his duty was compassion. To make his point was enough; whether she heard or not, immaterial. All this had been fairly recent, and he still wore black, but then, he had usually worn black when she was alive. The habit of uttering phrases had also survived her passing, but now he could permit them to be audible and distinct, since he was the only beneficiary, and they helped dispel an occasional feeling of loneliness, which was not the same as a not disagreeable solitude.

His detached house stood a little way outside Geneva, between Bellevue and Versoix, and although it boasted a pleasant garden, full of flowers, fruit, and vegetables, it was within feet of the railway line. Inevitably friends and acquaintances had asked him if this proximity to the Paris – Milan line, among many others of a more local nature, was not a nuisance. M. René was a great man for minute calculation, and the question automatically brought a smile to his lips. 'A good question,' he would reply. 'I have calculated that I am incommoded for three point 57 minutes a day. Do you think that is too high a price to pay for this glory?', and the sweep of his arm indicated the extent of the garden. Before the guest had time to digest this impressive figure, a train would inevitably pass with an impeccable sense of timing, rendering all conversation momentarily impossible. The smile on M. René's face had soured by the end of the interruption, but he carried on gamely with some such remark as, 'A case in point. Twelve seconds of interruption. The local train, Geneva – Lausanne, stopping at Nyon, Rolle, and Morges.' And that was always that.

Now there had not been a train for quite a time, and he began to miss the familiar sound. He glanced at his watch, a gold one presented to him on his retirement from the hotel circuit, and inscribed with a message of goodwill from his peers. Every time he consulted the watch, he lingered for a moment to sense once again the sum of his achievements. Then he was reminded of the extent of his guests' lateness.

The crunch of gravel on the drive changed the private person, with his own way of wiling away the time, into the public one, which he had been for most of his life. He rose and went to the door, a trace of a smile on his face. He opened the door. A small man with a grey crew-cut came towards him. It was Monsieur Alonso.

'You are late, dear friend,' M. René called.

M. Alonso was visibly surprised. 'Late?' he cried, slightly out of breath. 'I had no idea that an invitation to come between eleven and twelve entailed punctuality.'

'I was joking,' said M. René, who had a habit of saying basically unfunny things, and then protest that he had been joking.

'It is not as though it had been an invitation to dinner—'

'Forget it.'

'It's not as though I had so much free time to spare.'

M. René rose to the bait.

'You told me it was your day off,' he snapped, as factually as possible.

'Yes, it's my free day,' M. Alonso explained, laboriously.

'In any case, the others are not here yet.'

'They are still later?' M. Alonso allowed himself a moment of sarcasm, then realized what had been said. 'The others?'

'Yes. I have invited Monsieur Arrigo, Mr Butler, and, of course, my nephew Louis.'

'What is it all about?' enquired M. Alonso, sensing some kind of occasion.

'I will have to wait for them. Sit down. Can I serve you a drink?'

'Ten past eleven is a little early for me.'

'Even on a day off? How about a Cocktail Monsieur René?'

'Ah, there you tempt me!'

While M. René began to mix all the prepared ingredients, lemon juice, angostura, crème de cacao, vodka and Italian vermouth, a mixture which had curiously enough never really caught on among those who still drink cocktails, this neglect only served to make his concoction more exclusive in M. René's eyes. M. Alonso watched the ritual with some foreboding.

There was the noise of a motorcycle revving up.

'It's unusual that my nephew Louis is not last,' M. René grunted as he shook his cocktail in its shaker. Still shaking, he went to the front door on an impulse.

'Not on the grass!' he shouted. 'How often do I have to tell you?'

'Why don't you have a proper parking place like everyone else?' called the nephew, having some difficulty removing his crash-helmet.

'I've never had need of one.'

'Am I the last?'

'Funnily enough, no.'

'Where did the others park their cars?'

'M. Alonso knows the property. He obviously left his vehicle outside somewhere,' and he returned inside to his guest.

The manner in which he referred to his small allotment as his property irritated Louis as he propped his motorbike up on the path, and followed his uncle into the house. Mr Butler followed moments later, and then Monsieur Arrigo. When they were all seated with their cocktails, all, that is, except Louis, who preferred a Coke with ice cubes in it, M. René seemed ready to explain their presence to his strange assortment of guests. His nephew Louis wore his hair long, and affected the black leather costume which has become almost a uniform among the motorcycle community. He sat with his garish white crash-helmet in his hands as though already thinking of his departure. M. Alonso toyed with his cocktail, staring into what depth it had for inspiration. Mr Butler was English, with a craggy red face and blue eyes which frequently watered. He sniffed intermittently like someone who had been swimming, and his hands had a tendency to shake. M. Arrigo, the last to arrive, was almost indecently handsome, a fading blond from the North Italian lakes, erect as a ramrod, with the movements of a dancing master. Now that they were all there, no one broke the silence, which drew excessive attention to them so that they were not gulping their refreshment, and eagerly asking for more.

Since M. René himself seemed tongue-tied, it was left to M. Alonso to start things off.

'May one ask how the autobiography is going?' he asked.

'The ideal question to start this meeting off,' blurted M. René, as though so full of information to impart that he did not know where to begin. 'I have abandoned it!'

'Go on,' said Louis, incredulous. 'I thought that young woman was a permanent fixture in this house.'

'She was a young person sent by the publisher to ghost my words into an acceptable literary form,' M. René announced drily.

'Yes, but she was not a bad looker, and I would have thought it only natural to drag out the pleasure of dictating your life story . . .'

'I don't know how you can say that, so soon after your aunt's passing,' M. René interrupted testily, to which Louis shrugged his shoulders like a sulking child. The mention of the bereavement cast a pall of embarrassment on the others, who stared at their cocktails without drinking.

It was M. René himself who broke the silence.

'The fact that I sent the young person packing is no reflection on her competence or on the choice of the publisher. In fact, she did all she could to be agreeable, and although she was of a different generation, she made every effort to understand my motivations. No, no. The fact is, I have been thinking—'

The others exchanged looks. It was always a bad sign when someone has been thinking, especially in a profession where excessive thought is more of a hindrance than a help.

M. René studied their faces with an omniscient expression.

'You all have superb anecdotes to tell from different branches of our profession – superb and dangerous anecdotes.'

'Dangerous for whom?' asked M. Arrigo.

'I am coming to that. All of you are as capable of having autobiographies ghosted for you as I am. It is perhaps that as Permanent President of the International Brotherhood of Concierges and Hall Porters, I occupy a position of particular eminence in the record books that I was chosen for this – this honour.'

He awaited momentarily for confirmation of this declaration. None was forthcoming. He went on mournfully.

'When I think of the confidences which have passed your way, M. Alonso, and which you absorbed out of a sense of the tradition of our métier, I marvel at the waste.'

'The waste?' It was the last reflection M. Alonso expected.

'And you, M. Arrigo, while the diners were studying the menus and talking as your minions were serving them, what a mine of scattered information, which, when pieced together, is a woven tapestry of the history of our times.'

'When you come to think of it, yes,' M. Arrigo admitted.

'I repeat. What a waste. And you, Mr Butler, all the items left in the pockets of statesmen wanting their suits pressed for the next day's conference or meeting, all the idle words expended while the influential were standing before you, unguarded because trouserless. What an opportunity for exclusivity of information!'

'I always made it a matter of principle to place all papers found in pockets to be pressed, small change, stray telephone numbers, scribbles, in a plastic envelope, to return unread, to their owner.'

M. René's eyes gleamed. 'Need I say it once again, what a waste!'

Mr Butler was mystified. 'If I understand rightly, M. René, you are rebelling against one of the fundamental laws which make our profession so unique in a world of constantly shifting values. Trust is the word I had in mind. Being trustworthy, being known to be trustworthy, is more important to me than anything else in this world. Are you now asking me, after a lifetime devoted to an ideal, to betray my trust?'

'How was your trust compensated?' M. René snapped.

'By personal satisfaction.'

'By tips.' M. René was merciless.

'By both,' Mr Butler conceded.

'Tips are common to us all. Satisfaction is up to the individual. Tips are things we pool, by tradition. There I was as scrupulous as anyone else. Even when some Eastern potentate, deprived by birth of a sense of values, slipped me thousands of dollars in breathless gratitude for having found him a couple of willing call-girls, I pooled the money with the rest. That is, indeed, a law in our profession, and I respect it. But what kind of satisfaction was his generosity supposed to engender in me? An inner glow that a couple of wretched girls had gone through degrading antics to bring His Highness to a state of ecstasy? And thanks to me?'

'They chose their profession, not you,' Mr Butler argued with his weak voice. 'By their own rights, you did them well. If he could afford to slip you thousands of dollars, they probably found even more on their pillow.'

'Don't you believe it. They were only women, to be used. Worse, females. I was the man, the natural accomplice, the silent conspirator. Should my satisfaction spring out of playing this role?'

There was silence.

M. René continued with the utmost gravity, measuring his words.

'You see, my friends, the Bible is right in one respect at least. Three score and ten is the expectancy of life. After that, it is borrowed time, and urgency. Much that had been taken for granted is suddenly questioned. In a sense, it is a rebirth. Only the other day, I passed by the Law Courts, a magnificent building you will say, but dedicated to the poor fools who get caught. This whole massive structure, and the learning that stands behind it, is never visited by the really culpable. The whales and sharks of industry and international intrigue wallow in the open sea, only the minnows are caught in the nets. And who are the big tippers, Mr Butler, the minnows? No, dear friend, the whales and sharks, those who are never caught, and we are their accomplices, because only they can afford to stay in the best hotels. Should that be a source of pride in us?'

M. Arrigo laughed, if somewhat nervously.

'Can it be that the great M. René, defender of all that is conservative, has become a revolutionary?'

'If by revolutionary you mean one who examines all he expected in life to be worthy and finds the very opposite to be the truth, yes, then I am a revolutionary.'

Louis balanced the crash-helmet on his knees, and clapped.

'You are too young to understand.'

'Then why invite me here?' Louis was insulted.

'You are the only family I have. Isn't that tragic? Louis and his Motoyama, all I have to leave behind.'

'If you hadn't sent the girl packing you might have had some decently written memoires as well.'

'The very point I am making,' declared M. René to the others. 'Why did I send her packing? Because she failed to interpret my thoughts correctly? Because her literary

style displeased me? That was not the principal reason.
I reflected, what is the point of recollecting items which
have lost all urgency, all focus? And are not memories
full of an old personality, worthy of confidence, eager to
whitewash and beautify some of the outstanding scoundrels
of this century who have passed close to our ears and to
our pockets? The Emir of Djabbadieh, for instance.' The
others, Louis apart, smiled a little grimly at the mention
of the Emir. 'He travelled, if you remember, with eight of
his wives. It was always such a business to find him a suite
of eight adjoining rooms, seven for himself and one for the
wives. We all thought at the outset that the wives took it in
turns to pleasure him. None of us could guess that he always
enjoyed eight at a time. His people lived in misery, while he
whiled away years at a time far from the minarets and the
abstinence, living like a pig, too idle or too exhausted to use
the abundance of toilets at his disposal, and roasting lambs
on the hotel verandah. Why should his story only appear
years after his death of a series of massive heart attacks, only
a colourful anecdote instead of the stinging condemnation
he deserved while he was alive?'

'You are surely not going to pillory the few lunatic
eccentrics who pass our way, and who add colour to our
otherwise drab lives? For obvious reasons, most of these
eccentrics are rich. Most eccentricities cost money. Eight
wives are certainly dearer than one. His habits may have
been dirty, but are the quirks of an old fool really worth
the venom you waste on him?' asked M. Alonso.

'I agree,' said M. René reasonably, 'there is absolutely
no use in castigating dead horses. I had the Duchess of
Calamayor to cope with over the years, a seven time
Grandee of Spain in her own right, only three more

than the right of her husband, the Duke. She liked to confide in me that she had married beneath her. I used to shrug fatalistically, as though life is like that, with ups and downs. She used to praise me for my profound philosophy, and then demand an endless supply of straws to be sent to her suite.'

'Straws?' asked Louis, intrigued despite himself.

'She drank wine in quantity, at times water, even gazpacho, through a straw. She had a morbid hatred of the marks of lipstick on glasses or spoons, and in no way wished to be guilty of lapses of taste of that kind. Thick soup she adored, but avoided it on the grounds that the stupid manufacturers catered mainly for adolescents, and had not yet developed a straw of sufficient diameter to permit the passage of small vegetables or chunks of meat. I used to reflect that in this world, everyone has this cross to bear. She used to sigh, nod, and thank me for my solace. She was utterly harmless, and certainly not worth getting excited about. We all must have culled thousands of stories of a like order.'

'I remember Lord Harry Cyplemore, the Earl of Isay's eldest boy—' Mr Butler's eyes watered with affection.

'To the point,' M. Arrigo interrupted. 'What exactly are you after, M. René, so that we may take positions? Money?'

'Money?' M. René recoiled. 'You surprise me, M. Arrigo. Is it likely that one who always made it a point of pooling his tips, even when his tips were far above the average – I repeat, is it likely that such a man would suddenly develop a taste for blackmail? For that is how money would have to be made if it is uppermost in our minds. Of course not! I live frugally, and enjoy my way of life. I have no desire to ruin it all by wealth.'

M. Arrigo laughed. 'There is no reason to appear so outraged, dear friend. I was at no time moralizing, merely asking for clarification. Personally, I am not averse to blackmail.'

'A great one for jokes, our M. Arrigo,' cackled Mr Butler, tears cascading down his cheeks.

'Power,' said M. René soberly, striking a sinister note by his choice of word and his manner of saying it.

'Power? Us?' echoed M. Alonso, incredulous.

'Power. We left the power to others, out of obsequiousness. And what have they done with it? Destroyed the earth,' M. René said coldly, quietly.

'We never had the power,' M. Alonso spoke, as reasonably.

'Listen, friends, they call this the age of information. Why? Because information is power. All the world fears it, secret knowledge, as useful for insider trading, fraudulent dealing on the stock market, as it is in the jockeying that takes place in international affairs. Everyone is trying to find out more all the time, to have the edge on the competition. Now, I ask you, who is in a better position to deal in information than we are?'

'How?' M. Alonso felt it his right to ask.

M. René bent forward, and spoke with unusual intensity. 'By listening, by overhearing, by pooling information as we once pooled our tips, by remembering points in the conversation of the highly placed as they indulge themselves in second helpings at banquets. It is always at table that statesmen are at their most unguarded. Waiters have golden opportunities for this kind of work, which they never take. Concierges are well placed for a different kind of intelligence work, which I suspect can be a perfect complement to the work of waiters and maître d's. Then there are the valets, and the small shreds of evidence left inadvertently in clothes. You objected when I brought the matter up, Mr Butler, but I persist in believing that the carelessness of celebrities can play a vital part in penetrating the rules of the games they have invented for humanity's discomfort. I don't give a damn for picturesque anecdotes of the kind we exchange with each other over a glass of wine after a day's work. I don't give a damn for scandals either. Who is sleeping with who, or where. Power lies in information about dirty tricks and deliberate deception in a world in which every denial is a silent confirmation and every outburst of injured innocence is a tacit confession of guilt. I want to know what these people know, and make proper use of it.'

M. Alonso was aghast. 'But your plan, even if feasible, requires the most enormous organization!'

M. René smiled. 'The organization is already in place. Who needs spies if they have waiters, concierges and valets? All they need do is to keep their ears and eyes open, and conquer their scruples. Then we pool our knowledge at a central command post. For the moment, I put my house at your disposal. Later, it may become too dangerous.'

'Too dangerous?' M. Arrigo exploded. 'Why?'

'Oh, I'm not speaking of physical danger. I mean the success of my venture depends on a high degree of secrecy. And, to start with, very careful recruiting. Don't try to enlist gossips, drunkards, drug-takers, or womanizers. Go for discretion and intelligence.'

'Do we vote, or what?' asked M. Alonso.

'There are too few of us to vote yet,' M. René conceded. 'Between ourselves we can speak openly. Later the vote – the secret vote may become a necessity.'

'As you know, I have my doubts, not only about whether your plan can succeed, René, but whether it ought to succeed. I need some time to examine my ethical position in all this.'

M. René grinned. 'You have dropped the Monsieur. That is a good sign, Alonso. Take what time you need. I can accept no other head of department. Think of it this way, if you will. Endless secret meetings take place in Geneva. This city asks no questions. The sick and the politically sick come here for treatment in obscure clinics. Statesmen drop off here casually on the way to somewhere else. Conspirators come in on false passports to prepare their coups and to acquire their weapons. All these people have to eat, sleep, and have their smalls washed. And they have to meet. We may well have it in our hands to prevent assassinations, secret clauses in treaties, all manner of chicanery which costs the lives of the innocent. Our potential is enormous, since no one in his right mind thinks of waiters as threatening or valets as political animals. That is our strength. Our reputation is that of being menials, before whom it is safe to talk, because we have not the mental wherewithal to understand.'

'So your purpose is moral?' asked Mr Butler.

'Exclusively,' insisted M. René. 'Mr Butler, there are other satisfactions, beside obedience.'

'How about women?' enquired M. Arrigo, with a debonair simper.

'I have thought about them, and at the risk of offending those rather tough and, dare I say it, masculine ladies who consistently uphold women's rights, I would say that certain elderly maids and established housekeepers are invaluable adjuncts, but I would be most careful in their selection. Finally, the same rules apply to them as to men, but remember, the keeping of secrets is a masculine propensity rather than nature's gift to the fair sex.'

'And chauffeurs?' asked M. Alonso.

'Not as good an idea as it at first seems. Obviously chauffeurs have the possibility of overhearing longer and more coherent conversations, but the kind of people we are targeting rarely employ rented drivers. They usually have their own, or they use those of embassies and of international organizations. And it is not an ambition to corrupt, merely to listen.'

'So what is the overall plan, given we are in agreement?' M. Alonso said, and added: 'And I must say, up to now I am most intrigued by the idea. Whether it works or not is in the lap of the gods, but I suspect it is all a question of attitude. It is true to say that only on our days off are we really ourselves. The rest of the time we are, as you say, obsequious by nature. It is part of our profession in the same way that an omniscient smile is the necessary part of a priest's equipment. There are things we don't morally discuss. They are there, facts of hotel life. If now we managed to uncondition these reflexes, to unplug the automatic pilot which programmes our existences, then anything is possible. With a little luck, your Quixotic vision of our duties to humanity may become a reality, at least part of the time.'

M. René extended his hand. M. Alonso took it. They looked each other deep in their eyes, as though each had placed a foot on an unexplored planet.

'Finally, M. René, what do you want us to do?' M. Arrigo asked.

'I ask no more than this, think it over for a week. Test the water. Talk only to real friends, ones you can trust. We meet again next Saturday if that is convenient. If there is one or the other of us who feels, after mature reflection, that he cannot live with this idea, there is no harm done. All you need do is not turn up. But all I would ask you is, give my child a chance to grow and prosper. Keep silent. Don't give us away.'

Slowly they rose and looked at each other to get a premature hint of the other's decision. Then they shook hands and left in silence, conspirators already, leaving the filled cocktail glasses behind them as the only evidence of their presence. M. René accompanied them to the door and noticed Louis' massive motorcycle on the path, its front wheel leaning over the grass like the mouth of the victim of a stroke, and he reflected that he had rarely seen such ugliness. He returned to the drawing room and saw Louis still sprawling in his arm-chair, spread over his allotted place like treacle.

'Well?' he enquired.

There was a pause, which grew to almost insulting proportions.

'You really want to know?'

'Yes.'

Louis rose to his feet as though the arm-chair were trying to detain him, and placed his gleaming white helmet on his head. 'I think you're nuts. Bonkers. Cuckoo.'

'Everyone is entitled to their opinion,' M. René replied stiffly, and added as his nephew reached the door, '—at least you will keep our secret!'

'Who would believe me anyway?'

'That is not the point. Swear.'

Louis smiled quite warmly, but it was invisible inside the helmet. He held up his hand.

'I swear it. Satisfied?'

'How are you enjoying the Ecole Hôtelière?'

'It's hell.'

'Will you pass your exams?'

'That, I won't swear to.'

M. René laughed as pleasantly as he could. 'I never thought I would pass them either. Give my love to your mother.'

'I'll give your love to your sister.'

And on that heartwarming note, Louis left.

M. René sat, and contemplated the events of the morning. He noticed the abandoned cocktails, and tried one. He pulled a face. He was over seventy. Had he forgotten the receipt? Bonkers, eh? Ah, the young! Young and drab, dressed in that odious black leather, with metal studs, the pretentious aesthetics of evil. Still, it had been disturbingly successful, the meeting of those groping for the last vestiges of youth in their hearts. Second youth must be authentic youth, the rebirth of enthusiasm. Certainly, when compared to the verve of that morose idiot. Cuckoo indeed.

His thoughts were interrupted by the explosion into life of four cylinders, barking for release like dogs with the odour of the hunt in their nostrils, and then the crunch of gravel, small rocks displaced by wheelspin, all over the grass no doubt, and then the receding wail of the superbike, drowned out by the civilized prattle of the 12.11 from Paris to Milan. Life was more than good, it was interesting. And then he went into the bathroom. In his hurry to receive his guests, the latecomers, he had neglected to trim his pencil-thin moustache. No detail is too small to deserve attention, not in our business.

# II

HE TRIMMED his moustache earlier a week later, in case
any of them arrived before eleven. Almost invisible bits of
hair fell into the sink, no bigger than a hamster's eyelashes.
A casual observer would probably not have noticed the
difference, but it had a disproportionate effect on M.
René's morale. Before he had quite finished, the doorbell
rang. One of them was early! Usually M. René heard the
visitor before it was necessary for the bell to be rung. Was
he losing his grip? At his age one had doubts, doubts
about all sorts of things. One also had wonderful and
unexpected ideas, an Indian summer of the mind, a store-
house of valuable bric-à-brac which had seemed impractical
or unsuitable before the great liberation of the third age of
man, or was it the seventh? Shakespeare was meticulous
in most things, but then he can never have known the
emotions of horizons rediscovered. First of all, he hadn't
lived long enough, and secondly, his ever-present poetry
had never been forced into submission by a life in captivity,

as it would have been had he been a hall porter and not a gentleman farmer.

The doorbell rang again. Oh God, his thoughts had been pursued at the expense of the first bell. Had there been a first bell? Of course there had. He remembered thinking that one of them was early. 'Coming!' he called. He replaced his moustache-trimming scissors in their étui. His voice sounded robust, at least to him, which was a source of satisfaction. He glanced at his watch, with its message of gratitude for long and faithful service. Whoever it was was a full eleven minutes early. Interesting. He opened the door. It was Mr Butler, as usually streaming with tears and drops from his nose and moisture at the side of his mouth. 'Didn't you hear the bell?' he asked dramatically.

'Of course I heard the bell,' replied M. René. 'I called out that I was coming.'

'I didn't hear you!'

It's you that is old, my dear, thought M. René, not me. But he refrained from saying it. What he did say was not much better.

'I suppose you know you are eleven minutes early?'

'Oh, I do beg your pardon.' Mr Butler exaggerated his remorse. 'I have to come from the other side of Geneva, remember! What am I expected to do if I inadvertently arrive early? Loiter on the drive? Smell the flowers? There aren't enough of them, you know, for eleven minutes.'

M. René begged him not to excite himself, and then reflected soberly that, in view of his scruples at the first meeting, it would not have been entirely surprising if he had elected not to come at all.

'I've given the matter a great deal of consideration,' Mr Butler explained, 'and I've come to the conclusion that what you are intending to do could be characterized as a public duty.'

M. René beamed incredulously. 'You are the first to understand.'

Mr Butler looked no happier than usual, his baleful eyes gathering water visibly, and his hand quivering. 'I'm over seventy myself, you see,' he said, playing for sympathy.

'You don't look it,' M. René said, and it was almost true.

Mr Butler grew hostile. 'I want to look it!' he wept. 'Once I am it, I want to look it!'

'I know that honesty has always held a place apart in your code of conduct. You made that abundantly clear at our meeting last week. I suppose a desire to look what you are can be construed as an expression of that honesty—'

'Oh, you don't know what you're talking about, René,' sighed Mr Butler in a resigned way. 'It's you who don't look your age.'

'So I have been told,' admitted M. René, not without satisfaction. 'The fact does not depress me as it seems to do you.'

Mr Butler sat down and began to talk on a different level, quietly and reasonably.

'You have your own interpretation of old age, and I respect that. You speak of it in a very positive way. You see retirement as a new beginning.'

'A second childhood, isn't that what they call it?'

'They may do. They may even know more or less what they're talking about, the length of time people have been getting older on this earth, and however hard the individual tries not to conform to a pattern, he never really succeeds. The weight of precedents is just too much for him. He

begins to recognize in himself many of the things that most
irritated him about his parents, but there's no one else to
share this grim discovery with. They might have understood
what he's talking about, but they've gone, haven't they . . .
long ago. They've left you to irritate your own children, if
you're lucky enough to have any.'

'Have you children, Mr Butler?'

'I have a son, Arnold. He's getting on now. Oh, he never
gave me anything to complain about. He's a moderate
drinker, doesn't smoke, never was attracted by drugs, like
too many of his generation. He's done rather well, in fact,
by the usual standards.'

'What is he, if I may ask?'

'He's a Labour Member of Parliament. Socialist, you
understand. And I've never voted anything but Conservative all my life. I couldn't vote for them. Can you
understand that?'

'I don't have that problem,' said M. René, without
emotion, 'I have no children. I have a nephew, who you
met last week.'

'So nobody is satisfied.' There was a pause while Mr
Butler shed a tear.

'My motivation is different from yours, René,' Mr Butler
said at length. 'Young Arnold – I call him young – he's
forty-eight – he always said to me, the trouble with you,
Dad, you've got no ideals, just principles. You don't look
forward, he'd say, there's no distance, no scope, just what's
there, under your nose, and that's good enough. Why?
Because it's always been good enough, that's why. You've
always believed what you've been told, and you called that
keeping the trust. You've expended all your devotion, all
your loyalty, on pairs of creased trousers, and never asked

yourself any question about the men inside them. Oh yes, René, young Arnold had a sharp tongue. He could hurt,' and he continued slyly, gently, 'I'd dearly love to make him eat his words before I go.'

'Is that your motivation for joining the movement?' M. René laughed. 'Must I thank young Arnold for your enthusiasm?'

'Put that way, I suppose you must,' Mr Butler conceded, wiping his face with a handkerchief.

'Well, at least you've kept your idealism in the family.'

'Ah, good point, good point,' laughed Mr Butler. Then he grew suddenly serious. 'I've asked around,' he murmured.

'Asked around? And?'

'I've had a most surprising green light from Agnes Schanderbach.'

M. René's eyes narrowed. 'Schanderbach? Schanderbach? The name rings a bell.'

'She may have been a little after your time. She's Chief Housekeeper at the Bellerive Davel.'

'In Geneva?'

'Exactly.'

'That's a responsible job.'

'And she's a responsible person. But then, people like her teach you that which you've really known all your life. Never judge by appearances.'

M. René was on his guard. 'What does she seem to be?'

'A perfectly conventional hotel employee. Scrupulous in all her ways, of impeccable morality and probably devout.'

'And—?'

'I didn't know before sounding her out – her grandfather fought in the Spanish Civil War on the Republican side.

He was a lifelong communist, with, as she puts it, an unswerving belief in the inherent goodness of man.'

'In that case, he didn't die a natural death,' said M. René.

'No. He was captured by the Fascists, and shot by a firing squad.'

'For his beliefs.' M. René nodded. 'And her father had better luck?'

'Concentration camp. She and her mother escaped to Switzerland. She was only a child at the time.'

'Most of the Germans are so disciplined that when, on occasion, they break ranks, they make formidable revolutionaries. They bring an element of order to the disorder of civil strife.'

'That's what worries me slightly about Agnes,' admitted Mr Butler. 'She swallowed my bait so thoroughly that after only a minute or two she was eager to know what was expected of her. She hoped the tasks allotted to her would be active ones.'

'Active ones?' asked M. René. 'What on earth does she expect?'

'Search me. I don't think she can possibly mean plastic, or car bombs and the like, yet you never know. She's not lacking in enthusiasm, as you can see. All she kept asking was, "When do we start?" I think she is worth cultivating.'

'What does she look like?'

'If I had to describe her, I'd say she looks like the Chief Housekeeper of a large Swiss hotel.'

M. René heard a distant footfall on the path. As he went towards the door, he asked Mr Butler: 'Any other contacts?'

'Not yet. I proceeded with caution.'

'Quite right.'

MM Alonso and Arrigo arrived together, giving the impression of having met earlier in order to discuss the situation before confronting M. René. Now they all accepted coffee which M. René had prepared in advance, and which was eminently drinkable. He did not make the mistake of offering them an alternative. When they had expended the usual ration of small talk to warm up the atmosphere, M. René began the more formal proceedings by saying: 'Well?'

Alonso and Arrigo exchanged looks, then M. Arrigo said that they had both thought about the scheme, and wondered if the recruiting of others was not a little premature, since they had not yet acquired a focus for their activities, and perhaps that was a more urgent necessity than swelling their ranks. In the light of their conviction, they had made casual enquiries among their friends in the large hotels in Geneva, discovering that the Emir of Djabbadieh was back in Geneva for a cure and a complete rest at the Clinique Ma Joie.

'Isn't it a little late for a cure?' asked M. René. 'He's dead.'

'On the contrary, it may be a little early for a cure,' M. Arrigo replied. 'It's his grandson, aged twenty-two.'

'The new Emir? God help us all.'

'Yes. Meanwhile we have made discreet enquiries at the Clinique Ma Joie. The Emir is registered as Emir Mustafa el Mahali al Salaam el Talubi, but his room is occupied by a bodyguard who sits there all day, on the bed, not in it, reading pornographic strip cartoons.'

'Where is the Emir?'

'There is a mysterious booking at a leading hotel, but

no one is willing to tell us who it is. The staff is still obedient to the old tradition, before you came along.' M. Arrigo smiled.

M. Alonso took over. 'I phoned M. Boisferrand, the Concierge, who told me, in confidence, that the verandah overlooking the park has been roped off, presumably for the roasting of a lamb.'

M. René's eyes narrowed. 'Boisferrand? That is the Bellerive Davel?'

'Precisely.'

M. René and Mr Butler exchanged looks, and grinned. 'We have a mole in the hotel,' M. René announced curtly.

'Already?' M. Alonso was surprised.

'Already. What do you imagine the Emir is doing here, and why would he register ostentatiously in a clinic and slip unnoticed into a hotel? He must be alone in that case. No man with several wives could be as discreet.'

'There are rumours that this grandson is homosexual.'

'Oh dear,' said Mr Butler.

'That in no way affects the quality of the oil, you understand.'

'You think he is here for negotiations of some sort?' asked M. René.

It was M. Arrigo who replied. 'Why else would a young man in perfect health come to Geneva, of all places, for a complete rest? A rest from what? Casinos, hammams, siestas? And why should a bodyguard occupy a room at the Clinique Ma Joie, the most expensive in the world, just in order to look at dirty pictures? This doesn't appear to me like personal indulgence, but rather as a clumsy way of assuming anonymity. Why would he need anonymity – he is practically unknown as yet – only his oil is famous, owing to Petroco, Flortex and other major interests from the West?'

M. Alonso consulted bits of paper. 'I agree. I have a friend – a personal friend, truth to tell, if you understand me – who works in the VIP section of the airport. I asked her to find out for us the VIP arrivals of the week. They include, on flights from Washington, Dorothy Labell, a Chief Negotiator for Economic Affairs. She is staying with personal friends in what is described as a private visit.'

'Sounds suspicious,' observed M. René.

'Indeed. The Panamanian Minister of Public Health, Senora Gomez O'Malley, came in from Panama City. She is staying at the Pension Geranium. I don't imagine we will ever have a mole there.'

'Hardly.'

'Then there is a Nobel Prize winner from Zimbabwe, an estranged wife of a member of the British Royal Family . . .'

'Which one?'

'My friend wouldn't say. There are some things which are sacrosanct. Two papal nuncios, travelling separately. Feruccio Lipinelli, the Italian judge involved in several concurrent scandals. And a man called Ivanov, described as a scientific worker from Kazakhstan. He is booked, guess where? In the Bellerive Davel.'

'That's a Russian name, the equivalent of Smith or Dupont – so common one is free to doubt its authenticity – and he comes from Kazakhstan? In their present financial state, they can't afford lodgings of that class unless he is a very high official indeed.'

'He may not be an official at all,' remarked M. Alonso. 'Who else could afford a luxury hotel? The mafia.'

'Is there a mafia in Kazakhstan?' asked M. René.

M. Arrigo reassured him. 'There is a mafia everywhere. And it is quite conceivable that Ivanov acquired his VIP status from his government and the luxury treatment from the mafia. In many parts of the world, the two are not incompatible. I will go further and say that if, in fact, Ivanov was sent by his government as a high official, he would rate VIP treatment, but would probably be in the Pension Geranium with the Panamanian Minister of Public Health, queuing for the use of the bathroom down the hall. For that reason, I think there may well be the mafia in the background of whatever mission he is on.'

'Is there anything I should be doing?' asked Mr Butler.

M. René spoke quietly. 'Arrange a meeting with our mole as quickly as possible. Today, if possible, or tomorrow. Whenever she is able to get away, and meanwhile question her discreetly about the presence of the Emir and of Ivanov. The phone is over there.'

'She?' asked M. Arrigo.

M. René made a gesture of silence while Mr Butler dialled the service number of the Bellerive Davel Hotel with an unsteady finger. M. René indicated that all would be explained if they listened.

'Hello . . . Est-ce que c'est le Bellerive Davel?' Mr Butler's French accent made everyone wince. 'Je voudrais parler à Madame Agnes Schanderbach, s'il vous plaît.'

He nodded to the others, suggesting that she was being fetched. His hand shook uncontrollably for a moment. His humourless smile broadened as he sensed her approach to the telephone on the other end.

'Hello!' he said. 'It's Lambert Butler, remember? That's it, valet extraordinaire. Can you speak freely?' (His voice dropped.) 'Oh, you can't. Can I speak freely, if you

understand me? . . . You're not sure . . . I see. Can we
meet? . . . As soon as possible . . . tonight? . . . It's all right
with me . . .' (M. René nodded urgently.)' . . . Say eight
o'clock . . . you'd prefer seven thirty . . . How about Le
Mouton Enragé . . . Rue Pangloss, in Onex . . . it's quiet,
and the food's good, and there's adequate parking . . . have
you a cough? . . . You're being asphyxiated? . . . What by?
. . . They're roasting a lamb on the spit? . . . At this hour of
the morning? . . . Oh, it's for lunch . . . I won't ask you any
more questions for the time being . . . that's right, if you
can't answer them, it's merely frustrating for us both . . .
till tonight then . . . Auf wiedersehen.' Mr Butler replaced
the receiver with a little difficulty.

'It's all right for tonight. How many of you can manage
it?'

'I'm afraid—' M. Alonso began.

'We must be flexible, otherwise nothing will ever work
between us. We can only be truly efficient according
to availability. After all, before we all grow too excited,
we must realize that all this information may just be
coincidental. There may well be no connection whatever
between Ivanov and the Emir of Djabbadieh. They may
easily have just selected the same hotel to stay in,' M. René
warned.

'It's unlike you to be a wet rag,' M. Arrigo observed,
'especially having stimulated us to partake in this game
of yours.'

'It may well turn out to be a game if we enter it in a
spirit of unprincipled adventure, but it may be an act of
real significance if we do not try to force the pace. We
are not the police, and we should never try to behave as
though we are. Our strength is that the façade remains

what it always was. Our purpose has changed, but not the
manner in which we achieve an end. If M. Alonso cannot be
there, that is unfortunate, but we will inform him in good
time, and never be tempted to run before we can walk. Any
questions?'

They rose to go.

Mr Butler remarked that Louis, the nephew, had not
turned up.

'I'm quite glad, really,' M. René sighed, 'he's too young,
and I fear he always will be too young. Would you count
on the discretion of someone who rides around on an earsplitting motorcycle, with art nouveau graffiti all over it?'

Mr Butler smiled. 'We never realize the size of the gap
between the generations until we're getting on ourselves.'

The guests walked down the drive talking among themselves. M. René watched them go with a sense of satisfaction. Already the organization was taking on a life of
its own. The final aim would be to have hundreds of
members of this loose band of hotel and restaurant staff, all
overhearing as a second nature, contributing mosaic stones,
often incomprehensive in themselves, to a pattern which
was clearly decipherable to a central control. The path was
bound to be a difficult one to tread. There would be the
reticent, and the mendacious, filling in by pure invention
what they had failed to understand. And there would be the
over-enthusiastic, wishing for results before the spadework
had been done. The idea was so hugely ambitious that it
needed, above all, serenity. It needed high expectations,
with a resilience which made allowances for continued
disappointments. To put it in a word, it needed strategy.

Now that he was alone, he sat down on a chair which
was not his favourite, and meditated. He wondered briefly,

before losing himself in thought, why he had chosen an ordinary dining-room chair to settle in rather than the battered easy chair which had adapted itself to his shape over the years. Perhaps, he reflected, it was because he was not looking for comfort or reassurance, but rather stimulation and contradiction. Once he was lost in the surrealist world of semi-consciousness it became a chair like any other. Why, he wondered, in the pleasant haze of a daydream, had he suddenly thought the moment was ripe for such a drastic change of outlook, which had knocked all his friends back on their heels? Was it entirely due to his three score and ten years? That was hardly credible. The seeds for this late blossoming must have begun to burgeon under the soil of his consciousness some time before.

It was a cumulative conclusion he had come to, in a flash, when the pot of circumspect behaviour boiled over. It could be that Switzerland, the land of his birth, was just the right size, and with just the right mixture of diehard tradition and emotionless modernity to give such an experiment precise definition. If not Switzerland, at least Geneva, a stout upholder of accepted values, with every now and then a mayor who was nominally a communist, bearing no resemblance whatever to any other communist in the world, a city of frugal balance sheets and miserly budgets, catering to the luxury-loving and the spendthrifts, the celebrated anonymities and anonymous celebrities of society; a city of evident grace and permanence, reflected in the shifting surface of lake water, a doubt reflecting every irrefutable fact, names indistinctly visible behind the reassuring stronghold of numbers.

Before returning home in order to retire, and occupy his place at the accepted zenith of his profession, M. René had

risen as far up the tree as was possible, having been the
Chief Concierge at the Hotel Waldo Emerson Towers in
New York, an icy finger poking the clouds from the heart
of Manhattan. All the thoughts he now entertained had
developed in America, but no practical realization such as
the one he now envisaged was within reach over there.
Over there, he had learned, tips were not only a token of
thanks for the past, but an advance on services expected
in the future. A good memory was more important there
than in most other places. He had enjoyed his time in the
United States, and the Fairweather Group, who owned the
Waldo Emerson Towers among hundreds of other hotels,
had been good to him in the sense that the terms of his
agreement had been scrupulously respected. At the same
time, he never had the remotest idea to whom he should be
grateful. The President of the company had changed three
times during the period of his employment in the course
of palace revolutions, without him feeling even the most
infinitesimal repercussion at his level. At each ousting of a
President, the incumbent had left his office with a golden
handshake of immense proportions, which suggested that
despite constant complaints of times being hard for the
industry, times were far from hard for certain individuals
squeezed out of it.

At all events, America was certainly an extraordinary
land of opportunity for some, while being a land of hope
inevitably lost for others, whose horizons had been shattered
by an overpowering indifference. He had little to complain
about, however. The tips had been generous, even if what
was expected in return was sometimes on the extravagant
side. Still, rarely as wild as the Emir of Djabbadieh, who
took the biscuit in this respect.

But, he remembered with a smile, at the threshold of sleep, that he had been mugged at night in a lonely New York street. At least, the intention had been to mug him. A gentleman of indeterminate origin with a sock on his head had brandished a knife at him, and demanded his wallet. M. René had adopted the stony stance of a Swiss reserve officer called on suddenly to defend his frontier. He had told his assailant in a quiet but unambiguous tone that there would be no money forthcoming if the man didn't sheath his knife. The man, deprived of the initiative for one surprising moment, did the only thing he could, which was to threaten M. René's life. M. René had pointed out that if that was his intention, he should go ahead, since there was no argument against stupidity.

'Stupidity?' the man had roared, incoherently. The word was a little long for him in whatever condition he was.

'You want me to tell you why?' M. René had asked, and had prudently not given the man time to reply. 'When the stuff you sniff, or inject into your vein, comes out of the ground, it's dirt cheap. By the time you buy it at street corners, it costs the earth. Who makes the profits? The growers, the smugglers, the dealers, all the guys driving around in Cadillacs while dudes like you are forced to steal or kill in order to keep the Cadillacs in gasoline. Does that make sense to you?'

During M. René's sermon in the dimly lit street, the man began chanting like a litany: 'You're lying, man!', until he reached a point of dangerous clairvoyance about the intolerable truth of the drug trade, when he tore himself away from M. René as a sinner might stagger out of a confessional, now eager to stab his habitual dealer for overcharging him. But not before receiving a tip of ten dollars, which M. René had enough experience to dispense with elegance, and a small Swiss Army knife he was never without, because it had an attachment for pushing back the cuticles.

He lost consciousness with a grin on his lips, and woke, fully clothed, in his dining-room chair at around two in the afternoon. He felt much refreshed, went into the bathroom and clipped a couple of wayward hairs he had not noticed in the morning from his moustache, splashed some toilet water over himself, and settled into his habitual chair for a siesta. He tried to resume a dream which had given him pleasure, although he could scarcely remember why. Sleep refused to come. He rose and fried himself an egg. Lunch in Switzerland stops at 1.30, even for widowers alone at home.

# III

'LE MOUTON Enragé' was difficult to find, but they were all on time. M. René had arrived early to arrange a table, and had selected one in an alcove in which a certain privacy could be assured. The manner of the three men was affected by the presence of Agnes Schanderbach, who turned out to be quite attractive. At least, she inspired in many men a slight regret that they had not encountered her earlier in life, when her attributes would have benefited from a greater freshness. Even as it was, there was a warmth and softness to her which made a careworn quality at moments pleasantly mysterious. But her greatest attraction and reassurance was her voice, wonderfully melodious and gentle. The men indulged in an aperitif, offered by the owner in recognition of new clients. There were not that many old ones, one of the reasons it had been selected by Mr Butler. Another was that he lived a stone's throw away. Fräulein Schanderbach revealed that she didn't drink, perhaps another point in her favour.

Once they had ordered their food, they got down to business. M. René outlined his plan in a slightly weary voice, but with a crystal clarity he could now afford. He had disciples, who did not hesitate to correct him whenever they felt he was being too diplomatic, or else too philosophical, to be understood by someone hearing the proposition for the first time.

'If I understand you rightly,' Agnes said at the conclusion of the exposé, 'you wish me to take over the housekeeping section?'

'We first need to know if you accept our idea in principle,' M. René said reasonably.

'There is no one in our profession who would not, in their hearts, approve of your aims,' she said quietly, 'perhaps especially if they protest the contrary to be true.'

'You equate our profession with hyprocrisy?' asked M. Arrigo, smiling.

'Very much so,' retorted Agnes. 'There is scarcely another profession which relies as exclusively on the use of hypocrisy.'

'And you believe that a saturation point is eventually reached?'

'Mine was reached before I ever started work.'

'Why did you choose to give your life to hotels?' asked M. René, every inch the examiner.

'We were desperate,' Agnes answered, softly. 'My father died in the furnaces of a concentration camp. I hardly remember him, except that he was the very opposite of a hypocrite. He remembered his own father, and followed in his footsteps. His father, my grandfather, died in the Spanish Civil War, before a fascist firing squad. He was a lifelong communist, as was my father, old-fashioned men of a kind you don't see any more. Enthusiastic, believing in the brotherhood of man, eager to give away anything they had to those less fortunate. The Nazis broke the tradition. My mother, with me in her arms, managed to enter Switzerland on compassionate grounds. We lived here on charity for a short time. My mother was an expert seamstress, and made her way by taking in extra work. I am German, and housekeeping comes naturally to me. I started here, it was easier than for Mother. I had never known anything else. My only glimpse of another world was when my mother used to sing me to sleep with some of the old songs from the Thälmann period, or even before, the Spartakists. Some of the songs were too militant to be of much use as lullabies, even when sung softly, and when that happened I remained awake to see my mother's face streaming with tears. She never noticed that I was not asleep.'

She told her story, which Mr Butler already knew, without a trace of self-pity, but with a kind of tough acceptance of natural forces which impressed the others.

'So you wish to throw in your lot with us?' M. René asked.

'I will do what I can in the hotel in which I work.'

'No one can ask for more, for the time being.'

A trace of a smile lit up her melancholy face for a moment. 'I am surprised that a group of men should be ready to put their trust in a woman.'

The men glanced at each other guiltily.

'Why not?' asked M. René.

'Why not indeed?' she replied, and cleared her throat. 'You wish to know about the Emir of Djabbadieh?' she enquired. 'He has dirty habits.'

'They are hereditary,' declared M. René.

'Housekeeping, maintenance and room service take it in turns to go to his room. There is always more than enough for them to do.'

'Does he have eight rooms as his grandfather did?'

'No, he has a normal suite. I have noticed no visitors apart from a masseur.'

'A masseur? A male?' M. René asked.

'Oh yes, otherwise it would be a masseuse,' she explained, with a twinkle suggesting that the Emir would not be seen dead with a masseuse.

'Does he go out much?'

'Not at all, as far as I can see. He had a few friends in to share the lamb at lunch, all in traditional dress. Oh, one curious thing. He sent a suitcase over to the Clinique Ma Joie. I happened to be near the desk when he phoned in his request. M. Boisferrand was furious. The Emir demanded an armoured car to take the suitcase to an Arab whose name I can't remember. "Why an armoured car?" M. Boisferrand fumed, saying they all had complexes, and how simple life used to be.'

'I must compliment you, Agnes,' Mr Butler said, trembling slightly with a sense of occasion, 'you are quite an observer, and what a memory!'

'Not really. When I knew you were after some information, I gathered as much as possible without knowing what in particular interested you.' She produced from her bag a couple of typed sheets. 'Before coming here I made a copy of the list of guests and their room numbers from the hotel computer.'

M. René nodded in admiration.

'For instance, the Emir is in suite 476, overlooking the park, the one with the verandah.'

'And—' M. René looked conspiratorial, 'Mr Ivanov?'

Agnes Schanderbach consulted her list.

'Ivanov,' she said, 'Mikhail, from the Ministry of Foreign Relations, Alma-Ata. Room 312.'

'Interesting . . .' M. René reacted as he imagined detectives would. 'They are on different floors. Is the hotel full?'

'About forty per cent occupied.'

'They did not insist on being on the same floor?'

'If I was either of them, and I had shady business to perform, I would not insist either,' reflected Fräulein Schanderbach. 'There is always the lift, and the stairs.'

'And the telephone,' added M. René.

'And the patient man in the clinic, with nothing but comic books to read,' said M. Alonso, who had been able to come after all.

'Oh yes,' echoed M. René, 'I had almost forgotten him . . .'

'In this kind of work, it doesn't do to forget anything,' reprimanded Fräulein Schanderbach gently, very much the housekeeper.

The others looked at her in admiration, already enslaved by her professionalism.

'What should we do next?' Mr Butler asked her, to M. René's discreet annoyance.

Agnes smiled sadly. 'What can we do but watch and wait? Evidently, you do not wish to take more positive action.'

There was a momentary silence.

'More positive action?' enquired Mr Butler. 'What more positive action could there possibly be at this stage? Come to that, at any stage?'

'No, I merely asked.' Agnes hesitated. 'I mean, there is

no intention of harming any parties we find guilty of – of what are known as crimes against humanity.'

M. René was quick to respond.

'It is not up to us to sit in judgement on such people, merely to bring their activities to the attention of the appropriate authorities.'

'Then how does our work differ from that which is done in any case by the police? And, forgive me, but in order for it to be worth our while to bring our findings to the attention of what you call the appropriate authorities, we sit in judgement on them whether we like it or not,' countered Agnes.

M. René frowned. 'We have no mandate to do more than open up entirely new channels of investigation,' he said, with a certain intensity.

Agnes was delightfully casual. 'What you are really trying to tell me is that we have no mandate to kill,' she said, smiling.

This was so surprising an affirmation that the others treated it as a joke, laughing at the wonderful absurdity of the statement. Agnes laughed with them.

'I merely wish to know the terms of reference of any work I am offered,' she said. This brought back a note of uncomfortable sobriety.

'If there were really any activity of the kind you envisage,' murmured Mr Butler, 'it would certainly be surprising for a group of grown men to – as you put it – place their trust in a woman.'

'How wrong you could be,' replied Agnes, almost coquettish.

'Could be – or would be?' asked M. Arrigo.

Agnes considered her reply. Softly, she decided: 'Could be.'

There was a long silence while they digested the disturbing tone the conversation had taken.

Eventually M. Alonso rediscovered his words. 'Crimes against humanity,' he muttered. 'There is absolutely nothing – no evidence – to point us in that direction.'

'Absolutely none,' snapped M. René.

'We must have suspicions,' countered Agnes, 'otherwise what are we doing here? What kind of country is Djabbadieh?'

'Djabbadieh,' laughed M. Arrigo, 'is not a country at all, but two American oil companies and an Emir floating on a sea of the stuff. I know, I was in charge of Western food at the Scheherazade Calypso forty years ago.'

'There must be people,' said Agnes.

'People? I suppose so—' reflected M. Arrigo. 'Over ninety per cent illiterate, with a magnificent, if empty, National University named after the late Emir. Education is forbidden for women, and felt to be unnecessary for men, therefore free.'

'There are no schools?' M. René was appalled.

'They are irrelevant, once there is television.'

'Television?'

'When I was there, there were already five channels, two of them religious. Today, there must be thirty, all of them religious.'

'Well, we can probably rule out drugs, don't you agree, gentlemen?' smiled Agnes. 'As our good Karl Marx might have said, with so much religion around, who needs opiates?'

'In any case, if that were the Emir's additional vice, what an absurdly complicated way to indulge it. All you need is money in this day and age, and certainly the Emir has enough of that,' laughed M. Arrigo.

'I'll hazard a guess it's weapons,' said M. René.

He embroidered mysteriously on the masses of Soviet hardware he had read about, rotting helplessly in their silos in the former republics of the Union, the nuclear warheads protected only by guards who hadn't been paid for months. The whole regime, reflecting the pain and confusion of its even larger neighbour, Russia, was now open to the new opportunism necessary to the survival of the individual. An appearance of normality was pursued by the acquisition of a national flag and a national anthem, sung without much enthusiasm by football teams predestined to defeat and mumbled by a populace too indolent to learn the words. As an adjunct to these symptoms of independence there was also, of course, a worthless currency battered into submission by rampant inflation, and to go with it, the worship of the distant and elusive dollar.

'These people are in desperate need of selling their assets, and cotton is not enough,' M. René concluded.

'That explains one side of the equation,' commented Agnes, 'but why should Djabbadieh be eager buyers?'

They all looked to M. Arrigo.

He cleared his throat, and took a very Italian approach towards complexity. He explained that the very fact that a country is small does not mean that its political reality is simpler than that of a large country. Sometimes, the very opposite is true. Djabbadieh has been ruled for a long time by a single family, the El Talubi Emirs, who treat the Emirate as private property, leasing bits of it to American oil interests for their pocket money. They have long since sunk into degeneracy through excessive inbreeding, peppering the landscape with illegitimate off-spring, while allowing only the legitimate a share in the profits, and a place in the long line of succession leading to the throne. There is always trouble seething under the serene exterior of visionary architecture, oil rigs, electric minarets and swimming pools. The old, notorious Emir had to withstand numerous attempts to get rid of him, all of which he side-stepped by cunning, overpaying his bodyguards more than any potential rival could match by bribery. His eventual successor, the Emir Taieb el Mahali al Salaam el Talubi, was side-stepped because he was mad even by the standards of the ruling family, and replaced by the young pervert who was advancing his nation's interest in the Bellerive Davel Hotel, the Emir Mustafa.

'I still fail to see what such people should want with weapons,' remarked M. René. 'I have the distinct feeling that a car backfiring might cause a national panic.'

M. Arrigo continued with his exposé by revealing that Djabbadieh was the home of a remote sect of Islam, neither Sunni nor Shi'ite, which was so extreme that death by stoning was only reserved for criminals of proven piety in order to facilitate their entry into heaven. Criminals of an irreligious or agnostic tendency were flogged regularly to the very portals of death, and then allowed to recuperate until the next ration, and so on until a merciful deity allowed the ignorant floggers to go too far. In such a depraved atmosphere there were inevitably those, possibly spawned by princelings in the wombs of the lowly born, with fiery ambitions for Djabbadieh and its 80,000 inhabitants. But from there to nuclear warheads? Why should anybody of sound mind be shopping for such things in any case?

The conversation spread to general politics, under

a growing feeling that dinner was over, they having accomplished as much as was possible under present circumstances. Only Mr Butler was emboldened to ask Agnes a question which had been gnawing at his strictly circumscribed mind.

'Agnes,' he said, as they were on the point of leaving, 'are you still a communist?'

She laughed merrily. 'Who is still a communist?'

The others grunted in approval of this evidence.

'You haven't answered my question,' Mr Butler persisted, 'and I think we deserve to know.'

Agnes paused to give a more sober reply. 'Communism was a way of life in a world which no longer exists. It protested against conditions which were common in industrialized areas, but where everything has changed through technical development. In agriculture, communism was a disaster at the best of times. Solidarity at the workbench is entirely different from solidarity among the crops, and it was always more difficult to build up a head of steam in the countryside. But, even if communism is a relic of the industrial revolution, idealism is not so volatile. Ask me if I am still a communist, I will answer that I doubt if I ever was. I was born too late to be like my parents and grandparents. Ask me if I am an idealist, I will answer: more than ever, even if it is temporarily out of fashion to be one.'

The others looked at Mr Butler as though he was unusually lucky to get such a skilful reply to such a dreary question, and stood up to leave.

As they proceeded to the exit, M. René noticed another diner in a booth, who seemed to bury his head in his hands as they passed. Once in the open air, M. René stopped dead for a while. Then, without giving any reason, re-entered the restaurant. This time, the other diner had no opportunity of adopting an attitude, meeting M. René's penetrating look. In fact, he seemed to have returned to his seat from elsewhere, not the toilet, insufficient time having elapsed.

'Should I know you?' asked M. René.

The man was thickset, with, one would have thought, a certain indolence imposed by nature. He did not smile. 'M. René,' he said, 'the world famous concierge.'

'Thank you,' replied M. René tersely, 'but I have no difficulty in recognizing myself. My question is, who are you?'

'Ah,' sighed the stranger, 'perhaps you are unaccustomed to seeing me out of uniform.'

M. René thought for a moment. 'M. Mildenegger?'

'Your Chief of Police, at your service.'

'I am surprised to see you at the Mouton Enragé.'

'People are usually surprised to see me anywhere. That is, if they recognize me.'

'You probably live near here,' shrugged M. René.

'I could hardly live further away. And now, I suppose you will want to know why I chose this bistro?'

M. René allowed his silence its own eloquence.

'I make it a rule to discover every nook and cranny of my bailiwick. Just as a taxi driver needs to know every small alleyway of the city, I need to know every potential meeting place of the city which is my responsibility. Satisfied?'

'And today just happened to be the turn of the Mouton Enragé?'

'Precisely.'

'However,' M. René went on, 'I will refrain from asking you your opinion on the food.'

'And why is that?' asked the Chief of Police, a little taken aback.

'There is no cutlery on your table, just a used cup. No trace of the merest crumb, not the smallest sign of disorder.'

M. Mildenegger responded with a gruff laugh. 'Who is the Chief of Police, you or me?'

'And who is the concierge?'

'Congratulations,' Mildenegger conceded, 'I never eat dinner. The food is not what interests me. However, I am a coffee addict. I dropped in for a cup of coffee.'

'Dropped in? You will have noticed that a bell rings whenever the door of the restaurant is opened, to attract attention to the fact that there is a new client. The bell has not rung since my dinner party's arrival.'

'Ergo?' asked the Chief of Police.

'Ergo, you must have been here when we arrived nearly two hours ago.'

'I said I was a coffee addict. I had several cups.'

'But you weren't seated here when we entered.'

'Oh?'

'I would have noticed you.'

'Where do you think I was?'

'Not in the toilet. I sat where I could see both it and the entrance to the restaurant. Perhaps you were in the kitchen. That is my guess. That was the only door in frequent use, and therefore virtually impossible to observe.'

M. Mildenegger grew suddenly truculent. 'Now it's my turn to ask the questions, M. René. Do you always go to restaurants with such an arrantly guilty conscience?'

'Guilty conscience?'

'What have you to hide? Why do you elect to sit where you can keep an eye on the entrance and on the toilets? Do such considerations help the digestion? What are you up to?'

For a moment, M. René was at a loss for words.

'What do you think I am up to?' he asked.

'I will ring you in a day or two and tell you what you are up to,' said the Chief of Police.

'I am most interested to know.' M. René reached into his pocket.

'Don't bother to give me your number. I know where to find you.'

M. René bit his lip. He needed the initiative again and, on an impulse, went back to the table he had previously occupied instead of leaving. Seated once again in his alcove, he groped under the thick oak table, and after the usual brief encounters with ancient chewing-gum, turned to stone with the passage of time, he found a fresh piece of Scotch Tape, which curled itself round his finger. Pulling it free, he went back to where the Chief was sitting, immobile.

'It's a pity to waste good tape,' he said. 'One of the maxims of hotel life is: Always be sparing with essentials, never with luxuries,' and he went, leaving the tape on the Police Chief's table.

Outside, the others were waiting obediently.

'Come on,' he directed, 'walk on as if nothing had happened.'

'What has happened?' they were eager to know.

'That hunched figure by the door was the Chief of Police. By all evidence, he taped our conversation.'

'We said nothing to be ashamed of,' Agnes protested.

René waved them into silence.

When the Chief of Police emerged into the lamplit

evening moments later, he was in time to see a group of relaxed figures ambling into the parking area. The Chief gestured for his driver. The driver noticed at once that his boss was in a foul mood.

# IV

M. RENÉ found sleep difficult that night, simply because his
mind had been overstimulated by events. He dreamt, only
to find he was not dreaming, because awake. He relived
every moment of the meeting at the Mouton Enragé, everything very precise, but in a wild disorder. Had anything
been said which could give a lead to a third party, starting
out from a position of total ignorance, and listening alone
in a room, retrospectively? Some voices will have been, if
not loud, at least clear, his own, for instance. And that of
M. Arrigo. Those of M. Alonso and Agnes, by nature, less
carrying. That of Mr Butler, hard to decipher at the best
of times, even with the man before you, so extensive was
the wavering, and the English suburban accent, always a
challenge for foreigners.

At length, M. René gave up the struggle, put on his
aged but beautifully dry-cleaned Thai silk dressing gown,
a relic from his stint at the Celestial Kingdom Riverside in
Bangkok thirty years ago, and shuffled to the front door in

his slippers. It was too early for the crisp croissants, but the morning paper was already there. He settled down with it while waiting for the water to boil for his coffee. A small item caught his eye at once, the Geneva papers having a tendency to encapsule all the latest news on the front page in small sections, extensively commented on elsewhere. The item he spotted was followed by a question-mark, as though the news were still breaking at the time of press. 'Palace revolution in Djabbadieh?' it read, and went on to say that spasmodic firing had been heard at night, presumably between legitimate and illegitimate family members. Sheikh El Awabi bin Talubi bin Talaat was the name on every lip as the new pretender, a fifty-five-year-old graduate of the University of New Mexico, according to the wire services from neighbouring Emirates. The American oil companies were on full alert.

The kettle whistled, and a rustle at the front door suggested the arrival of the croissants. Once M. René settled to his frugal breakfast, it was time for the rest of the paper. Another item, to which greater space had been accorded because it was local, added to the chapter of morning mysteries. It was the arrest of an undisclosed foreigner referred to simply as S at the Clinique Ma Joie, charged with transporting goods of unusual danger to the public. Such is the rigid code of anonymity governing charges levelled by the authorities in Switzerland that the one thing you could be sure of was that the name of the party charged did not begin with an S.

The idea of calling the clinic entered M. René's mind, but then he imagined that M. Mildenegger might easily expect such a precipitate gesture on his part, which made him, instead, put in a call to Agnes, which was, in fact, no wiser.

As it happened, she was not available, but sent a message to say she would call back. M. René tried M. Alonso, but was told by the switchboard at his workplace that he was indisposed. Indisposed? Is it serious? We think not. He was all right yesterday. So were many who died this morning.

M. René hesitated before calling M. Arrigo. He guessed ahead of time that he would not be available to take calls. He was right. He decided not to call Mr Butler for a while. He was the most difficult to understand, the least coherent, the most prone to panic. M. René imagined they had all been contacted by the police. Only he had been left to marinate in doubts. He saw himself falling into a trap, and decided to do precisely nothing in order to preserve a very limited freedom of action. He washed up with all the serenity he could muster, even singing as he worked. He was just drying his hands when the phone rang. It was Agnes.

'Where are you calling from?' he asked.

'A cellular phone,' she replied. 'I always carry it with me. Of course, it can be bugged like any other, but I believe it to be less likely.'

'I have the feeling all our friends have been told not to accept calls from me.'

'They were all called by Mildenegger, but I don't know what he told them. I only know what he told me. Nothing.'

'What? He called you too?'

'Oh yes. That's quite usual. We're old enemies. He knew that I had seen him, sitting alone near to the door, in the restaurant. There was no escape. He had to call, to explain.'

'To explain? What kind of ongoing relationship do you have with him?'

'Oh, it has lasted for as long as I care to remember,

but I don't want to discuss it here, in case ... you understand?'

'Yes, yes,' replied M. René urgently, 'but apart from that?'

'Apart from that? Ivanov left during the night, by taxi, paying his bill in cash, and forgetting the extras. M. Boisferrand is six hundred francs out of pocket.'

'Plus the tip.'

'A tip from a Kazakh civil servant? Six hundred francs is enough.'

'And the Emir?'

'He was fetched an hour ago by a car small enough and shabby enough to be owned by the police for covert operations.'

'No other details?'

'I saw him briefly. He was in tears, of rage. He had a cluster of faxes in his fist as he was led away by plain clothes men.'

'No wonder. You read the paper?'

'The palace revolution? Of course. And Mr S in the Clinique Ma Joie. I thought it wiser not to call my contact for the time being.'

M. René smiled somewhat grimly.

'We are all learning fairly quickly whom not to call. At length it could lead to total paralysis.'

'Not really. We only have to be cleverer than they are. Remember most of the time, we hold the initiative.'

How interesting. Another person who saw life as a series of initiatives, lost, and regained.

'Why do you say that?' he asked with an interest which was not just coincidental.

'Do you ever go to the cinema?'

'I have been known to.'

'Have you ever seen a car chase in which the police are in the leading car?'

'No,' he said, after momentary reflection.

'There you are,' she said. 'We are always in the first car, not the second. We can choose the direction we wish to go in. They can merely follow. That's why they're usually in such a surly mood.'

'We can make mistakes.'

'With the advantages we have, it is up to us not to make mistakes. Incidentally, I have another lead. We will discuss it when we next meet.'

'Another lead? Do be careful!'

'There's no harm in their knowing we have another lead. It gives them more to worry about.'

'When do we meet again?'

'I will call you when I am ready. I may have to take you by surprise. Meanwhile, do nothing.'

There was silence on the line. She had given him an order. She had actually given him an order. How strange, he ruminated. The whole absurd odyssey had been his idea, a whim so powerful he did not even question it before inviting his acquaintances, who followed their self-imposed leader, at first a little tepidly, then with a boyish sense of adventure, and now, suddenly, here he was, under observation like some captive animal, accepting instructions from a person he had known for several hours. And a woman at that! Well, it was no use speeding up events which pursued their own logic. To do so would be foolhardy in the extreme. In that sense, her peremptory instruction was no more than obvious. He reasoned himself into a state of mind in which the police were all avidly waiting for him to make a move, and it was precisely on that level that he was refusing to give them the remotest satisfaction. Seen like this, he held the initiative again, not they. It was they who were awaiting his pleasure, and not the other way round.

He sat back with a kind of grim satisfaction. But then the doubts began again. A new lead? What did that mean? An extension of the Ivanov-Emir affair, or something entirely new? Of course, in order to keep the police in suspense, she also had to keep him in suspense, the identical suspense, as it happened. What a pity that was, for his peace of mind, but it was, in the circumstances, inevitable. What if the new lead was a pure invention, just to foment questions if they happened to be listening? That would be gratuitously cruel, although justifiable, and a perfectly legitimate way of retaking that initiative. And if the lead was to a new scandal, easier to explain, fresher in the mind, then every means was in order. He gave her the benefit of the doubt, deciding to be mature as his age demanded.

The Paris – Milan Express flew by, boring a large hole in the wall of silence, which grew together and hermetically sealed itself to its previous integrity in a matter of seconds. M. René automatically reached for his fob watch, but he did not wear it in his dressing-gown. He shuffled to his bedside. 9.42. He grimaced. It was almost two minutes early. It would have to loiter outside Lausanne to put it back on time again. Punctuality was all important in running the railways, as everywhere else. Somewhere, in the attic, there was a carefully preserved web of miniature railroads, with marshalling yards, control boxes, and stations, with which he had played as a boy, a habit which had only hibernated during his active years, but which he could easily fall back into at any moment now that his daily chores had made way for all manner of dreams.

He showered briefly, fidgeted with stray hairs his eagle eye identified, and dressed in working clothes. Then he took his expandable metal ladder as well as his powerful torch, and climbed towards a cover which, when pushed open, revealed the poky attic in his unambitious house. He saw a row of gleaming engines as he had left them years before, rails still laid out through pastoral landscapes, rural stations with eternally awaiting passengers, a tunnel carved into sheer rocks. He leant in to the signal boxes, trying the switches, but there was a whole schema to remember, plugging into a central switchboard. He was amazed to see how much space it took up, laid out as it was, with no effort to confine at least part of it to boxes. And he shuddered as he realized how much expensive electricity it must eat up, considerations which had hardly bothered him as a child.

Carefully he replaced everything where he found it, including the entrance to the attic. He descended the ladder, stored it, shaved as though he were trimming a hedge, splashed himself liberally with aftershave, and dressed with the kind of formality which gave him confidence at difficult moments. He had showered with the bathroom door open so as not to inadvertently leave the telephone unanswered, and even when the hour of midday struck he determined to concoct a meal from bits and pieces left over in the icebox, rather than risk missing a call.

It was only well after his frugal meal that he began angrily to throw caution to the winds. He abruptly felt exactly that which he had been trying so assiduously to avoid, a victim of circumstances. The hell with the others. It would serve them right, potential friend and potential foe, to find him out when they rang. He therefore went walking to the electronics shop, and bought himself a cellular telephone. He paused at the post office to fill up the requisite forms. Soon he would be accorded an individual number and be up to par with Agnes, with a command post all his own. There had been no need of a fax up to now, or access to the internet, luxuries he had only vaguely heard about, but it was the imagined expense which put him off. His time of life was not the signal for incursions into the fastness of lifelong prudence. He understood the utility of a travelling, cordless telephone, but found it more difficult to countenance dramatic improvements on communication where mankind had done little to improve the quality of what was said. Technique by itself did nothing but underline the basic poverty of communal thinking, the famine of constructive ideas.

It was while musing on these depressing verities that he reentered his drive, to find the gate wide open where he had shut it, and Louis' hideous motorbike taking up the entire width of the path, leaning drunkenly over the lawn. He closed the gate, silently, and went to investigate, walking on the grass. The front door had not been tampered with, the windows were all hermetically sealed. He fancied he heard the rhythmic sounds of lovemaking, a sound he was able to identify without having more than a casual experience in the matter. He crept round to the back of the house, where, in the high grass surrounding the workshed, he spotted a naked backside heaving up and down, black leather trousers and skimpy underwear pushed down over the back of the knees. From further down in the grass came female squeaks and moans which might as easily have been those of asphyxiation as the conventional expression of an orgasm.

M. René was caught awkwardly between legitimate fury and the need for propriety under such circumstances. At least, in a hotel room, there was a door to knock on.

Here, nothing. He cleared his voice instead, calling out in a way which made no effort to conceal his anger: 'If you want to see me after you have finished your copulation, use the front door. I will leave it open.'

Louis became furious, and reckless, standing up, revealing his bony, adolescent frame and his dangling manhood. 'Fuck you, Uncle!' he shrieked. 'Copulation indeed. Trust you to make something natural sound disgusting!'

M. René looked round anxiously. There is something hostile about neighbours. They cannot find it in themselves to resist satisfaction in the distress of others. 'Pull your trousers up at once. Join me indoors if you have something to impart other than this disgraceful behaviour,' and he turned to go, as though he were disowning his nephew.

'Christ,' exploded Louis, without making any gesture towards decency, 'I came here with the best intentions. All I wanted to do was to introduce you to my girl.' It was her turn to struggle to her feet, as unaesthetically naked as he, but with a seductive grin plastered on her face as though she were auditioning. She extended a hand, which she expected M. René to walk back to.

He contained his annoyance, looked around again for inadvertent eavesdroppers, and turned on his heel. 'You can both use the bathroom if you feel so inclined,' he called, as quietly as possible, and made for the front door.

Once inside, he waited in a cold fury for an unconscionable time. Eventually they entered the house sheepishly, advancing slowly with bits of earth and grass sticking to their black leather outfits.

'Don't sit down on my furniture like that!' he warned, treating their appearance as an emergency of sorts, in order to disguise the extent of his rage. They made ineffectual efforts to shed the bits of the garden clinging to them, but the moisture defeated them.

'I hate to advise you to get undressed again,' he said, 'since you do so all too readily, but I would suggest a good shower for both of you, and hanging your clothes in the boiler room downstairs until they are dry.'

The girl, whose name was Kuki, or something of the sort, was of Greek origin, according to Louis. He brought the matter up hoping it might move his uncle's thinking onto a different plane.

'Modern, rather than ancient,' was the only reaction the information allocated.

'The Greek word for doll is—' she declared.

'Kukla – I know,' interrupted M. René.

'Yes. My mother used to call me her doll. I tried to say the word too, but couldn't get my child's tongue around it. Kuki, I used to call myself.' And she laughed.

'Your mother, I presume, was not Greek.'

'Why do you say that? That's interesting . . .'

'She would have pronounced it better. Kukla.'

The girl smiled. 'No, Mum was from Plymouth. Come to think of it, Dad wasn't much of a Greek either. I never knew him properly.'

'He is deceased. I'm sorry to hear it.'

'Why? You never knew him. Why should you be sorry to hear it?'

M. René spoke icily. 'It is usual for a person to commiserate with someone who has lost a close relative.'

'Dad's not dead,' she explained, 'he's in prison.'

'Oh.'

'I don't visit him. I can't, really. He's in Bangkok.'

'Bangkok? You think, no doubt, that he was innocent.'

She was more than casual. 'I don't even know what he's supposed to have done, but the one thing you can be sure of is that he's guilty. That's to hear Mother talk, anyway.'

'And Mother is—'

'Oh, she's alive all right. Very much so. Married again. A Greek.'

'Ah, hence the Greek origin.'

'I suppose so, yes – except I'm not sure Mother ever married Father. And I'm not sure she's married now. Hates bureaucracy, she does. Can't be doing with bureaucracy.' Louis looked from one to the other with a grin on his face, convinced they were hitting it off famously.

M. René caught the look, and it spurred him into action. 'Now, you take your shower first,' he said, 'and dry your clothes in the boiler room. You know the house.'

'OK, Uncle. Meanwhile Kuki has something to tell you.'

M. René nodded his head in acknowledgement of this information, which filled him with foreboding. A pregnancy in the family? It seemed as likely as marriage seemed unlikely.

'You called me Uncle before, I seem to remember.'

Louis laughed merrily, as did Kuki.

'Yeah, fuck you, Uncle. I was mad then. No hard feelings, René,' and he left the room. There was a long pause. M. René cursed his sister, Charlotte. In a moment of mental aberration she had spawned this idiot boy, and left him with the tangled consequences. Prepared for the worst, he sat down.

'And what do you wish to tell me?'

'D'you want me to take my clothes off first?'

M. René started in horror. Brashness of this order was something he had not expected even from the youth of today.

'What on earth for?'

'I don't want to spoil your furniture, remember?'

'No, no.' M. René rose with a snatched sigh of relief. He laid down yesterday's newspaper on the piano stool. She sat with quite unnecessary precaution, even lifting a particularly long stem of grass from the seat of her pants, and looking round helplessly for somewhere to put it.

'There is a waste-paper basket over there.'

He would have shouted had he not controlled his voice. He stood up, fetched the bit of grass, and threw it in the waste-paper basket. It fell short. She rose to pick it up.

'Leave it where it is!' he cried, as if it could sting.

The pause resumed. He assumed an air of cordiality with the greatest difficulty, reminding himself that Louis was a relative. 'You said you wished to tell me something,' he reminded her.

'Oh yes.' Her eyes narrowed as though she were making a meticulous assessment of something.

'You must have had a fascinating life,' she said at length.

'Fascinating,' he admitted, a little surprised. 'And you may have noticed that it is too soon to speak of it in the past.'

She smiled, and began to ask him why he had never put any of it down. He replied evasively that he didn't think it was worth it. As though she was letting the cat out of a bag, she mentioned, en passant as she put it, that Louis had told her about his plan for espionage on customers of hotels.

He stiffened. 'He did? He shouldn't have done.'

She went on volubly that he had thought the plan idiotic, saying it would never work in any case. She had disagreed from the outset. She thought it a wonderful idea.

'It has nothing to do with espionage,' M. René said.

'It has to do with going through people's pockets, doesn't it?' she asked. 'Overhearing conversations, putting two and two together? What's that if it isn't espionage?'

'It is not to do with spying as a profitable pastime,' he remarked. 'It is not sordid.'

'That's the bit I didn't understand.' She knitted her brow, and assumed a tone of earnest innocence. 'Isn't everything done for profit these days? Haven't the powers that be seen to it that the world has become one large market place, and all in the name of freedom?'

'What have you against freedom?' he enquired.

'It's all right if you can afford it. It's expensive. Like food and clothing and fun. Fewer and fewer people can afford it. They're told they're free, but they're not. That's what I like about Louis. He doesn't give a shit. He's supposed to pay for that motorbike in seventy-two monthly instalments of 1200 francs. He signed the agreement a year ago. He paid the first instalment, and that's it.'

'Good gracious. Why haven't they caught up with him yet?' asked M. René.

'No fixed address. Louis is on the run. Now listen, I'm not telling you this hoping you'll pay for the bike.'

'I wouldn't dream of doing anything so stupid.'

'Oh, you know, for the sake of the family and all that. All that pompous crap older people take into consideration.

Understand me. Louis gets a kick out of riding a bike which doesn't belong to him. It's as good as stolen property. Knowing that, the roar of the engine goes to his head like a drug. And I feel it, riding pillion, clinging to his leather jacket, sensing his spare body in my arms at 150 kilometres an hour in a built-up area.'

'It seems you do quite adequately without a bike, when you are relatively still.'

She smiled. 'That's what I like about the elderly. They've got sarcasm.'

'Probably because we spend so much time feeling embarrassed.'

'You've also got the power.'

'Power?'

'Power to pay the bills, power to insist on things remaining as they are, power to pay the police, too.'

'All your ideas are frightfully silly, if I may say so,' remarked M. René, stifling a yawn.

'And that just after I've praised you to the sky!' cried Kuki.

'You like my ideas because you fail to understand them—'

'I understand them only too well, except I don't agree with the idealism which motivates them,' she interrupted, very sure of herself. 'Leave the idealism to the young fools, for God's sake, those raving idiots on unpaid motorbikes. A person your age knows the value of things – knows his way around the world he's inherited and doesn't want to change it because he understands it, a world like a tidy room, everything in drawers and cupboards, so that you know where to find it.'

M. René smiled. She went on.

'Your image frightens us because you are what we are destined to become once you have gone and the motorbikes are in the scrapyards. Dull. Deadly dull, living lives that aren't worth living, lives without surprises. And you still think I don't understand? You're trying to break out of your cage, before it's too late. You're trying to escape the prison you've created yourself, simply by living and making what you call a success out of that life. Go ahead and do it. I'm a hundred per cent with you. Break out, but don't do it for the sake of some silly ideals. Leave them to the likes of us. Put down your experiences. Tell your story. Use that sarcasm in you to a constructive end. Throw a spanner in the works. A hall porter tells all. Jesus. You saw fifty times what the butler saw. A spotlight on the corrupt society you know better than any of us – not by instinct, by experience – by surviving it. But, for God's sake, reap the benefit. Make them pay through their noses for your wisdom, don't throw it down the drain and let others get rich!'

He looked non-committal. When you put the pieces of her jigsaw puzzle together, it had more coherence than he had expected. Also, her position was unusual, in that, within a somewhat strident venality, there lurked a kind of compassion, even a humility, which was unexpected. He had no desire to make fun of her. He even grinned at her.

'Every person is constituted differently, whatever their age.'

'So?'

'It's not in my nature to regard my life as some sort of financial investment.'

She returned his smile.

'How wrong can you be.' It was no question.

'Perhaps. But even if there's some merit in your low

opinion of the kind of freedom people allow themselves to be satisfied with, I am still free to keep my own counsel. Why? Because it's my life, and no one else's. OK?'

'OK.'

Louis came in, flushed with the joys of the bathroom. His complexion was what in babies would be called bonny. Even the occasional spot on his face seemed to have vanished in the glow. 'Your turn,' he said, slapping Kuki playfully, 'there's nothing like a shower, except . . .'

'Louis!'

'I didn't say it,' and he held up a finger to make a point.

'When was your last shower?' asked M. René.

'A week? Two weeks? Somewhere between the two.'

'Is that sufficient?'

'It has to be, doesn't it? I've no permanent address.'

'Because of the back payments on your motorbicycle?'

Kuki had left the room in a hurry.

'She told you?'

'Yes, which obviously means that you have dropped out of the Ecole Hôtelière, thereby forfeiting all hope of winning a diploma.'

'Why?'

'Because the police could always know where to pick you up. It stands to reason.'

Louis thought for a while.

'I have no ambitions to be a head waiter at the age of forty-five.'

'I'm sorry to hear that. It's the only branch in which I have any influence, to help you. I know nobody in the motorcycle industry.'

'What did she tell you?'

'You made a down payment, leaving seventy-one instalments unpaid.'

'That's a lie!'

'Then tell me the truth.'

'I've got enough together for the second payment – almost.'

'But you haven't made it yet.'

'No.'

'Then, seen from the point of view of the motorbicycle distribution, it is not a lie at all.'

'Whose side are you on, your nephew's or the dealer's?'

'Must I answer that? The dealer's, of course.'

Louis was reduced to a glum silence.

'Another, more disturbing item is that you breached the confidence I invested you with by telling your mistress of our plans.'

'Oh shit. Kuki's not my mistress. She's just a great lay. And utterly reliable.'

'That I can believe.'

'So you should. I thought your idea was God-awful. A lot of pathetic old fogies getting their own back on society. I thought it stank. Lots of better things you can do to society. Or rather, worse things, know what I mean? It was she took your part. Thought it was wonderful. Are you going to blame me for that?'

This conversation brought no benefit to either of them. Like an old married couple, they played their parts without giving them much thought, linked by some kind of association which had become obscure with the passage of time. In short, they nagged rather than spoke, and spoke rather than listened. All M. René discovered was that Kuki was the kind of call girl who needed no second calling, and that their relationship was as impermanent and as hard to nail down as the seasons. He also discovered, without much surprise, that his young relative had a bent for larceny. At length, M. René was forced to remark, mainly out of desire to occupy his mind with other, more urgent matters, that the concubine of His Majesty devoted an awfully long time to her ablutions.

There was no need for Louis to answer, since she announced her return with one of the latest hits, sung in a reedy voice, like all those who find microphones indispensible. She came in brimming over with well-being, and even René had to admit that she looked surprisingly attractive in her ramshackle way, hair all over the place, still wet. She gave an emphatic thumbs-up sign to Louis, who exploded with excitement. To M. René it seemed as though they had discovered the joys of the hot shower for the first time.

'Well, time we were off,' cried Louis, springing to life. 'We've wasted enough of your—'

'My door is always open,' René said, as they gathered their voluminous clobber together, 'except, of course, when I am out. Then it is closed to everyone, without exception.'

'We won't bother you again.'

'It's been real,' professed Kuki, a phrase she had picked up from a recent lyric.

'But remember, if you are arrested by the police, don't expect me to bail you out.'

Louis answered from the depths of his helmet, which was already in place. 'In this life, it's every man for himself. You taught me that long ago, Uncle René.'

'Every woman for herself too,' laughed Kuki.

'Aren't you going to wear your helmet?'

'No, speed's much more exciting without one. And then, how am I to dry my hair?'

'They could pick you up for not wearing one.'

'Come on. Andiamo. We're under starter's orders!'

M. René accompanied them to the door, taking care to remain inside the house, as if disowning them.

'One final word,' Louis shot back from the foot of the stairs.

'You don't have to tell me,' replied M. René quietly, and added, with evident distaste, 'Fuck you, Uncle René.'

'I would have left the Uncle out.'

Kuki waved as René shut the door.

Now, where was he when his train of thought had been interrupted? He grimaced as he anticipated the infernal racket of the superbike on his drive. As it happened, the local train, stopping at all stations between Geneva and Sion, rattled by. It was while M. René was consulting his watch that the motorcycle sprang into life, and moved off slowly but noisily, its wheelspin as usual scattering pebbles onto the grass in negligent profusion. The noise took a long time to vanish, going from static revving-up to a gathering whine, a change of gear, and then a cradle-song for Wagnerian monsters as it attacked the upper register of the scale through a multitude of other gears. At last, silence, and a good riddance.

M. René entered the bathroom, which was, to his eyes, in a deplorable state. Water was still dripping from the shower head, soap had fallen to the floor, there was wetness everywhere. The radiator on which they had dried their clothes was covered in bits of grass and earth, and an odour of warm leather hung disagreeably in the air. He would

have to explain the unusual circumstances to Mme Radibois
when she came to clean, every other morning, without, of
course, going into details. A reflection on the youth of today
was a sufficient gesture towards the truth. Mme Radibois,
not the most original of women, would certainly counter
with examples from her family life, which had to be avoided
at all cost.

He glanced at the telephone, and sat by it, remarking
that he was awaiting a call. He also unpacked his new
acquisition, fondled it as though it were a musical instrument, and read the detailed instructions. It was during this
highly concentrated task that another image invaded his
consciousness, that of Kuki entering the room after her
shower, and that elaborate thumbs-up sign. He remembered Louis' febrile reaction, and immediate desire to leave.
Why had they come in the first place? Kuki was the kind of
girl one hides from one's relatives, not the sort one parades
before them. It made no sense.

# V

THE NEXT day, early in the morning, the telephone rang. It was the Chief of Police, Urs Mildenegger.

'Have you been expecting my call?' he asked.

'No,' lied M. René, 'should I have been?'

'It doesn't matter one way or the other. Are you free for lunch?'

M. René hesitated. 'Not really,' he replied. 'But I can always wriggle out of something.'

'I wish you would,' said the Chief. 'One o'clock? Le Mouton Enragé?'

'Must it be there?'

'I know it is one of your favourites.'

'I had never been there before.'

'Is that so? Well, I'm sure it's one of your favourites now.' And he hung up.

M. René resolved not to be over complicated. Perhaps he was wrong to have said that he had had an appointment. He had not even convinced himself, and the secret of lying was to convince oneself. It is the first step to convincing others. He sighed. How often he had had to lie in his life. It was part of the job, part of the vocation. 'Your husband, with a girl? But Madame, I assure you, when he left the hotel, he was alone. He said he'd be back in half an hour. That I can't say, Madame, I go off duty at eight o'clock. That's not what who said? The detective? Madame, if I have to testify in a court of law, I will be forced to say that he left the hotel unaccompanied.' And so it went on, protecting reputations, and receiving emoluments in a cupped hand without embarrassing the donor by looking down before he had gone.

And invariably, the compensation was far from commensurate with the invaluable service rendered. One thing which experience had taught him was that what those who succeeded in business and those who cheated on their wives have in common is their stinginess. Basically, they are animals who are satisfied with a life in two dimensions. An added dimension, that of humanity, only complicates the issue, and gets in the way of success by conquest, by outsmarting, success at the expense of others. He rediscovered the roots of his revolt, a life dedicated to the service of the base desires and bulging pockets of others. He smiled grimly, pleased with himself in a quiet way, and determined to arrive early, in order to forestall any new low tricks.

It was half past twelve when he arrived at the Mouton Enragé by taxi. In the parking lot, he saw a single car with a driver reading a newspaper at the wheel. Half an hour early? It was not to be believed. He went to the door of the restaurant on tiptoes, and after a pause, pushed it open violently, half expecting the Chief of Police to be on all fours, affixing another microphone under a table. Instead he found him seated, as before, with a half-finished cup of coffee before him. He was half way through a malodorous weed described as a Swiss stump. He attempted to rise laboriously.

'Don't get up.'

'This table all right for you? It doesn't carry too many memories?'

'Memories? We sat over there, as you know. You're very early.'

'So are you, but I was earlier.'

The Chief smiled, and did not stop when M. René reached under the table to feel for obstructions, examined the cushions, and shook the salt and pepper to make sure they were not microphones in disguise. He even rose to examine the lighting fixtures. When he finished, Mildenegger produced a tape recorder from his pocket, and laid it on the table. 'I prefer to use this under normal conditions,' he said. 'Have you any objections?'

'I have,' replied M. René, tartly.

'In that case—' Mildenegger prepared to return the recorder to his pocket.

'No, no. Once it is out, leave it out, please. On the table.' M. René made sure it was switched off.

'Anything else I can do for you?'

'Have you another one on your person?'

'No. You can go through my pockets if you wish.'

'I prefer to take your word for it.'

'I only have my service revolver in a hip holster. Would you feel happier as its custodian for the duration of lunch?'

'I wouldn't know what to do with such a barbarous toy.'

'I have never used it. I agree with you.'

Just then the owner of the restaurant appeared with two immense menus, with comic strip drawings of enraged sheep on the cover. 'Benvenuti, Signori,' said Vittorio Campella, the owner, 'I am glad to see you both back. It gives me great confidence.'

M. René spoke, while pretending to study the menu, and thereby take the curse off his words. 'It shouldn't,' he said quietly, 'because however excellent your cooking, this is the last time I shall ever come here.'

This was like a slap in the face.

'The last time?' stammered Campella.

'The last time. And I am only here today because I was invited, under the mistaken impression that this was my favourite restaurant. I will not fall into such a trap a second time.'

'Were you treated badly?'

'Extremely badly. You had no right to become an accomplice in a trick which I believe incidentally to be perfectly illegal.'

'Perfectly illegal,' confirmed Mildenegger.

Surprised, M. René continued, 'You allowed your restaurant to be bugged, so that a private conversation could be overheard without the knowledge of the parties concerned. You must have received the Chief of Police long before the arrival of your first clients. He had all the time in the world to install a microphone under our table, the quiet one we booked by telephone. Then he must have enjoyed your hospitality by sitting in the kitchen, out of sight, until we had taken our places, and begun our dinner. Then, and only then, did he creep out and take his place here, where we found him on our way out.'

The Chief shook with silent laughter. 'You should be the Chief of Police, not I. It is an excellent analysis.'

'Am I right?'

'In every detail, but all this is not poor Campella's fault. It's entirely mine.'

'You understand, the police,' pleaded poor, distraught Campella. 'Everyone wants to help the police. There is such crime all over the place. It only needs someone to show us a document, and we become slaves of law and order, eager to help. Remember, I had not seen you then. I did not know what the Chief was expecting. Looking at you now, I would never think of you as a criminal, and I might even have raised my voice in objection—'

There seemed no way to stop the flood of Campella's determination to justify his complicity in this illegal action, other than to order.

'I'll start with the pâté de campagne, and then the boeuf bourguignone.'

Campella took the order.

'As to my friend here,' M. René went on, 'he doesn't eat, if memory serves me right. I notice he's already on the coffee.'

'Who told you I don't eat?' laughed the Chief.

'You did.'

'Did I? Oh yes, quite right. That is the only detail missing from your analysis. I ate in the kitchen before your arrival.'

'At six in the evening?'

'I can eat at any time.'

'In other words, you lied about coffee being your staple dish?'

'I lied. Is that so dreadful?'

'No. In the course of the day, I am forced to lie fairly frequently.'

The Chief leaned forward to a disagreeable proximity, and muttered: 'That adds spice to our conversation.'

And without elaborating further, he said in a louder voice: 'I'll take the Iranian caviar with blini, and then the rosbif à l'Anglais.'

'Caviar?' echoed M. René.

'Would you care for some?' the Chief enquired. 'It is the police which pays. The civil authorities know better than to question any accounts.'

'No, I'll stick with my pâté,' insisted M. René, after a pause for temptation. His decision seemed to give him some moral advantage, at least in his own mind. The Chief was probably insensitive to such niceties.

The meeting of very different minds only really began when the food arrived.

'Perhaps you can enlighten me about the reason for this invitation,' asked M. René, not without a glimpse at the caviar being heaped onto the blini.

'What are you up to?' asked the Chief, munching.

'Up to?'

'And what do you constitute?'

'We are a group of independent citizens who have broken no law.'

'Admittedly, but your final aim may be entirely different. It may even, conceivably, interfere with the work of the police. You have done nothing to be ashamed of, or even to be proud of yet. I am only concerned about the future.'

'Is it usual for the police to be involved in the detection of non-existent crime?'

'Put like that, no,' chuckled the Chief, but immediately

adopted a much harder tone. 'I'll put you out of your misery. The Emir of Djabbadieh was expelled from Switzerland the day before yesterday. As you know, there has been a palace revolution. Several of his cousins are wrestling for the throne.'

'You sent him back to a certain death?'

'Portugal has accepted him. They have always been very good about exiled rulers. He should be safe in Estoril, with plenty of sheep to devour, and we won't mention the rest of his appetites.'

'But what was he doing in Switzerland?'

'You were right. There was a link with Mr Ivanov, via the Clinique Ma Joie. Kazakhstan is eager to sell some of its old Soviet hardware before it rusts into dust and creates local havoc. They also want to survive by making a legitimate profit out of stuff nobody in their right mind wants any more.'

'Are you saying Djabbadieh is not in its right mind?'

'It is full of romantic hotheads of the kind at the moment struggling for power. The Emir seemed to share their ambitions, and so came here himself to undergo a complete check-up. One whiff of hospital discipline, and he moved out to the Hotel Bellerive Davel, in order to indulge the joys of an infinitely wealthy life in relative freedom. He rather forgot his mission.'

'Which was?'

'To arrange a transfer of samples as the first step to a large armaments deal.'

'This is where the poor idiot sitting on his bed in the Clinique Ma Joie and reading pornographic magazines comes in.'

The Chief nodded approval. 'Once again, excellent

analysis. He left the clinic for a long walk in the Parc des Eaux Vives, wearing blue jeans and a checked shirt instead of traditional Arab dress. He sat on a bench, where he was joined by Mr Ivanov. They had an animated conversation, which was not surprising, since Mr Ivanov speaks no Arabic and the fellow in jeans speaks neither Kazakh nor Russian. English, which should normally be the lingua franca, is only vaguely comprehended by either, and their accents are so defiantly different that it precluded all possibility of communication.'

'The police followed them?'

'We now have extensive photographic evidence of the contact.'

'And what is it all about? Nuclear fission?'

'Even uglier, if that is possible. Chemical warfare. Poison.'

'Good God.'

'We arrested the fellow in jeans, with the trunk full of samples which Ivanov had sent over. They were never detected entering Switzerland because they were covered by diplomatic immunity. They were carelessly enough packed to have killed a sniffer dog. It begs many questions.'

'The case is closed?'

'More or less. Ivanov will be expelled to Kazakhstan, and the Federal Council is bound to protest. As to the pornographer of the Clinique Ma Joie, he is under arrest, enjoying no kind of immunity, and being found in the possession of highly dangerous material.'

'What will happen to him?'

'Oh, several months or years in prison. Years, more likely, as an example.'

'An example?' said M. René wrily. 'The ex-Emir enjoys

massages in Estoril, Ivanov waits for another assignment in Alma-Ata, and the poor patsy found in possession of the samples pays the price. Knowing the high moral posture of Swiss institutes of correction, he won't even have access to more recent copies of dirty magazines.'

'Tragic, isn't it,' smiled the Chief. 'And how do you feel, now that I have let you into every secret?'

M. René thought for a while. Then he looked the Chief straight in the eye.

'You have not let me into every secret,' he said, quietly.

'Perhaps not. Every relevant secret.'

'How do I feel? Mixed emotions. On the one hand, a certain sadness that an episode is over, unresolved as far as I am concerned. On the other hand, a certain satisfaction at having arrived at conclusions not so different from yours without any professional help whatsoever.'

'It's true. There is a considerable power of deduction evident in your conclusions, but I still fail to understand why you go to such lengths. There are several references in your . . . rather, in *my* tape, to your desire to help the police. Am I right?'

M. René became as factual, as down to earth as possible. 'It has always been clear to me that it is not in our power to affect arrests or to punish crimes. All we have are means of furnishing proof, of sniffing out trails, of informing – by means as scrupulously legal as yours are, at times, illegal.'

'Our power, you say. Whose power? And whose idea was this arbitrary collection of elderly justicers?'

M. René smiled. 'It was my idea. It still is my idea. Why do you ask?' The smile lived on, but it was grimmer than before. 'I'll tell you the reasons behind it, but perhaps you'll be too young to understand.'

'I'm 59, on the verge of retirement. That's as old as a civil servant gets, before beginning his second childhood on half pay.'

'Well, I'm past 70. That's the end of life as prescribed by the scriptures. That's the moment borrowed time begins. You look back at the journey and begin to question the values which governed it. I worked my way up from kitchen help to office boy to lift operator at a time when lifts still needed humans to guide them. I ended up Concierge, then Chief Concierge, finally elected, democratically, as Permanent President of the International Brotherhood of Concierges and Hall Porters. A success story if ever there was one, within the narrow limits of an accepted way of life. But what lies beyond those limits? Desires begin to manifest themselves which have never existed before. One knows the map by heart, where one is, where one has been. All that's missing is the scale. And without a scale there is no way of knowing where one is going, in the little time which is left. What is the purpose of existence? It's as banal, as conventional, as that. Is it part of life to endlessly twist the facts for the greater serenity of the paying customer, to cater to the whims of despicable imbeciles whose only claim to fame is their extravagant solvency, to be the sugar daddy of call girls? I earned the gratitude of a tiny fraction of humanity, but at what cost to the soul?'

The Chief sighed. 'I think I know what you mean. After all, I listened to your conversation, quite illegally. We did far worse to those poor imbeciles, the Emir, Ivanov, and the other. Perhaps it's because I'm so close to retirement that I'm a little casual about details like strict legality. Put it this way, five years ago I would not have used such methods against either of them, or against you. I would have been too obedient to the rules. As a result I would not have been in a position to nip a sinister plot in the bud, nor would we be having this delightful lunch at this moment. I recognize that the chaos is upon me, but since the chaos brings results, must I be opposed to it? Anarchy is a wonderful relief after the bondage of duty. Don't you agree?'

'I don't know. I don't know. Anarchy has its dangers, one brick displaced is followed by another. God only knows where it may lead.'

'Relief, as I said.'

'The kind of relief that ends up in madness, beating up of prisoners, the shooting of those alleged to be attempting escape, the executions in self-defence?'

The Chief shrugged briefly. 'Perhaps,' he said.

Then, he resumed his casual, investigatory tone, consulting a note. 'The gentlemen you call Mr Butler, Monsieur Alonso, and Astigas, is it?'

'Arrigo.'

'Arrigo, I can understand. You are all men of a certain age, and with a certain, very similar experience. I can imagine that they all rose to your bait. But Fräulein Schanderbach?'

M. René admitted that she had not been his idea, in fact, that she was a recent acquisition.

'Who found her?' asked the Chief.

'Mr Butler.'

'Mr Butler? Interesting.'

'Why?'

The Chief explained that she was rather younger than all the other participants, and then, of course, she was a woman.

'I had noticed. I got the impression that you are old acquaintances.'

The Chief grunted. 'Yes.'

There was a long pause, which seemed to refine M. René's thoughts.

'She's a remarkable person,' the Chief said at last. 'Not always the most reliable.'

'Oh?'

'Not in a professional sense, you understand. From all I hear, she is exceptional at her job. Many hotels would be only too ready and glad to tempt her away from her present job. But she is also extremely loyal, and of quite exceptional intelligence.'

'Well then, in what way is she unreliable?'

The Chief sighed deeply. 'How many times have I heard the story of her being sung to sleep by her mother, singing old marching songs dear to the communists of the period, and her mother not realizing she was not asleep, because her mother's eyes were overflowing with tears.'

'You mean it's not true?'

'The truth is much more terrible, and far less flattering to our nation.'

M. René searched the Chief's inexpressive face for clues.

'Does the name Otzinger mean anything to you?'

'Otzinger? Wasn't there a trial?'

'Yes, and Major Imthal?'

'Yes, wait a minute. Something that happened during the war?'

'Colonel Otzinger was in command of a frontier crossing on the German border. Major Imthal was his second in command. There was no love lost between the two men. They were of completely different temperaments. Otzinger a military automaton, of a kind who, while being profoundly Swiss and patriotic, wished in his heart that he had an army as large as the German one to serve in, and on which to vent his devotion to duty. He was, if you like, as far from our anarchy as a man can possibly be.'

'That is merely a lack of imagination.'

'That in any case. Major Imthal was the opposite, a humanist, a romantic, open-minded. The order came from above, hard-hearted and panic-stricken at the same time, to return refugees to their destiny at the hands of the Nazis.'

'Oh my God,' muttered M. René, who saw what was coming.

'Agnes was five years old at the time, and very advanced for her age. She had seen horrors, and had managed to hide them in a compartment in her heart. She has always had the same unruffled exterior. She preserves it to this day. Well, despite the fact that Frau Schanderbach and her daughter had found refuge in Switzerland, Otzinger decreed that, together with many others, they would be returned to Germany. The mother pleaded at least to be able to leave her daughter on Swiss soil. According to evidence which emerged in court later, Otzinger is alleged to have said, before witnesses, that it would be inhuman, even under these circumstances, to separate mother and child. Imthal had been deeply shocked by this perversion of elementary norms of compassion, and spirited the child away from a dormitory, the refugees' last night on Swiss soil. He had found sanctuary for the child in the home of friends and sympathizers.

'Imthal's secret organization was evidently at least as well organized as Swiss intelligence, and thank God for it. A considerable number of refugees, Jew and Christian, had already slipped through the official nets. Imthal promised to attempt a similar coup with Frau Schanderbach, and it was not his fault that he failed. The events were playing on Otzinger's nerves. He felt himself responsible for the evasions. His bad temper gave a dangerous edge to his vigilance. Even at the expense of sleep, he tried to be everywhere at once, not to trust his assistants. They were Lieutenant Bompoz and Captain Zocco. They turn up again later in the saga. As the refugees were lining up to enter the buses which were taking them back to the border, waiting, praying – a scene heartbreakingly ugly – Otzinger was counting them aloud from a list on a clipboard. They were already numbers rather than people, or indeed bank accounts. Frau Schanderbach hung back in the hope that Imthal would work his last minute miracle. She was clinging to a large object wrapped in a blanket. Otzinger spotted her, and yelled: "Get in line, you!" And then, more contorted: "I know you, you and your pleading – what's that in your arms? Your child is old enough to walk."

'Despite her efforts, he seized the object, tore away the blanket, and revealed bundled brown paper, which fell to the floor. He looked down for a moment, then struck her face with all the power of his arm. A Swiss soldier made an instinctive gesture to protect her, a movement which Otzinger caught out of the corner of his eye. Otzinger froze, like an animal which suddenly recognizes danger. "What do you want?" he asked in a small, almost timorous, voice. "Sergeant, put this man under arrest!" he shouted, beside himself, and he addressed the refugees, who had interrupted their exodus to watch these events with a mixture of despair and hope. "In case any of you have any questions, this is Switzerland, not Germany. We mind our own business and let Germany mind hers. According to the instructions of my superiors, you are Germany's business, not ours! March!"

M. René hardly dared to ask what happened next.

'Next?' The Chief shrugged his shoulders. 'Frau Schanderbach disappears from the story for ever. Imthal doesn't survive much longer in his role of guardian angel. He is arrested and court-martialled. It became a *cause célèbre*. His defence he conducted himself, basing it on human instincts alone. That, and simple morality. You know how powerful such platforms are when opposed by the logic of military law. He disobeyed orders, it came down to that. He was disgraced and kicked out of the army, despite the efforts of a few politicians, intellectuals and priests, who disliked the peremptory nature of the judgement. They managed to keep their contentions alive. Suffice it to say that Imthal died, unexonerated. Some time ago, the army, while not admitting that there had been an error of judgement, at least conceded that there were two sides to the question. The reason for this change was that an enquiry had opened, questioning the comportment of Otzinger at the time – nearly thirty years after the events. Isn't that typical of the Swiss? Our fault is never our lack of courage or our cowardice. It is quite simply our incredible slothfulness at being anything at all. We simply cannot be hurried into either heroism or villainy.'

'Was Otzinger tried? – I can't remember.'

'He didn't live long enough. He died in his hotel room, poisoned. The poison was arsenic.'

'Was it murder?'

'The matter was never resolved. Suicide seemed probable because of the likelihood of his disgrace. The autopsy brought us nothing except the cause of death. But it always seemed to me strange that a career soldier, especially one who bore an unfortunate resemblance to some of the villains in the Dreyfus case, should choose such a means of suicide. A smoking revolver seemed much more likely. There is something feminine about arsenic as a solution.'

'Feminine?' M. René looked piercingly at the Chief.

'Oh, I forgot to mention,' said the Chief, avoiding the look, 'the hotel in question is the Bellerive Davel.'

Slowly, M. René asked: 'And you suspect—?'

'I suspect no one yet. I have no reason. But, of course, I have had ideas at the back of my mind for years.'

'Just a minute. Agnes was saved by Major Imthal at the age of five. How could she have known about the identity of her mother's tormentor?'

'Good question. The little girl was a source of amusement for the short time she was detained at the border because, unlike most girls of that age, she had a handbag, of which she was inordinately proud. It was a miniature handbag, of course, of atrocious quality, expressive of all Germany's basic misery at the time, ersatz leather, with a tarnished metal chain. But she handled it with all the premature assurance of a lady, occasionally taking out a mirror to look at herself, licking her lips, arranging her hair. She was never without that handbag.'

'Where is it now?'

'God only knows. At the time of Otzinger's death, we conducted a thorough search of her belongings. It was nowhere to be found. Her patient indifference to our investigations convinced me that we would not find it.'

'What do you think it contained?'

'Some sort of message from her mother, identifying her three tormentors.'

'Three?'

'You remember I mentioned Lieutenant Bompoz and

Captain Zocco? Lieutenant Bompoz died trying to protect
his dog from the gendarmes. He failed. Soon after, they
found him dead.'

'Arsenic?'

'Yes. He was also under investigation. This time the
matter was simplified by the fact that he left a letter which
could be construed as a suicide note, although there was no
hint of any rash act in view. He wrote that he had difficulty
in sleeping, that his military advancement had come to a full
stop. The letter was addressed to no one in particular. This
added to the impression that it was written to be read after
his disappearance.'

'And the other one, what's his name?'

'Zocco. A different case altogether. He was a witness to
all those events, and was probably also for the high jump.
He took leave just before the investigation began, with his
people in the Ticino. He drank some wine in the village
café, miles away from here, in a place called Magadino. He
toppled over and died.'

'Arsenic?'

'One of the ingredients.'

'But it happened, as you say, far from the Bellerive
Davel.'

'Yes, at a time when our friend was on holiday too.'

'Where?'

'With friends, in the Valais, near Sion. People called
Stobs.'

'They confirmed it?'

'Yes, but she had her car with her, and was not often in
for meals.'

There was a silence.

'To come back to the handbag—' said M. René.

'Ah. It's only a supposition, but what if it contained a scribbled note from the mother, with the names of the three Swiss officers who carried out the order to send them both back to Germany? A note which the child would gradually understand as she grew up. It is a somewhat wild guess, I know, but a woman in desperation might well do the equivalent of committing a message to the sea, contained in a bottle, a last sad effort to make her protest heard. One thing is sure, from Imthal's evidence at his court martial and the evidence of the kind people with whom the child was secretly lodged, the Bruetschi family, who told investigating journalists that the little girl caused much amusement by being categorical in her utter refusal to be separated from her handbag, even hiding it or keeping it in sight during bathtime or supper. It was this which led me to the idea that there must be something in it of particular importance to the child, which the child was still too young to understand.'

'And you never succeeded in finding it—'

'Never. My theory may be utterly worthless. It could have been discarded long ago, like a toy which has been outgrown.'

There was a long silence.

'Well, it has been an excellent lunch, and most instructive.' The Chief rose with difficulty, the shape of the booth standing in the way of his corpulence. 'Have I your permission to replace my tape recorder in my pocket?' he asked.

'Don't be silly.'

'Oh, before I forget.' The Chief produced a cassette from the same pocket.

'What's that?'

'For you. The offending tape of your lunch here. I made a copy for you in case you wish to refresh your memory about things that were said here, and the manner in which they were said.'

M. René took the tape. 'That is most thoughtful.'

'My car is outside. May I give you a lift?'

'No, thank you,' replied M. René, pleasantly. 'If I am seen in a car with the Chief of Police it might damage my reputation irrevocably.'

The Chief spotted the drop of wine in his glass. He raised it. 'To anarchy.'

There was no wine left in M. René's glass. 'To anarchy,' he replied. 'Such a toast is safer without wine.'

# VI

When he returned to his house, M. René immediately sat down to listen to the tape the Chief of Police had given him. As he suspected, the sound was dreadful. It was difficult to make out anything at all. After much searching, fast forward and rewind, he managed to find the portions which interested him. He heard Agnes say, not very clearly, but recognizably: 'What can we do but watch and wait? Evidently, you do not wish to take more positive action?' He stopped the tape, ran it back, listened to the words again. The Police Chief had done his job of stimulating doubts too well not to inspire resentment. It was clearly absurd, although he recollected very well the astonishment which had greeted her observation at the time. Nothing was clearly said by Mildenegger, but the implication was clear. Agnes was an unpunished murderess. Unpunished because uncaught. Too clever by half, not that that was much of an achievement. He ran the tape forward.

'It is not up to us to sit in judgement on such people,'

he heard himself saying. 'Merely to bring their activities to the attention of the appropriate authorities.'

Pompous idiot. In his mind, he could see the Chief of Police nodding weightily, giving him a good point, that is if he could decipher the result of his own technical inadequacy. But first things first. Could Agnes indeed be a poisoner? How far fetched was the theory of the little handbag? Very far fetched if she and her mother were indeed separated when she was only five years old. No, it was preposterous. Although . . .

He left the tape aside for a while and looked at the sky. It was a neutral enough background for thought. The high clouds were moving lazily against their blue background, without haste. 'This is where we came in,' reflected M. René, almost aloud. The whole promising adventure had come to more than a grinding halt, all those painfully acquired clues, with their titillating aura of conspiracy, now confiscated like toys from children at bedtime. All their work, pre-empted, no point in going on with this arbitrary collection of peculiar ageing professionals, who were admittedly acquainted, but who had no reason whatever to know each other better than they already did. M. René shuddered at the idea of seeing M. Alonso again, or M. Arrigo, or above all, Mr Butler, with his appalling dignity, his wavering, and his almost unbelievable son, the socialist Member of Parliament.

Only Agnes was different. She had another dimension, no doubt the consequence of tragic events, but kept alive by a striking independence of spirit, as though the pain had been sublimated into irony. As much as he did not wish to take up where he had left off with the men, too easily led for comfort, a little short on intelligence, so, he admitted to himself, he wanted to see her again. To satisfy his curiosity? He guessed that the curiosity would last a long time, there would be much to satisfy. No, he reflected, he was not even eager to know if she had taken the law into her own hands. He didn't care. He smiled to himself, a little recklessly. Some people are incurably inquisitive about details of that kind. He was not, he made up his mind. He just wanted to see her again. Why, and to whom did he have to give a reason? Contact with the police always caused the mind to function in an unhealthy way. The good guys and the bad, with no provision made for the vast majority bent on survival in between.

Just then, the phone rang. It was Agnes. His first reaction was not to listen to what she said, but to take a private pleasure in the sound of her voice.

'What did you say?'

'It's Agnes.'

'I know that. I thought you said something else.'

'How funny you are! What's the matter? Have you been asleep?'

'No. No, daydreaming.'

'That's what I do too.' (A merry little laugh, a mite breathless.) 'Listen, we must meet.'

'Whenever you wish.'

'Have you spoken to the Big Chief?'

'Yes. He invited me to lunch, in fact.'

'I was sure he would, sooner or later. Later rather than sooner. To let you sweat it out, incommunicado. Did he mention me?'

'Listen, is it better if I ring you back?'

'What difference does it make?'

'I have a mobile phone now. I haven't used it yet. Let me try it out.'

'Very well.' Agnes was amused by this.

'Where are you?'

'In the street.'

'OK. Right away.'

He was slightly nervous, trying out this new intrusion into his isolation, and therefore was especially irritated when a disembodied but authoritative voice told him that the number he was looking for did not exist, and advised him to consult the phone book. He thought he had committed the number to memory. Had he remembered the numbers in the wrong order? He had to search among his credit cards to find the slip of paper on which he had noted the number. This time she answered. 'What have you been up to?'

M. René mumbled some excuse, not the truth, and suggested a meeting in a public place.

'We cannot meet before darkness has fallen, and I suggest I come to your place.'

'To my place?'

'Yes. I have a very good idea. I will cook you dinner. I will bring everything with me, wine, bread, butter – everything. You can sit and watch television. I'll call you when it's ready. Shall we say eight o'clock?'

'Very well, eight o'clock, if you insist. But, in that case, don't spoil everything by parking outside my place.'

There was a moment.

'Do I give you the impression of being stupid?'

'Anything but.'

'All right then. Till then.'

Once again, she put an end to the conversation in almost peremptory fashion, as though the last word belonged to her by right.

He switched off in silence. Instinctively, he disliked the idea of having his privacy invaded, like when the young

people decided to use his garden as a lupanar, on the simple
pretext that he was not home, and they had to do what
came naturally to while away the time. As a consequence,
everything in the house was dripping wet, towels used which
would have lasted him two weeks or more, bits of soil and
grass in the waste-paper basket, stuck to other refuse. He very
rarely invited people for drinks – or only a few – like the
friends who had to a man rejected his special cocktail, but that
was different. Four glasses to wash out, and the episode was
over. But she would bring everything with her, tidily packed
as only a housekeeper could, a strange table cloth, bottles,
condiments; a regular picnic, and it meant only one thing
once no account was taken of the possible pleasures of such an
event: mess, disorder, a spanner in the silent works. But then,
on the other hand, he was to dine tête-à-tête with a suspected
murderess. That held its own nefarious excitement. Would he
survive the encounter? Would the wine she promised to bring
be laced with arsenic, to taste, as they say? His thoughts were
more by way of amusing himself. He did not take any of this
heavy handed hint dropping of the Chief of Police seriously,
while always leaving a door open for any possibility. If his
life had taught him anything, it was that there is no law
against either cretins stumbling upon the truth, or wise men
making fools of themselves, just as there is nothing to prevent
a proven criminal from having an idea of genius, or one of
established uprightness from causing injury or even death to
many innocent people. Judgements which aspire to finality are
invariably open to reversal after the passage of time has played
havoc with assessments of the circumstances surrounding the
crimes. For M. René, the police were always under pressure
to prove a point, and therefore as unreliable as all others under
such an obligation, stockbrokers, entertainers, industrialists,

lawyers, all of those wedded to evidence of success as a motivating force. In that sense, tramps and drop-outs are far more reliable witnesses of the moral scene. Only their appearance stands in the way of their objectivity, of their wisdom.

He went to the dining room, and began planning his contribution to the coming events as a grand master might contemplate a chess board before the pieces are out of their box. Many different scenarios suggested themselves to him in the course of the afternoon, some of them indefinably erotic, which he rejected out of hand, even chiding himself for such unexplained waywardness. He drew the curtains a little earlier than he normally would have done, lighting the room softly and subtly. He passed the whole house in review, as one does when a visitor is expected, seeing it through fresh eyes. Anything too personal, like a photo of himself and his wife crossing Lake Leman on a paddle steamer in summer clothes, he put into a drawer. Then, he went out onto the little porch at the back of the house in order to further analyse his thoughts in darkness. There was only just over an hour to go, and yet time had not gone too slowly. He had not watched the pot. There was no shortage of things to think about.

It was not really the sanctity of his place of residence which made him nervous, as he had for a moment supposed. He had not been alone in it for long enough to warrant such a feeling. Admittedly, during his wife's life, especially during her decline, he often succeeded in imagining that he was alone, until interrupted by an unmusical croak from her bedroom. When he answered the call, he always knew what he would find. A face both sleepy and self-indulgent, moist with perspiration, tangled hair spread over the pillow like the springs of a light car, steeped in oil. And then, demands which were difficult to decipher, breathless and disjointed, uttered without so much as a glance in his direction. That podgy hand with its huge wedding ring, biting into the flesh, an insult to the sanctity of matrimony, trying to help the hesitant flood of words with circular motions in the air. It was a sickening sight, an antidote to all thoughts of tenderness, of duty even. The solemn row of medicine bottles, coloured like miniature tallboys in a chemist's shop, and a spoon, upturned, a little sticky liquid still inside, made solid by specks of dust which had settled there. Many memories were preserved not with the veneer of affection which permeates even difficult moments of a relationship, but as exhibits in a range of the indifferent and the insensitive. The moment of her death, for instance.

He had gone to her room simply because she had not uttered her characteristic croak for rather too long. He entered her room without knocking, and noticed her, immobile, her eyes riveted onto a spot on the ceiling. Only a spilled bottle of blue liquid suggested that something was wrong. He recognized at once that she was dead and, quite unsurprised, wondered what he should do next. He had frequently seen in the cinema how to close the eyes of the deceased, by drawing a hand across the lids. The idea filled him with revulsion, and he thought in terms of words he would have used had there been any need for them. 'Let them do it!'

He had to look up the number of Dr Uelsheimer.

'You think she's dead, M. René? Good God, man, can't you tell?'

'I've nothing to compare her condition with, Doctor. I have to do largely with the living.'

'Have you felt her pulse?'

'No. She seems to be staring at something on the ceiling.'

'I'll be right over.'

Half an hour later, Dr Uelsheimer was there. And what did he do?

With his hand, he drew the lids down. She now gave the requisite impression of peace.

M. René quelled his desire to laugh out loud.

'It was only to be expected,' said Dr Uelsheimer confidentially. 'Did her requests become more and more irrational?'

'Yes,' admitted M. René, with a sinking feeling in his stomach. At no time should her passing be interpreted as a relief for him. Now would come the intolerable chore of accepting condolences, of looking lost, of hiding his relief.

He banished it from his mind. He had shaken all the requisite hands, accepted pecks on the cheek from those who had never had the idea before, or since. He was alone, as though he had never been anything else. Alone, but preparing to hear another footfall in the house, even for a moment. A voice, humming in the kitchen. Another presence. He did not know.

Was man meant to be alone? Certainly not. But was man meant to be with the wrong person? Ah, there we come to all the misinformation of priests, those of the community deemed to be experts in the matter because totally lacking in experience. What nerve, to suggest to the adulterer that what God had united, let no man put asunder. How can even God, in His omniscience, know if a passing fancy or a moment of distraction is the real thing, or not? Hasn't God got enough to do without breaking His head with individual cases, sifting love from lust in the bleakness of a celestial sorting office?

Did he believe in a supreme being? Was it not playing to the gallery, like the rituals of death and posing for holiday snaps and all the dreary protocol of existence in communities? When people are driven together, they lose their identity voluntarily, in order not to be apparent. Be it a church, in which they all sing together, or at least move their lips, or an angry street demonstration, when they all shout the same slogan. It gives a wonderful feeling of security, this possibility to forget the words, because the others all know them. It's like a hot bath for the spirit, the splendid anonymity of a crowd. Congregations, that's what dictators need to survive, along with bishops. That's what they rely on, belief, trust, gullibility. But, honestly now, in the secret of his mind, and however he was brought up – raised is the fashionable transatlantic word – raised, like Lazarus – can a concierge sincerely believe in God? Is such belief compatible with the profession? St Peter, perhaps – the Concierge of Heaven – but God?

It was while his stream of consciousness was rippling away on its own, irrigating the channels of his brain, that the bell rang. Already? He looked at his watch. It was, in fact, one minute after eight. Strange. The 7.57 from Domodossola, stopping at Sion, Montreux, Vevey, Lausanne and Nyon, must have passed during his prolonged reverie without his noticing it. He entered the house, closed the door to the porch, and was on his way to the front door when the bell rang for a second time.

'All right, all right,' he cried out, infusing his voice with good humour. He opened the front door.

There she was, looking slightly different from how he remembered her. In the white light of the street lamps, she looked almost glamorous. A smile lit up her face.

'I saw no light from the outside,' she said, 'I thought you might have forgotten.'

'Forgotten?' he laughed. 'You underestimate me, and indeed yourself.'

'Can I come in, in case they are seated in the hedge, pursuing their enquiries?'

'Here, I'll take that.' He lifted her heavy suitcase, and closed the door behind her. 'My God, from where did you carry that?' he asked. 'Your car?'

'I didn't bring my car. I came by taxi. But only to the corner of the next road.'

'And you carried this all the way—?'

She interrupted him, by suddenly saying: 'Good evening, stranger,' embracing him, and forcing him to take her in his arms. He felt her ice-cold nose against his cheek, and sensed a subtle whiff of perfume.

'You must have carried that damn thing a hell of a way!'

'It'll be much lighter when it leaves,' she laughed, 'it's our dinner. Help me to take it to the kitchen. Then you're to show me where a few things are, and leave me to it. You're to sit in your den or whatever you consider your inner sanctum, watch television, or read, do whatever you like to do most. I don't want a peep out of you until I call you. All right?'

Here she was, giving orders again. A habit which could become obtrusive in the long run. But her face was so coaxing, so mischievous, it was hard not to take some pleasure from obedience. 'All right,' he agreed.

He put on his slippers as she insisted, and sat in the shadows, the images from the television flickering on his face. She had turned it on before retiring to the kitchen, turning the sound up. His only disobedience so far had been to turn the sound right down to nothing. He enjoyed sensing that the house was occupied again, and deciphering the noises as they came out of the creative workshop which a kitchen should be. There was running water, sizzling, chopping, stirring, a voice talking to itself, a laugh or two, not humorous, just to make a point, to express abstract delight. And at last Agnes herself appeared, dressed in a kind of kimono, with heavy earrings and a necklace, restrained in its modernity, a free interpretation of rock formations, with pearls, crystal and semi-precious stones cascading down what appeared to be golden lava. Her hair was up in a kind of petrified wilderness. M. René was not sure that he really liked what he saw, but she had certainly taken trouble. Perhaps a little too much trouble for his taste, but, of course, she belonged to the kind of people to whom one must give their head. She could be right in the long run. Who knows, what might be momentarily surprising, even shocking, could turn out to be an acquired taste? No, he told himself, not like Camembert or even oysters. More like Picasso.

'You look marvellous,' he heard himself saying.

'I'm not sure you approve,' she said coquettishly.

'I do. I do.'

'I made a bet with myself that you would not approve, but that you would say that I look marvellous.'

'Must you always win your bets?' he asked.

'No. No,' she replied after a moment's reflection. 'No, I sometimes prefer to lose them.'

And she searched his face with a slight frown of misgiving. He failed to understand what she meant, and so smiled reassuringly.

'You've certainly lost this bet,' he said. His remark sounded as empty, as unconvincing, as any innuendo of hers. Their hands found each other at this moment. Their fingers intertwined. 'Hungry?' she enquired.

'Ravenous,' he admitted.

'Come in.'

She steered him into his own dining room. A white lace cloth was spread over the table. Two crystal candelabra holding pale orange candles and a silver bowl half hidden under a mountain of pastel-coloured roses and a profusion of leaves were the centrepieces, surrounded by an army of glasses for different wines, and an unusual array of cutlery for only two people. A bottle of champagne on ice stood on the sideboard, and a Burgundy of the richest red had been decanted. M. René laughed in surprise.

'How many of us are there?' he asked.

'Two,' she replied. 'You don't really think I'd make this effort for more than two, do you?'

He looked into her eyes, suddenly too moved for words. It was she who lightened the atmosphere.

'Come and sit down. Where is your usual place? There may be only two of us, but tonight I am the waiter, the head waiter, the sommelier and the cook. Now, are you ready? Spread your serviette on your lap then. We start with caviar, blini, sour cream, chopped eggs, onions, and Russian vodka.'

'Are you out of your mind?' he asked.

'You wouldn't have it at lunch the other day because the police were paying for it. I trust you'll be my guest?'

'How do you know this?' he asked, startled.

But she had already returned to the kitchen to fetch the entrée.

# VII

THE MEAL itself was a culinary triumph, gradually shedding the tensions, the result of her desire to do well by an expert, and his futile efforts to help, which invariably led to a febrile command to relax, and allow things to happen as she had planned. When it was over, he found himself in what she had decided was his favourite chair, sitting in unwilling comfort with an unlit cigar between his fingers, which she had bought from a reputable tobacconist in case he smoked. He didn't. On an occasional table, a coffee, a balloon glass with cognac, and a tray of after-dinner mints. From the kitchen came not the noises of eager preparation, but the rather less exciting ones of washing up. She had, of course, refused to allow him to participate. At last it was over, and she came in, discarding her apron, a look of happy accomplishment on her face.

'Sit down. Sit down.' He tried to rise and pull up a chair. She pushed him back gently, and settled by his side, on a footstool.

'I will sit here, at your feet.'

'Listen, I'm embarrassed—'

'You shouldn't be. If you only knew what pleasure it gives me.'

He glanced at her upturned face.

'At all events, thank you for a memorable event in my slightly monotonous life,' he said, a little stiffly.

'How did you celebrate your last birthday?' she asked.

'I didn't. I don't.'

She laughed. 'Now you have. And do.'

'At my age, there's not much to celebrate,' he grunted.

'It has nothing to do with age,' she replied. 'When a person is alone, there is nothing to celebrate at any age. If there are two people, there's more and more to celebrate the older you get.'

'What, for instance?'

'The fact that you've succeeded, against all odds, in being as old as you are.'

M. René chuckled ruefully. 'I suppose so.' Then he changed his tone to one far more down to earth. 'Listen,' he went on, 'the dinner was far too good to discuss serious matters during it.'

'I agree.'

'There are meals of a quality which even kill conversation, but in that case, a prerequisite must be an inherent incompatibility between the diners. In this case, out of the question.'

'I hope so.'

'Oh yes. But I must say, you intrigued me when you phoned by saying that you had another lead. I presume you know that our amateurish plans linking the Emir of Djabbadieh to Mr Ivanov are all blown away. We played at detectives to no avail. We were too inexperienced. Yes, you must know this. If you know that I preferred the pâté to the caviar at lunch, you must know at least this.'

'Yes, but it's a pity to give up so easily. The police are not infallible. Far from it. They're often reduced to picking at dustbins for clues, like homeless tramps. Don't forget, most people, even those without guilty consciences, try to avoid them. They are not popular. They don't fit seamlessly into the community. That's why I found what you call the amateurism of our group so attractive.'

'Attractive? That's an odd word to choose.'

'I don't think so. Seen from the outside, that's what you were. Remember, I was the last to join you. And you did very well, for amateurs, without a secretariat, without anything the police need, weapons, fast cars and the rest. It would be a crying shame if you gave it all up now, because of a tiny reverse.'

'No, I have no stomach for it any more. Not one of them has bothered to call me since our dinner, with one solitary exception. You.'

'They were warned off by Mildenegger. You were quite right in your supposition. He made them feel they were doing something slightly illegal, and they dried up like clams. They all testified that you were the initiator, the ringleader, as Mildenegger put it. Don't let it worry you. He's pathetic.'

'Pathetic is not a description that comes immediately to mind.'

'You're not a woman.'

'Oh, I see.'

'At all events, I have another lead, as they say. There is a conference between various factions in ex-Yugoslavia

which has been in existence for several months now in
Geneva. They make no progress, which doesn't worry them,
since they are lodged in comfort, fed regularly, and paid
expenses in Swiss Francs. In short, it is not in the delegates'
interest to reach any positive conclusion, which would be
the regrettable outcome if the conference were to succeed.
They have their working lunches in a derelict palace by the
side of the lake, the staff being supplied in shifts by the Ecole
Hôtelière.'

'The Ecole Hôtelière? In other words, apprentices.'

'Exactly. As you can imagine in this day and age, fewer
and fewer of these apprentices are Swiss.'

'None of the new generation wish to work in jobs which
used to be dignified in my day, but today are considered
menial.'

'And so, who are the apprentices? Albanians, Cypriots,
Nigerians, Zimbabweans, Bosnians, you name it.'

'And so—?'

'I've been asking around, and there's a young Croatian
waiter from Istria, who passes for an Italian. They all had to
be checked by Serbian, Bosnian and Croat intelligence for
suitability. He badly wanted the job of serving at the lunch
table, and thought himself more likely to be accepted if he
pretended to speak only Italian. His name is Fiorino, which
helps the illusion. Well now, he claims to have overheard a
plot to kidnap the Bosnian delegate for ransom, or else just
to kill him. The latest version was that kidnapping is more
satisfactory, because it is less likely to hasten the end of the
conference.'

'The plotters were, of course, plotting in Serbo-Croat, or
whatever the language is called today.'

'Yes.'

'And while they were concentrating on helping themselves to green peas and string beans, it never occurred to
them that the waiter understood their words.'

'Right.'

M. René clapped his hands with excitement.

'That's what I had always imagined. That is what we are
really gifted at, by nature. Nothing complicated, like putting two and two together. Nothing which needs excessive
discretion on our part – we are not devious enough for that.
All it needs is the modicum of propriety which enables us
to profit from the indiscretion of others.'

'It's wonderful to see you enthusiastic again.'

M. René sobered up very quickly. 'Let me ask you
something.'

'Yes?' Agnes seemed concerned by this change of mood.

'You seem to have very close contacts with the police,
whatever you say about them, and about Mildenegger in
particular—'

'I never said anything.'

'You said that he is pathetic.'

'Oh, that.'

'If you have discovered a plot to kidnap a Bosnian
delegate, why not take the information where it belongs,
instead of bringing it to me?'

She grew harder. 'So long as the diplomat has not
been kidnapped, it really doesn't matter who has the
information. I have no confirmation that the report is
true. I referred to it as a lead, and no more. If I can
avoid contact with Mildenegger, I would prefer it. I never
call him. It is always he who calls me.'

'I don't wish for a moment to upset you.'

'You haven't upset me. I only slightly resent the fact

that we are spoiling the atmosphere after a lovely dinner by talking about him. You will have guessed by now that he is not my favourite subject of conversation.'

'I also guess that he has bothered you pretty consistently in the past, harassed you even, in today's jargon.'

She smiled sadly. 'A lot of good it did him.' She looked up at M. René, who appeared both young and old in the half light of his study. The lines on his face spoke of authority, of decision, but there was something boyish about the shape of his head and his spare frame.

'I think *Les Misérables* is probably his bedside book,' she said at last.

'Because he is convinced that you murdered three Swiss officers whose names escape me.'

She laughed and shook her head. 'Look, there's something I want to show you,' she said, and produced a hideous little handbag of ersatz leather with a corroded chain.

'That is the handbag you clutched to you as a child, and wouldn't let anyone look at.'

'Yes.'

He took it from her, only because she reached out for him to take it. 'May I open it?' he asked.

'Of course,' she answered casually.

He opened it. There was nothing inside, but the lining was frayed and torn in places. It was so fragile that he shut it again carefully.

'What did you expect to find?' she enquired.

'Nothing,' and then, as an echo, 'nothing. Did it ever contain anything?'

'Oh yes, a broken pencil which went for lipstick. The top of a biscuit tin, my mirror. A bunch of safety pins, my front door keys. Make-believe was necessary in the last days of the Third Reich. We had to imagine everything, not only playthings, pleasures, victories, everything.'

'I remember. It must have been terrible.'

'It was terrible for everyone. You must remember that too.'

'Worse for some than for others.'

'I wonder. Do you think I murdered those men?'

'No.' The question was so surprising, he wondered how to make his answer sound convincing. It was too late. He was stuck with a flat denial. The pause went on for ever.

She cajoled him. 'Be honest, now that it is over. Didn't you wonder if the champagne had a curious taste to it? Wasn't the Burgundy bitter on its first impact? Or the vodka? Was it more like kerosene than usual?'

In a flash, he knew how to respond. 'Yes. I will be honest. But I know that I have a permanent phobia about being poisoned, nothing to do with you. I'm never without litmus paper in my breast pocket, to dip into the alcohol when my host is momentarily out of the room.'

'What happens to litmus paper when dipped into poison?'

'I have reason to believe it becomes wet,' he said, with gravity.

She took his hand in hers, and studied his face gratefully.

'Thank you,' she whispered, 'you make me feel so free from pressure.'

He deemed the moment to have come.

'It has been a most wonderful evening,' he said, pressing her hand warmly. 'Now, how are we going to get you back? Shall I call a taxi?'

'They will be very surprised to see me at the hotel. I said I was away till tomorrow evening.'

'Why did you do that?'

'I don't know. Perhaps I thought . . . I really don't know. Have you a spare room?'

'No. I only have the room in which my wife . . . that is . . .'

'Didn't you share a room with her?'

'No. No, we had separate rooms.'

She squeezed his hand almost unbearably. It was, so it seemed, a gesture of solidarity, of commiseration.

All the alarm bells were ringing for M. René. He responded to none of her gestures.

'What is that room? The first on the right out of the door?'

'That is the room in which my wife died. It is locked. I never go in. It is miserably cold. And it smells of camphor.'

'No, I wouldn't dream – just find me a couch anywhere – anywhere except in your room. I'm sure you need your privacy. In any case, you're not used to anything else.'

'No, I'm not. And in any case, what are you going to do about all the necessary elements of an overnight stay? Toothbrush, pyjamas, all of that?'

'Forgive me.' She averted her eyes. 'I brought it all with me.'

He was profoundly shocked, but made light of his surprise. 'No wonder the bag was so heavy. Dinner, and a toothbrush as well?'

'But that's all,' she protested. 'I never wear pyjamas.'

'You sleep—?'

'—that's right, naked.' She laughed. 'What's so shocking about that? We didn't come into this world wearing pyjamas.'

'I wasn't thinking of that. You'll freeze to death. I keep the house well aired.'

'I have a dressing gown. I'm quite decent, except when I'm asleep.'

'Well—' He wavered slightly. A part of him felt betrayed, a part of him expected nothing else, one might almost say, hoped for nothing else. He rose a little awkwardly, and glanced at his study.

'There's no sofa in here. The Chesterfield would be far too uncomfortable.' He went into the living room, making sure that the curtains were drawn shut. 'I suppose I could give you sheets and a blanket, and make up a bed of sorts here.'

'Haven't I proved that I'm a better housekeeper than you?'

'That, in any case,' M. René laughed humourlessly.

He went to a cupboard, brought out sheets and an eiderdown, and laid them tidily on the sofa.

'It almost looks as though you were expecting me.'

'I was not.'

'You are just ready for any emergency.'

'Not even that. During my wife's terminal illness, I had to learn to do nearly everything myself.'

This successfully put an end to this phase of the conversation.

'Would you object,' M. René suddenly asked, as Agnes was rather unconvincingly making her bed, 'if I used the bathroom before you?'

'It's your house,' she replied, without looking up.

He hesitated. Reflecting that this sudden coolness had gone too far, being too great a contrast with the tentative warmth before, he remarked almost flippantly that it was

her fault; the superb cuisine and appropriate wines had
made him somnolent. 'Age catches up.' Since he evoked no
response, he went to the bathroom, and locked himself in.
It was a relief of a sort to be alone again. At least he was used
to it. He locked the door, then returned to ensure that he
had locked it properly. He washed, changed into pyjamas,
splashed some obscure English cologne on himself, from a
bottle embellished with several coats of arms, put on the
ancient dressing gown with a couple of rampant dragons
curling round his narrow hips, slid his feet into woolly
slippers, and was ready for the night. He emerged with
much rattling of keys in case she was changing. She was
not. Just sitting on her improvised resting place, glancing
casually at a magazine she had found lying around. She
failed to register his emergence from the bathroom. The
silence had acquired weight.

'What's the matter?' he asked.

'Nothing,' she said, without expression, as a matter of
fact.

He went to his door, and lingered there for a moment.

'Don't I get my goodnight kiss?' he asked, daring to
sound childish.

'I'm not sure you deserve it.'

'I got a kiss when you arrived.'

'That was a long time ago.'

'Well. Good night then.' He turned to enter his room.
She rose, and came over to him. She offered her cheek.
He kissed it dutifully, paternally. Her response was more
intense. He felt her hot breath on his cheek rather longer
than was comfortable, while her fingers dug into his arms
and back. Then she broke off and, as suddenly as she had
begun, picked up her toiletries and went to the bathroom,

shouting back as she went: 'I shan't be offended if you lock
yourself in.'

He flushed with anger.

'Don't be so perfectly ridiculous,' he said.

But she failed to rise to the bait, merely locking herself
into the bathroom as thoroughly, as ostentatiously, as he
had done. He lingered for a minute, then entered his room,
and shut the door. He was tempted for a moment to lock
it, but decided against it. It would, he felt, be playing into
her hands. He climbed into bed, turned out the light,
listened to every distant sound in the dark, and soon drifted
into sleep.

He awoke when he became aware of furtive noises in
the dark, accompanied by movements. A wavering light,
which he identified as a candle, concentrated his attention.
He had fallen asleep on his side, facing the door. When
the candlelight intensified, he narrowed his eyes to feign
contrived sleep. When it receded, he dared to open the
lids a little wider, in order to assess the new situation.
Good God, was she mad? He realized, as she was at
times silhouetted against the wall, that she was naked.
He watched her unashamedly for a moment. What was
she up to? He took a decision which seemed to him wise.
Making as much noise as sounded to his ears natural, he
gave the impression of a troubled sleep, culminating in a
twisting and turning, and an eventual readjustment, peace
rediscovered with his back to her. Now he could afford to
open his eyes wider, while taking care to breathe with the
serene rhythm of sleep. He saw the reflection of the candle
splashing weird shapes over the ceiling and the walls. What
was she looking for? And where had she found the candle?
As far as he knew, there was no candle in the house. Had

she brought it with her? Oh, of course – there were two
pale orange candles gracing the dinner table. Did they serve
a double function in this vast premeditated picnic? Or was
it much more than that? A seduction? A rape perhaps?

While he was thinking rapidly, the candle was suddenly
snuffed out, plunging the room into darkness. The smell
of smoke from the recently extinguished candle reached his
nostrils. There had been no sign of her leaving. No door. No
sound whatsoever. The silence was complete. Then, there
was the discreetest loosening of the covering blanket. Was
she out of her mind? His grip on the bedclothes tightened.
A tiny but inconclusive struggle culminated in an overt tug
of war. Being outside the bed, it was easier for her to liberate
the sheets on one side, and to infiltrate one bare foot. It was
cold and it made the pretence of sleep practically impossible
as it felt its way down his leg to the warmth he had created
for himself by his immobility.

'What's happening?' he asked, as though still half asleep.

'I'm cold,' she whimpered.

'This is a single bed,' he declared, more robustly.

'Double beds are for single people. Single beds for
couples,' she said, hoarsely, clinging to him in order not
to fall out, now that both feet were in bed, and the rest of
her body too.

He turned towards her, feeling, perhaps wrongly, that he
was less vulnerable in that position. She gave him no time
to think further. She clawed at him like a cornered animal,
tearing his pyjama top and ripping a button off. Despite the
desperate situation, he took a moment to think of how he
was going to explain the tear to Mme Radibois when she
came to do her housekeeping in the morning. That such
a thought should have entered his mind at all was a mark

of his discipline as a person, and of the priorities imposed by his profession. But it was not to last. Agnes, panting as though her life depended on it, tore at him, determined to attain a nakedness in him as complete, as irrevocable as her own.

Naturally, under such circumstances, logical reflection surrendered its priority to instinct, and almost to his surprise, his body began to react to both her passion and her proximity, undercutting all normal coherency. Abruptly, she mounted him, raising the bedclothes from their grip of the mattress, and carefully, almost daintily, steered him into her very being with a strange and challenging howl. He could think no further, all lucidity preempted by physical reactions outside his previous experience. A living thing, a weight and substance, was in communication with a part of himself he did not know existed. As the tension mounted, his instinct warned him that death was not far away, a death which was not frightening, but the logical end to the vac-illating adventure of living, something at last undeniable, something concrete, friendly in that it could be looked at in the eye. His hands explored the jockey who was riding him, the bones working within the pliant skin. He was beyond exhaustion, assailed by a breathlessness which seemed to be terminal. His only commensurate experience coming from his youth, cross-country runs, or during his military service, skiing through frozen forests until the heart was thumping audibly, beyond its highest level of possibility. Only time could provide a way back to normality. Was there enough of it? The utter strangeness of his condition was hardly helped by her wild shrieks, like calls from a primeval bog, and, even more disconcerting, the sound of his own voice joining in, out of all vocal control, suggesting at moments appeal, then mortal affliction, premonition of unexpected perils, at moments triumph. Slowly the volcano subsided, soundlessly, leaving behind only breath, subtler signs of life. And finally it petered out, with only amazement in its wake. Amazement and sleep, a sleep which did not last long, a foretaste of that anticipated death lasting half an hour or so. It was then he realized that, as usual, she had taken him over.

He had been a half unwilling, half hopeful victim of her conspiracy, moved by her industry, amused by her daring, astonished by her initiative, lulled by her wine, and finally hunted like a deer. She had virtually raped him, assuming the dominant position, riding him in the mad Valkyrie escapade across the lunar sky. Now she was pliable, as passive as a hibernating animal, content to breathe away quietly until touched by the first drop of a springtime shower. He moved her arms to where he wanted them, and then awkwardly climbed onto her, squeezing her breasts with his chest, and staring down at eyes that were open, grey-blue even in the dark, enigmatic, expecting moves which were no longer hers to invent. The relative coarseness of his hands was replaced in his quest for his answer to thousands of unformulated, abstract questions by his lips, in gestures of infinite tenderness, the all-important aftermath of the physical act.

As he explored the garden of his unexpected inheritance with his lips, he reflected on the incredible waste of young Louis' vulgar choreography in the high grass, going through the prescribed motions with his dancing partner, while singularly missing out on the essentials. It was hardly the moment to be thinking of that regrettable incident, but then the mind has its own rules of when to think of what. The wonderful gentleness of what follows the earthquake is the real entry into a paradise of the spirit, to the extent that it can even tolerate irreverent and frivolous reflections. Poor Louis, there was not and had never been the extraordinary peace of union in his lovemaking, merely a shower and a lot of playful splashing. But after all, he was seventy, and Louis a mere . . . how old was he? When he, René, had been whatever age Louis was, he had never dared to behave like that. He was far too good a pupil at the Ecole Hôtelière with real ambitions, not merely a quest for cheap thrills. And then, he could hardly visualize Louis at the age of seventy, nor believe that he could enjoy such a miraculous experience. Even if it happened, he would not be able to interpret it. Just as a chimpanzee cannot tell poetry from prose, Louis would stop at the physical level, believing that was it. For him there was no second act after the intermission. He just got dressed and went home, not realizing the best was still to come.

Why had he thought of chimpanzees in connection with Louis? Had he been unfair to the lad? Certainly, at this sublime moment, it was not the time to be unfair. He remembered how apes looked around them with a sort of quizzical melancholy, for ever observant without any real curiosity except about tactile objects, as though they knew it all, and what they didn't know wasn't worth knowing. Perhaps only they really did know the difference between poetry and prose, and that was the only reason for their impenetrable gloom? Was Louis then a poet, caught in the prison of his vision? Hardly.

The contact of his lips with her cheeks made him banish these inept reflections. He tasted salt. She had been crying. She still was crying. The last thing he wanted to do was to interrupt the deep silence with words, which would only dissolve the magic. He licked her tears away like a cat at its ablutions. Her cheeks swelled into a smile. Her eyes were shut, locking out the outer world, but she responded to his kisses with kisses of her own. It took a long time for sleep to overtake them. He lost consciousness under a mantle of the deepest contentment, only hesitating to find a position in which he could no longer hear his own heartbeat, knocking in his ear. It seemed at first faster than usual, then irregular, and finally he fell away into the most impenetrable oblivion, heartbeat notwithstanding.

It was in the early morning that he became conscious, almost surprised to find that he was not alone. He lay on his side, in order not to take up too much room. How unusual, to find himself sharing his innermost sanctum in a way he had never done with his wife, may her soul rest in peace, in a way he had never done before in the whole of his existence. To be with a loved one is an endless voyage of self-discovery, he reflected. He had learned more about himself during one short night of love than ever before, at least that was his guess. It had all been far too recent, far too massive and all-embracing to reach any conclusions which were worth analysing, but he felt enormously enriched.

He turned cautiously to face her. In the few beams of daylight which found their way into the room past the curtains, he could see her back arching away upwards from the middle of the bed, her head half hidden between two pillows, her hands under the pillow. She was largely uncovered. Fearing she might be cold, he pulled the uppermost sheet up. He did not wish to wake her up prematurely, having discovered the rare quality of sleep after such an experience. He nevertheless felt the pillow nearest her face.

It was wringing wet. She must have cried all night. He smiled briefly. Women are indeed astonishing creatures. Different from men. He felt he had slept with an embarrassing grin of gratification on his face, and here was the proof that ecstasy makes women weep. It is for that reason, he moralized to himself, that men and women are complementary, neither being able to claim superiority or inferiority. Except at times. And the thought irritated him briefly. He contorted his back to look at the fob watch by his bedside. It was just a few minutes after seven, another few hours of gratitude for long and loyal service from the Concierges of the World. His heart leaped. If only they knew!

A rustle and thump down the corridor suggested that the croissants had been delivered. The newspaper would have arrived by now. A few minutes after seven. He would get up quietly, put on his silk dressing gown for the sake of propriety. Even if we did come into the world unclothed, as she had said, we soon enough were wrapped in woollies, with pink or blue ribbons, according to the sex. He would go into the bathroom to relieve himself, shower briefly to freshen up, go to the front door, fetch the croissants and the paper, then to the kitchen, to slowly regale her with a cooked breakfast as ambitious in its way as her dinner had been, scrambled eggs and bacon, fruit yoghourt, a cereal, toast, cold cuts, cheese, a tumbler full of grapefruit juice. He smiled slyly, hatching a little masculine plot, the kind of plots husbands conceal from their wives. He would take his time with this spectacular breakfast. After all, she was still asleep. This would give him time to read his paper from cover to cover.

Passing back through the bedroom, he saw that she had not moved. Poor girl, she must have needed the sleep.

He entered the kitchen and locked the door. After all,
it had to be a surprise, this great breakfast. He settled
down to read the paper. The kettle was ready, the flame,
as yet, unlit.

# VIII

AFTER M. RENÉ had read the paper from cover to cover, an indulgence which brought him back to normality after the night, he squeezed three Florida grapefruits into a couple of tumblers, made the coffee and scrambled the eggs, and pushed the trolley with a feeling of distinct satisfaction into the dining room. On the way, he passed the bedroom, and noticed that she was no longer in bed. She must have woken up, and be in the bathroom. He laid out the breakfast as meticulously as she had laid out the dinner the night before. When he was ready, he drew the curtains and let the sunlight stream in. Then he called out: 'Frühstück! Breakfast! Le petit déjeuner!' He was only mildly surprised that there was no response. She must be showering. Still, it would be a pity to allow the coffee to grow cold.

He went to the bathroom door. There was no sound from within. He called out, 'Agnes.' No reaction. He tried the door. It was unlocked. He frowned. Where could she be? Had a morbid curiosity tempted her to open the locked door of his dead wife's room? He was momentarily annoyed, and crossed silently to investigate. The door was still locked. Could she be outside, in the garden? Would she risk such indiscretion? He went out in his dressing gown, looking around and calling out quietly, feeling the chilly wind and the dew-laden grass against his ankles. She was not outside the house. Worried, he returned indoors, and searched down in the cellar and up in the attic. At length, he returned to the bedroom, noticing in the corridor that her suitcase had gone. On the bed, among the chaotic sheets, he spotted her old child's handbag. He took it anxiously, raising it to his nose. He caught a whiff of her perfume, the sweet smell of her cupboard, of her personal belongings, and realized that he was in love. Why had she left it behind, an object so personal, which had accompanied her on most of her life's journey? He fingered it with some trepidation, wondering if it had not been an oversight on her part. Had her departure been so precipitate that she had simply forgotten to take it? Would opening it without her permission be an intolerable intrusion into her jealously preserved privacy, a wrong message for the future? His privacy was just as sacrosanct as hers, a respect which makes conjugal life possible. Nevertheless, he was tempted to open it. It might contain the key to her flight. He did so. Inside he found a piece of paper, untidily torn from a larger sheet. On it was written, in smudged lipstick, 'I do not deserve such happiness'. It was unsigned.

He sat down heavily on the battlefield of dishevelled bed-clothes. It was too soon to telephone the hotel. She could not have arrived there yet. He thought of breakfast. He would take his cellular phone with him, and at least do his half of justice to his excellent cooking. Then, as he munched his toast (or was it hers?), he began to physically shake until he could hardly hold his knife. It was an incomprehensible reaction, one of shock, this awful isolation after the high promise of the night, a chasm of black helplessness before him, deeply unfair, most unjust. Had he offended her in some way? That was another possibility. Hardly, since she referred to happiness. That is not a word to bandy about, to take lightly. It was even such happiness which suggested it was exceptional, incomparable, unique. Even if, for some reason, she did not feel she deserved it, she did not deny that it was a reality. On the contrary.

'La donna è mobile.' I'll say so. What goes on in their minds? By a miracle, that night, there had been no difference between them. Now, for the moment, the gap was immense, incomprehensible, as though all the old clichés were true. But then, he pondered ruefully, the old clichés *are* true. Otherwise they would never have become clichés. Had he lived three score and ten years to discover feminine waywardness for the first time? You could not have described his wife as a typical woman. As a typical anything, come to that. But then, seen from the other side, had he been too ingrown in his masculine ways for immediate comprehension by a woman, rendered oversensitive by a transcendental experience? Should he perhaps not have read the paper from end to end? Surely the sports and the market could have waited? At any rate, had he not reverted to such celibate self-indulgence, she might not have had time to abscond. He shook his head, and rang the hotel on his portable phone. No, they said, she was not expected back until tomorrow. He dared to call Mr Butler at his place of work. He was at home, ill. No, they hadn't seen him for a week, and hoped it was nothing serious. So did M. René.

M. René looked through his little address book, and found Mr Butler's number, and poked out the number. A grave voice replied. Mr Butler was resting. So early in the day? If younger people do not wish to speak to you, they are invariably in conference. The elderly are resting, for the same reason. M. René had absolutely no desire to talk to either M. Alonso or M. Arrigo. They represented a past error of judgement. Mr Butler was different. He had been the unwilling matchmaker. Matchmaker, that's rich! 'I do not deserve such happiness.'

He spent the morning restlessly, awaiting a sign of life. A noise outside the house made him start. His heart began pounding uncontrollably. It was Mme Radibois. Usually she had the great virtue of being unobtrusive. Today her presence annoyed him. He had engaged her on his retirement, and today she was one of the last domestics who were still Swiss, and who had no ambition to be anything but good at her job. After disappearing from sight for a while, she suddenly entered the study where he was seated, doing little else but seeking to conceal his impatience for news. She carried his striped pyjamas over her arm.

'I found these in the dustbin,' she challenged.

'Yes,' he said, as casually as possible. 'They are old. Not worth repairing. I stupidly tore a button off, and the fabric gave. It's beyond saving. I am throwing them away.'

'M. René,' she answered, in a tone of slight reproach, 'I know your clothes far better than I know you, even after all this time. These pyjamas were not in your wardrobe when I first came here. They are not old. I'm sure they're worth repairing.'

He felt like losing his temper, but spoke calmly instead.

'Madame Radibois, there are few enough things in life which one can really call one's own. Pyjamas are one of them. If I, as their possessor, decide I no longer want them, I am fully entitled to throw them away. I need no advice on the subject.'

Mme Radibois had not been taking in M. René's defence of his action. Truth to tell, it was a little complicated for her. Instead she stuck to what she could understand. Having pushed her finger through the tear, and looking at it with great application, she speculated: 'I wonder how you came to tear off your own button?'

'Never mind, I did, and that's that.'

'I mean, it's not like a coat button, which can always get caught in a door. This is a button on your chest. You couldn't tear it off, whatever the circumstances, without bruising or grazing your chest.'

M. René gulped in outrage. 'Now I suppose you wish to examine my chest in order to reconstruct the event? Mme Radibois, get it into your head that the pyjamas are torn beyond repair, and leave it at that.'

'I'm not so sure,' she said, and left the room. For two hours there was no sound in the house except those of Mme Radibois' activities. He tried the hotel once again, on the off-chance. There was nothing new. Then, towards noon, his ordinary phone rang. It was the Police Chief, very upset.

'I must see you at once.'

'Shall I come to you?'

'No, if I may, I'll come to you. I am on the point of retirement. My successor is here. I'm showing him the ropes. What I have to say is personal.'

'I won't be naive enough to ask you if you know where I live.'

'I'll be with you in ten minutes.'

Now what? M. René told himself he must avoid entering into any sort of complicity with this fellow. He must be kept in the dark as much as possible. Retiring? He was bound to use that to tug at the heartstrings. What did he want? He certainly sounded on edge. He was not good enough an actor to feign such emotions. He was cumbersome, clumsy, a man who fumbled, who dropped things. There was no further time for speculation. The squeak of the garden gate was followed by the crunch of shoes on the gravel. M. René opened the front door. They shook hands. He led the way indoors. Urs Mildenegger looked around as a policeman would, noticing everything and seeing nothing.

'Nice place you've got here.'

'Suits my purpose.'

A train passed to do what it could to damage the impression. They sat down in the study.

'Is there someone else in the house?' asked the Chief.

'No. Why?'

'I thought I heard sounds.'

'Ah, no. That's Mme Radibois, my daily.'

'I see.'

There was a pause.

'Can I offer you anything?'

'No, thank you. I hardly know where to begin. I was going to phone in any case to invite you to my retirement party.'

'When is it?'

'Tonight. A surprise, from the entire department. And then this had to happen!'

M. René waited, with an appearance of patience.

'She's given herself up.'

'Who?'

'Without any warning. This morning. Walked into my office carrying a heavy suitcase. She had been crying for a long time, so it seemed. There was not a tear left in her.'

M. René rose unsteadily. 'Who?' he asked hoarsely.

'Agnes. Agnes Schanderbach. After all this time. I was right. It's a most amazing end to my career. Confessed to the murders of Colonel Otzinger, Captain Zocco and Lieutenant Bompoz. Arsenic. I wanted you to know.'

M. René thought he might faint, something he'd never done before. Standing still used up all his energy.

'Extraordinary thing. There was nothing in her suitcase except pots and pans, candlesticks, vases. We wondered at first if she had stolen them.'

'And a toothbrush,' M. René managed to get out. 'She will not have stolen that.'

'Why do you say that?' asked the Chief, puzzled by M. René's odd tone of contained rage. 'We immediately conducted a thorough search of her effects in the hotel. Still no sign of that damned handbag. Just clothes, books of Asian philosophy, a little of everything.'

M. René left the room unsteadily, breathing deeply.

'Where are you going?'

After a full minute, M. René returned to the room. He placed the handbag daintily before the Chief, as though it was a priceless relic.

The Chief looked at it briefly, cast a bewildered yet enquiring look at M. René, and tried to open it by force in his usual, insensitive manner.

'Don't break it,' shouted M. René, and then added, with great docility: 'There is a clasp.'

The Chief opened the bag, manhandled the lining, so

that it tore again in one or two places, and shook out the stub of a pencil and the top of an ancient biscuit tin.

'There are no secret compartments. Save yourself the trouble.'

'What's it doing here?' asked the Chief, harshly.

'It was a gift.'

'To whom?'

'To me.'

'From whom?'

'From Agnes.'

'When?'

'This morning.'

'This morning? I'll take it along.'

'Over my dead body.'

'What?'

'I said, over my dead body. It's a gift. If she has . . . as you allege . . . confessed . . . there is no need of . . . of any further evidence . . . It's mine. It's all I have left.' And despite his resolve, the tears began coursing down his cheeks silently.

The Chief knitted his brow. 'I will have to make note of its contents,' he said, quietly.

M. René shut his eyes.

'One pencil stub, substitute for a lipstick. One tin lid, substitute for a lady's handbag mirror. Both taken from the imagination of a five-year-old child.'

'Very well, I will leave you the handbag for the time being, with a rider that you produce it on request should it be necessary.'

'No. It's mine, irrevocably. You are retiring today. What's it to you?'

'My duty doesn't end with my retirement.'

'Oh, then what are you celebrating tonight?'

Silence.

The tears were beginning to force a series of convulsions in M. René, like a pulse. The Chief was embarrassed by this unexpected show of emotion, and the intensely personal reaction to an event he thought would merely incite interest. M. René steered himself, half blindly, to his writing desk.

'Those two items were not the only objects in the handbag.'

'Ah—!'

M. René withdrew a sheet of paper from a drawer.

'The mother's instructions!'

The Chief read the message aloud.

'I do not deserve such happiness. What does it mean? When was it written? And what's it written in? Blood!'

'Lipstick. It was written early this morning.'

'This morning? Where?'

'Here. She spent the night here. It was . . .' M. René was no longer capable of coherent speech. His whole frame shook with a distress so acute that he was unable to exercise self-control. Not since his childhood had he wept as bitterly or as unreasonably, hearing the Chief's voice only vaguely through his torment.

'She stayed the night? You were lovers?'

'Damn you all. Damn you all. It's so unfair. So unfair,' shouted M. René, as much to give his jeremiad focus as anything else, but still the diaphragm went on tirelessly producing aftershocks and tremors without end. As with all things natural, sheer stamina eventually has its say, and M. René grew quieter, only to notice that the Police Chief was also at it, bawling like a child, after an unexpected fall. This sobered M. René like nothing else.

'What are you weeping about?' he asked, almost crossly, among the distant echo of sobs. Since there was no response, he went on. 'It's not like you to be weeping out of sympathy for me,' he charged, 'so what emotion do you feel to cause you to imitate me?'

The Chief rounded on him with a mad and liquid eye, an aspect of his character he had never had occasion to show before. 'Jealousy!' he roared, and relapsed into helplessness once again.

'Jealousy,' echoed M. René. It had been far from his thoughts.

'You have known the love . . . of a woman . . . who has tortured my loneliness . . . by her very existence . . . and now the dream is ended . . . impossible . . . the stupid bitch has given herself up . . . there was no need . . . we would never have caught her . . . never . . . and now . . . because she has known happiness . . . and you too, according to your words . . . she does something damned idiotic . . . puts an end to my hopes . . .' And suddenly, a statement which set off the flood anew: 'Unlike you, I have never known happiness. And I have deserved it!'

M. René, to whom the realization of his relative luck had come as something of a shock, reached for the opulent handkerchief which always blossomed from his pocket and passed it silently to the Police Chief, who blew his nose into it without expressing his gratitude.

Mme Radibois turned into the room. The sight of two men of a certain age, both in tears, made her reflect that it was not the moment to say goodbye, and she let herself out in silence. In her bag were M. René's crumpled pyjamas.

# IX

BY THE next morning, M. René had taken himself in hand. He was not of an age to blub like a baby, and the memory embarrassed him. He slept well, by sheer force of character. He was now himself, clear-eyed, facing reality as he always had done. Like a soldier, he sat before a blank sheet of paper, and wrote, as though it was destined to become part of the record: 'Objective.' Underneath, he inscribed: 'The release of Agnes Schanderbach.' A gap, then: 'Strategy.' Then, '1: Interview with the waiter Fiorino at the Ecole Hôtelière.' '2: Identification and Interview with Psychiatrists appointed to examine A. S.' '3: Identification and Interview with the Lawyer designated to defend A. S.' He read and re-read the sheet with cool satisfaction. Since no one but he had knowledge of its contents, he entertained the happy illusion that he had retaken the initiative. He replaced it in a drawer, and locked it. Fiorino. The name of the Istrian waiter at the Balkan conference was etched in his memory because he had no means of writing it down when Agnes first mentioned it.

Now it needed all his clarity of thought to plan for Agnes'
release, even against her will.

He phoned M. Robert Gailhac, the Director of the Ecole
Hôtelière at Lausanne. His prestige within the profession
counted in such calls. M. Gailhac was invariably in conference to most people, even if he was sitting in his office
thinking of things to do, but when his secretary told him
it was M. René on the line, he waited long enough to make
his allegations that he had laid aside some important activity
before taking the call. M. René spoke with a kind of weary
majesty as befitted his standing among his peers.

'I hear good things about a young fellow by name
Fiorino,' he said.

'Fiorino? On the young side, M. René,' replied M.
Gailhac, 'and good rather than exceptional.'

'I hear from sources I am inclined to respect that he is
potential sommelier material.'

'I frankly doubt that, especially these days, when there
is such a wide choice. He may indeed know his way about
Dalmatian vintages, even Romanian or Bulgarian ones, but
I wouldn't trust him with Bordeaux.'

'Perhaps not yet. I'd like to meet the lad, Gailhac. As you
know, I act as consultant for various hotel chains.'

'Very well.' He consulted a list. 'At the moment, he
spends most of his time at that endless Inter-Balkan
conference at the Villa Esperance. He even stays in Geneva
some nights if he's on dinner duty. I'll give you his portable
phone number.'

M. René raised his eyebrows. 'He has a portable phone?'

'Ah, who hasn't these days?'

'Quite. Quite.'

After lunch, M. René called Fiorino. He did so on the

verandah, using his mobile. He didn't want to feel himself at a disadvantage. They arranged a meeting. Fiorino seemed more than willing for it. There even seemed some urgency, in his opinion. He came to the house. M. René received him in the garden. He appeared very young, as M. Gailhac had warned, dark and pale, with a look which could be interpreted as either intellectual or else unwell.

'It was Mme Agnes who gave me your name, M. Fiorino.'

'I have been trying to call her urgently. The hotel tells me she is away,' he said, anxiously.

'She is not far away, although not readily available.'

'She didn't mention your name,' Fiorino said guardedly.

M. René produced his card with a flourish, looking away while it created its effect.

The young man whistled. 'Président Permanent de la Fraternité Mondial des Concierges et des Portiers d'Hôtel! That's like a Field Marshal!'

'Or a Master Sergeant's Master Sergeant,' said M. René, with studied modesty. They both smiled. 'Why did you wish to see Agnes so urgently?'

'I – don't want to risk betraying her trust.'

'We were working together.'

'Were?'

'We are working together,' M. René said, expressing a moment of annoyance at his own carelessness.

'Working – at what?'

'We were instrumental in the expulsion of the Emir of Djabbadieh the other day – and we nipped in the bud a deal between the Emirate and the Republic of Kazakhstan for chemical weapons. You may have read about it in the newspapers?'

'No,' replied Fiorino.

'You probably have your plate full with the Balkan conference,' snapped M. René, with some irritation.

'I wish I knew more about you,' said Fiorino, with trepidation.

'I feel exactly the same about you. I don't know whether I can trust you. I had no doubt before, from what Agnes told me. But now . . . ?' He shrugged.

'What have I done to alter your opinion, whatever it was?'

Tricky customer, this, M. René thought. Accustomed to life in a police state.

'I wish Agnes could have brought us together. Then there would be no doubt in my mind.'

'I wish the same. Unfortunately it is, for the moment, impossible. I ask you to believe that anything you wish to tell her could well be of immense help to her at this moment.'

Fiorino started. 'At this moment? Is she arrested?'

'Detained, for questioning.'

'How do I know you are not from the police?'

M. René shut his eyes for a moment. He tried a fresh start. 'There is no need to insult me. Agnes told me you are from Istria, despite your Italian name.'

'She told you that?'

'And she told me that, in your opinion, the conference has no chance of being successful. It is in everyone's interest to prolong it. Life here is more comfortable and safer than it is in Kosovo, in Bosnia, in Serbian Bosnia, in Croatian Bosnia, and so forth. In fact, the conference is the proof of the belief that a higher standard of living is the key to peace.'

'Yes, of course, but there are exceptions to the rule.

The head of the Croatian Bosnian delegation is in danger. Career warriors get bored. And endless conferences, however comfortable, are not to their taste. They begin to think again in terms of dignity, of exclusivity, of ethnic cleansing, and they grow restless.'

'Are you referring to something specific?'

Fiorino hesitated. 'Yes. That's why it's so urgent I contact Agnes.'

M. René grew intense. 'If it's as urgent as you say, you will kick yourself for your reticence. Someone may be hurt.'

Fiorino decided. 'It's worse than that. A booby-trapped car. There's a specific date and place.'

'When?'

'Next Tuesday. Eight o'clock in the morning, when he goes to work.'

'Who?'

'Miodrag Todorovic, the leader of the Croat-Bosnians in Mostar. He lives in a flat on the Rue de la Liberté Réformée, number 119.'

'And who are the plotters?'

'Bohumil Mlynic, of the Serbian Bosnian opposition, and Ali Bismilovic, of the Bosnian opposition.'

'How do you know this?'

'They always sit together at lunch, and I serve them. They think I'm Italian, and do not understand.'

'My God, my idea is vindicated,' cried M. René. 'Waiters can be much more than just menials in a world of reprehensible and careless people! That was the great hope behind my scheme. It didn't work first time. Now, the second time round, thanks to Agnes and you, it has worked, with a vengeance!'

'Ah, now I know who you are! The elderly, middle-aged man who first approached her?'

'Yes. You're sure of your facts, are you?'

'If they are sure of their facts.'

'Next Tuesday? That's the 14th.'

'Correct. He is brought to the conference in a small Opel. The car to be exploded will be parked behind it at his residence. It is already rented at the airport.'

'Fantastic. But why do they talk so freely in front of you?'

'They are bored stiff. Boredom has made them careless. And then, they are greedy. They always enjoy second helpings. I never look as though I am listening. I have trained myself never to look surprised. Every time they say "Grazie", I know I have succeeded for another day.'

M. René trusted this young man's information. He provided a link with Agnes. He represented her last positive action before madness overtook her. Now he had a weapon with which to taunt the police, information not in their possession, information he would attribute to Agnes. Fiorino reminded M. René of the danger he was in. He enjoined him, whatever happened, never to blow his cover. M. René reassured him, and accompanied him to the door when it was time for him to go. They made a date for Wednesday, after the failed attempt on Miodrag Todorovic.

Once he was alone, M. René typed out a resumé of Fiorino's information from the copious notes he made.

Once he had done so, he made two copies, and placed them in a drawer. Then he called Urs Mildenegger. He was somewhat surprised to find him out of the office. He was reminded by a police official, with amusement in his voice, that Mildenegger had retired. The official added that M. René would probably find him at home, nursing the mother of all hangovers. It had been a great party. M. René said that he was sorry he had missed it. 'Switzerland is a great country for reunions,' he added. 'Nothing ever happens, we put all our energies into celebrations of the fact.'

Since Switzerland accords no special privileges of secrecy to telephone users, M. René knew he could find the Chief's name in the phone book. He preferred this to asking for the number from Police Headquarters. Because he had asked to speak to the Chief in terms which suggested a degree of intimacy, he thought that asking for a home phone number might awaken some suspicions.

When he had found it, he called. Mildenegger answered with some irritation.

'Oh, it's you. You missed a great party. At least, it was a great party while it lasted. The aftermath is sheer hell.'

'A hangover, I understand.'

'More. It's a pity you couldn't come.'

'Thank you very much. I have no hangover. Listen, I must see you, urgently.'

'Don't ask me to go anywhere.'

'Can I come and see you?'

'As urgent as that is it?'

Twenty minutes later, M. René was in a small flat in a large modern block, completely devoid of character other than an aura of dirt and neglect. The Chief was as untidy as his home. He wore pyjamas, and a cardigan which had fielded soup and coffee in its time, without having had the traces eradicated. A woolly dressing gown with a vague tartan design of the type which accompany small boys to boarding schools, and worn slippers, completed the impression of slothfulness. Normally, his street appearance was a little more studied, and could always be put down to a temperament for whom outward appearances meant little, but today, with his washed-out complexion, his grey, moist skin, and his shifting, unfocused eyes, he could be mistaken for a recluse. Was this the much-feared, much-respected Chief of Police? That is, ex-Chief of Police. But, did the ex make all that difference?

'I've brought you these for the stomach. Dissolve two in a tumbler of water, every four hours if necessary. They can be allowed to dissolve in the mouth.'

'How can I thank you sufficiently? You are a real friend. I haven't many, as you will have guessed. I spent most of the night vomiting.'

'How very unattractive. I will prepare the glass of water.'

M. René went into the kitchen, and was appalled by the sight of plates and cutlery unwashed for days, lying in the sink like the result of a terrible accident. 'Where do you keep the mineral water?' M. René called out.

'I drink tap water!'

M. René washed out a tumbler, and returned with it filled with tap water. 'Is tap water safe?'

'I have no idea,' replied the Chief, dropping the pills into the glass, where they exploded into life, sprinkling the back of his hand with tiny, ice-cold bubbles. 'I remember that only last year we arrested the Chief Chemist and Chairman of the Acquaviva mineral water company after over fifty people were taken ill. The only common denominator in all fifty cases was their use of Acquaviva.'

'I remember the case,' remarked M. René, 'but I also seem to remember that they were acquitted.'

'Were they? I never have time to follow cases after we arrest the culprits. Whenever we finished one case, another was already in progress.' He sighed deeply. M. René came to the rapid conclusion that the regular purchase of mineral water was something far too complicated for a man as profoundly disorganized as the Chief. The tap was a far easier solution. The Chief successfully stifled a belch. He smiled.

'Mineral water makes you burp, tap water doesn't,' he said, and went on, making a sign for M. René to sit wherever he could find a place: 'What's so urgent?'

M. René pushed a pile of old newspapers onto the floor, sat on a stool, and consulted his paper. 'I must report a coming assassination attempt, next Tuesday the 14th, at 08.00 hours in the morning.'

The Chief pulled himself together. 'Who is the intended victim?'

'Mr Miodrag Todorovic.'

'A Serb.'

'A Bosnian Croat.'

The Chief brushed it aside. 'To all intents and purposes a Serb. And who is the potential assassin? Another Serb.' He said this as a statement, not as a question.

'Two men. Neither of them strictly Serbs.'

'You astonish me.'

'The accused will be Bohumil Mlynic, a member of the opposition in the Serbian Bosnian Parliament in Pale, and his co-conspirator, Ali Bismilovic, of the Bosnian opposition in Sarajevo.'

'Three Serbs. I may be oversimplifying things. If I am, I apologize. But these are hardly matters which concern me. If these people solve their problems by killing each other, I would do little to discourage them.'

M. René was tight-lipped. 'It depends on the methods used to kill.'

'Arsenic?' asked the Chief, with a wretched smile on his face.

'There is no reason to be tasteless. If it had been poison, I would hardly have specified a precise hour.'

'Did you?'

'08.00.'

'So you did. Wednesday the 14th.'

'Tuesday the 14th. Wednesday is the 15th.'

'And what method are these desperadoes preparing to use?'

'A booby-trapped car, causing considerable damage to Swiss property and other parked cars in the neighbourhood. You know about it now. You can never pretend you didn't know. I intend, before next week, to notarize the statement, and deposit a copy in a bank in the presence of the bank manager. Todorovic is driven to the Balkan Conference every morning at the designated hour. The car which is booby-trapped will be parked behind the small Opel used by the victim. The booby-trapped car has already been rented at the airport.'

The Chief began to stare at M. René, appalled. 'You're serious, aren't you? But I can't make use of this information without knowing its source.'

'Very well. Agnes.'

'Agnes?'

'The information was given me by Agnes. I wish it to count in her defence.'

'It may have precisely the opposite effect. It makes her active, rather than passive, resigned and contrite, which is her defence at the moment.'

'If her information helps avoid a catastrophe, it can only help, and I will do anything to help her.'

The Chief became thoughtful. 'Of course, one thing can hardly help another, if the other is a confession to three murders in the past. But, when did she give you this information?'

'During the dinner in my house.'

'The night of . . . then why didn't you come forward earlier?'

'She didn't give me the actual information. She told me where I could find it.'

'Ah . . . so it was not—'

'I cannot give the actual source. It may endanger lives. These are men who are used to thinking in terms of death.'

'But what if the information is false?'

'I think you should be thinking, what if the information is accurate. You will have condoned a criminal act without doing anything to prevent it. You, who were for many years Chief of Police.'

The Chief smiled. 'You have just reminded me that I am no longer Chief of Police. This information should go to my successor.'

'Who is it?'

'A miserable bastard called Beat Kribl, who spent the last eight years hoping I would put a foot wrong.'

'You have his ear. I don't know the fellow.'

'Go to him.'

'You go to him. This statement is for you. Show it to him. Until you do so, you and I are the only ones to know its contents.' M. René added slowly: 'You, me, and the bank manager.'

The Chief was thoughtful, and deeply perplexed in the face of this simple blackmail.

M. René added, slyly: 'At worst, you can encourage Chief Kribl to put a foot wrong.'

The Chief smiled humourlessly, and took the report.

'Feel better?'

'Thanks for coming.'

'Anything you need, don't hesitate to call me. After all, I have retired too. I never stop looking for things to do.'

On his way out, M. René was stopped briefly by an afterthought from the Chief.

'Incidentally, which bank is it?'

'Not mine,' replied M. René pleasantly. 'Another one.'

# X

THE DAY was Saturday. There were three days left before the assassination attempt, and M. René, conscious of holding a trump card if all worked according to plan, could scarcely wait for the time to pass. After breakfast, he began an extensive daydream, foreseeing in his mind all the possible twists and turns of events after the successful arrest of the would-be killers. His concentration was interrupted when he heard a key turn in the lock. Agnes! For a moment he entertained the thought before remembering she was incarcerated. He swung around to face the intruder. It was Mme Radibois.

'Mme Radibois!' he exclaimed. 'You don't usually come in on a Saturday!'

'It's raining,' she retorted, by way of information. 'No, usually I don't come in, but I thought I'd catch you when you were more relaxed, less on edge, in other words, the weekend.'

'Why do you wish me more relaxed than usual?'

'I want you to appreciate what I do for you.'

'But I do, Mme Radibois, I do. Without you, I'd be lost!'

'I wouldn't go as far as that, M. René, but I do believe I earn my salary, no more.' She hesitated, while he was silent. 'I want you to look at these in the daylight,' she went on, pulling out of an ample bag the striped pyjamas. 'I took them home to mend, and to clean. And I want you to tell me if you can see the merest trace of a tear.'

He concealed his irritation behind a twisted little smile.

'Take them to the window, the trousers too, and look at them close to.'

He obeyed, in order to get the ordeal over as quickly as possible. 'Amazing. Remarkable,' he conceded.

'And the pants,' she said, 'you should have seen the state they were in.'

He glanced at her, and fancied there was an expression of challenging insolence on her face.

'Thank you, Mme Radibois,' he said, as dismissively as possible.

'Stay where you are, in the light,' she instructed, pulling the sheets out of her bag in a tidy square. 'The sheets,' she declared, 'I wouldn't trust a washing-machine with work of such delicacy. There's nothing to replace the old-fashioned methods. Hard work and a sure touch. I can tell you, they were in a sorry condition. Now, they're like new.'

'I'm extremely grateful, Mme Radibois, more especially since you've taken the time on a day off to bring all this to my attention.'

'Oh,' muttered Mme Radibois, 'I know you well enough to realize that you wish me to leave. I'm going! I'm off!' She held up a hand, as though to countermand protests which were not forthcoming. 'You are not the kind of person who can be rushed. It may take even days to allow the significance of a remark to sink in. Oh, it's not that you don't understand things very quickly. It's no reflection on your intelligence, which is great. It's just that you have built such a wall around yourself.'

'Have I? That may well be so.'

'I didn't realize before only the other day that anyone could ever break through it.'

'Oh. And now you are satisfied?'

'More than satisfied,' she said quietly, as though wrapped in a dream. 'We will talk further when I judge the moment right – when what I have said today has sunk in. I'll just put the sheets and pyjamas back where they belong, and I'll be off.' She went to the door, and turned back. She always did. M. René was totally unsurprised.

'Incidentally,' she said, 'we will continue this conversation once you have fully digested what I have said. Meanwhile I will not claim overtime for today.'

She shot back a quizzical look which was very hard to interpret, and after a minute or so, it begged the question whether it was worth interpreting.

M. René heard the front door slam, and wondered if everyone had been infected by the happiness he had had inflicted on him. First of all, the retiring Police Chief of an important international city, crying his eyes out, and now a venerable charlady dropping suggestive hints about soiled and torn pyjamas as subtle as chords on a bar room piano. Why couldn't they mind their own business, these parasites with little independent life? And then, he remembered he had been just like them, his eye ever-ready for the keyhole, his ear for the rumour, his palm for the grease. All of

humanity lives by the grace of others, and knows hardship
when that grace is withdrawn. One cannot be too hard on
others without also being hard on oneself.

M. René went into the bedroom and crossed to the chest
of drawers in which his pyjamas were kept. Mme Radibois
had classified them, in the sense that pyjamas were her
documents. The repaired ones lay on top, with a little
home-made sachet of lavender neatly placed on them. Was
this a gesture usual for her, or was the sachet yet another
signal, yet another painfully dropped hint? He went to the
linen cupboard, and once again found the washed sheets.
They too benefited from a similar hessian sachet, with the
somewhat prim fin-de-siècle odour of lavender emanating
from it. What should he expect after the gestation period of
her double-entendres had expired? To hell with her. There
were other, more urgent matters at hand. It was probably
the menopause exerting its own cruel influence on her,
priming her for ridicule. Poor Mme Radibois. Thank God,
she was not to be taken seriously, however seriously she took
herself. There's a terrible thought. He dismissed it, and with
it, Mme Radibois.

He then did something he only very rarely did. Went
to the cinema, to see an American film called 'Backfire',
or something of the sort. He forgot the title as soon as
it appeared on the screen. It was an animated piece of
nonsense about the kind of policeman who sleeps with the
chief suspect, thereby separating himself from his revolver
for one fatal moment, and finds himself discredited in his
precinct by his arch-rival, who saves his life. The arch-rival
is, as far as M. René understood it, as corrupt as they
come, with a fine capacity for democratic double-talk,
which takes in the district attorney, the Police Chief,

and even the Governor of the State. The only one who sees through it is our poor naked detective, who falls for a well-shaped calf separating a high heeled shoe from a mini-skirt, thus ruining his chances of effecting a quick arrest, and ruining the film. It needed another hour and a half, several Ferraris and Lamborghinis over a cliff, bursting into the statutory instant flames, and the Chief of the Mafia caught red-handed beside his neo-Roman pool in a final shootout, in which the villain is pushed ignominiously into the deep end, staining the water a bright vermilion, for the simple-minded saga to stagger to an end amid a salvo of acrid trumpets and sobbing strings.

M. René emerged blinking into the daylight, with a sentiment that he had never wasted time more thoroughly in his life. Admittedly, his problems seemed minimal compared with those of the detective on the screen, the only difference being that his were real, and those of the detective cooked up by febrile script-writers, pacing an office like caged tigers, with as little in their minds. He remembered his meeting with the hooded hoodlum in New York, and how resourceful he had been compared to this cardboard assailant. Real life has at least an added dimension, which makes it formless, and wonderfully rich in surprises. The strange behaviour of Madame Radibois, the sordid living conditions of a high civil servant, the morbid anxiety of Fiorino, and the incomprehensible reactions of Agnes to a night of passion, all of them as yet unexplained and seemingly inconsistent, all belonged to life. They all possessed the necessary ingredient of mystery which begs solution, fully engaging the mind in its quest for answers. Compared to this the film was barely recognizable even as a frivolous commentary on the complicated patina of reality, froth posing as beer, lather masquerading as soap. But it did pass the time. And its inanity was, in itself, a commentary on the struggle of existence.

After the cinema, he went all alone to the Mouton Enragé and ate at the same table at which he had eaten at the first memorable meeting. The proprietor, delighted to see him again despite his previous anger, joined him at the table, and engaged him in a conversation which was hardly what M. René needed in his quiet quest for memories. The food, which he had never noticed to such an extent previously, was indifferent. He was grateful when the time came to pay the bill, and refused a digestive liqueur as gracefully as possible.

Sunday passed in silence. Rain fell, and there was a dull game of soccer on television, Switzerland versus Latvia, which ended in a draw. The rain persisted on Monday, and there was not even a dull game on television. M. René went to bed early in order to be ready for the morning. He rose at six, shaved, trimmed his moustache, showered, and drank a black coffee. He called for a taxi at 7.15, and asked it to go to 129, Rue de la Liberté Réformée, ten numbers away from the house in which Todorovic lived. He estimated that even if the odd numbers were all on one side, 129 was six doors away from 119, and should be far enough away for safety. On the way in the cab, he seemed to remember that the Rue de la Liberté Réformée was a quiet residential street, with benches, as always in Switzerland, catering for the repose of the weary rambler. Then it occurred to him the Liberté Réformée was a typically Swiss name, probably deriving from some local happening. What the hell is Reformed Liberty anyway? How can you reform something as fundamental to human happiness as Liberty?

He decided not to think about it further, but to accept it as a fact.

The cab arrived at 129 at 7.43. There was little traffic. M. René was warmly dressed. The weather was still uncertain. A few small pools in the roadway showed that it had rained briefly during the night. M. René strolled down towards 119. He saw the small Opel parked a little way along the road, and a Renault parked just behind it. He glanced at his watch. 7.46. He crossed the road slowly and retraced his steps to number 130, in front of which he found a slightly drunken looking concrete bench, and on which he sat. There was no movement in the street, except for an unhealthy looking jogger who passed by as though on his last legs. M. René looked at him anxiously. This was not the time or the place to require first aid. After a moment, an elderly gentleman with glasses emerged from a house quite far down the road. He was wearing an overcoat over pyjamas and bedroom slippers. He had a very small, inquisitive dog on the end of a long lead. M. René glanced at his watch again. 7.52. The dog was reluctant to decide on which patch of ground to relieve itself. It began searching in the direction of 119, and the old man gave it its head, following slowly. M. René could not bear to look, so settled with his head in the direction of the green Opel.

'Will that dog ever make up its mind?'

M. René turned in time to see Urs Mildenegger slide onto the bench beside him.

'What are you doing here?'

'I want to see your face when you realize you have been taken in.'

'Where were you hiding?'

'I have been here for the last half an hour, awaiting your arrival, in the porch of the house just behind
you.'

'Very clever.'

'We are not without experience.'

'You don't believe my information is valid?'

'Not for a moment.'

'Why not?'

'Your source is unreliable. I would be a fool if I were taken
in. I am not a fool.'

The Chief's smile was enough to make M. René wild
with anger. 'What's the time?' he asked.

'7.55,' said the Chief.

'I have 7.57.'

'Which just shows how impatient you are!' The Chief
laughed softly. 'At least we have achieved one little success,'
he said, indicating the other side of the road. 'The dog has
succeeded in finding relief.'

'Judging by its position,' said M. René, 'it's a bitch.'

'How observant! I told you you were the Police Chief,
not me.'

The old man retraced his steps slowly, still obeying the
bitch's whims, and at last vanished into a building, lifting
the animal to climb the stairs.

'They are both very old,' remarked M. René.

'They are not the only ones,' said the Chief.

There was a silence.

'How can you be so sure that you are right?' asked
M. René.

'I can't. I'm a gambler, like everyone else in my profession. Only, like the best gamblers, we know the odds. We
can make assessments. We don't react too soon. If you like,

we have cultivated instincts. And it is my instinct which tells me that you are a novice at the game.'

'Time?'

'7.57 my time. 7.59 yours.'

'You don't even think I may be right?'

'I'm not one for sticking my neck out. Everything is possible, but not everything is probable.'

A church bell sounded a sonorous and mournful eight. M. René managed a smile.

'Both of us wrong,' he said.

'From now on, I begin to be right and you start being wrong,' muttered the Chief, and added: 'A particularly quiet morning, I would say. No birdsong. Hardly a breath of wind. A speck or two of rain, just to show there's life in the sky.'

'You look like the winner,' conceded M. René.

'Don't be like one of those candidates who concede too soon after an election. It takes away too much of my pleasure.'

'You derive pleasure from being right?'

'No, I am used to it. I derive pleasure from your being wrong.'

M. René looked at him fixedly. 'Is that the extent of your jealousy?'

The Chief thought about it. 'I suppose so,' he admitted. 'I'm not usually a vindictive person. You must have hurt me very deeply.'

'I'm sorry.'

'To the extent of my searching for every opportunity to talk about it.'

'Oh, you know,' said M. René, softly, 'as my loneliness becomes intolerable with the passage of time, I will be searching for every opportunity to do the same thing.'

The Chief held out a hand. M. René took it, and they shared their absent friend for a moment.

'Time?' asked M. René.

'8 o'clock my time, 8.02 your time, 8.03 the local church.'

'I concede.'

'Not yet. Drag out the pleasure. They're anything but punctual in the Balkans.'

'We're not in the Balkans. We're in Geneva, the watch-making capital of the world.'

M. René rose. 'I know when I'm beaten. It's when I start to feel the cold.'

Suddenly the Chief grasped his wrist. His eyes were on the distance. M. René turned. Two men ran down the steps of number 119. They evidently felt they were late. One opened the back door of the green Opel, the other stepped in. Then the first sat at the wheel. A colossal explosion followed as the blue parked Renault literally disintegrated, blowing the Opel out of its way, and starting a fire. Windows everywhere were broken. One of the trees lining the road was blown out of its roots, and fell across the road. Both the Chief and M. René, who had instinctively flinched, were covered with dust the colour of terra-cotta from damaged and dislodged bricks. The Chief looked at M. René with shock and horror on his face. He was petrified. M. René hardly acknowledged the look, since something else claimed his attention. He found his notebook and pencil, and strode into the road.

Further down the street, a car, a silver Volkswagen, was having to turn round unexpectedly because of the fallen tree. With cars parked on both sides of the road, its manoeuvre was difficult and frantic. M. René had time to walk within convenient distance to begin taking down the car's number. There were two occupants in the car. It accelerated away, then came to a screeching halt. It backed in M. René's direction, halted again. The passenger half opened his door, then emptied a revolver in M. René's direction. The detonations sounded like caps from a toy pistol after the tremendous noise of the explosion. At all events, M. René, still deafened, could not take them seriously. He finished taking the number down in his own time as the silver car accelerated away and out of sight. Unhurriedly M. René walked back to where Urs Mildenegger was still cowering in visible shock.

'You never warned the police,' he said tensely.

'I did,' protested Mildenegger in a small voice.

'But they didn't believe you?'

'If I didn't believe you, how do you expect them to?'

People began to recover from the shock, some screaming from windows, others emerging into the street. One man had called the police, and was reassuring others.

'I'm so sorry,' Mildenegger managed to say.

'Here is the number of the car which drove away from the scene.' M. René gave the Chief a page from his notebook.

'They shot at you!'

M. René buttoned his coat, shook off the dust, and walked away in search of a taxi.

The two culprits were arrested later that day, and claimed diplomatic immunity.

# XI

THE PHONE began ringing hysterically and incessantly from the time in the afternoon M. René returned home. He could imagine why. After the police it was the time of the press to arrive on the scene. The idiotic ex-Police Chief was probably still sitting shell-shocked on his bench. How did he happen to be on the spot will have been the question. He had not known how to answer, even to his own people. He would probably invent some fatuous excuse, which would not ring true. Then, to extract himself from a tight spot, he would no doubt mention this respected doyen of the concierges of this world, who just happened to be passing, and who, with a total disregard of his own safety, calmly walked into the roadway through a veritable hail of bullets to take down the number of the getaway car.

He could already see the headlines in the local papers, not yet fully attuned to the wild excesses and total inexpressibility of the press elsewhere, but still pretty indiscriminate in turning courage into vulgarity and ordinary behaviour into

the extraordinary. 'A night porter in line for a medal', 'In
the absence of police, M. Le Concierge takes over'; a variety
of possible horrors suggested themselves to his imagination.
He stuffed his ears with cotton wool, and let the infernal
instrument ring. He then decided to close the shutters of
the house as though it were unoccupied. He used only
a small desk light in his study as a discreet comfort in
the darkness. Sooner or later there would be knocking on
the door as the press discovered where he lived. Knocking
and ringing and calls from outside. They materialized soon
enough, and when they stopped, there was no reason for M.
René to lower his guard. He continued to move cautiously
in the dark, even when the coast seemed to be clear. He
ventured into the entrance hall. The slats over the front door
were somewhat wider spaced than the others. He discreetly
looked out, and saw nothing. All the same, let night fall, he
thought, when the excitement will have died down, and the
news would be old.

He glanced at the floor, and saw that a message had been
pushed under the front door. He picked it up. Curiously
enough, it came from an address in Geneva, the registered
office of the International Brotherhood of Concierges and
Hall Porters. M. René snorted. He had virtually no contact
with the organization, despite the fact of being its titular
head. Perhaps because of that fact.

He read the note. It asked him to ring a number in
London urgently. London? Why London? The number
was that of the publisher who had tried unsuccessfully to
commission his memoirs. He had regarded the matter as
closed. Now here was the insinuating Mr Matheson – or
was it Matthews? – to open that fruitless dialogue again.
Full of resolution, he dialled the number on his portable.

What Mr Matheson or Matthews had to tell him was not reassuring, or immediately comprehensible. First of all, his name was Masters. Reggie Masters. He said that he had information that efforts were being made by an unknown party to sell portions of his unfinished memoirs to a British tabloid for a substantial sum of money.

'That's impossible,' said M. René. 'There are only two copies in the world as far as I know. Your copy and mine.'

Reggie Masters was open-minded about this. He thought it would still be possible to acquire an injunction against their use of the material, since the translation had been by Miss Whitlop, the young lady sent to Geneva to assemble his thoughts; but of course, the case would be immeasurably reinforced if they, the publishers, could announce that, far from having been abandoned, the book was being finished and would be published. With this assurance, the newspaper would not have a leg to stand on. M. René was still thinking of the lost manuscript. 'May I ring you back in ten minutes?' he asked.

'Not a minute longer. It's going to be difficult even now. Every moment counts.'

'Ten minutes.' M. René prepared to hang up.

'One final word. It is quite clear that the market potential for such a book is very great. Greater than we at first imagined. I believe it to be big enough to be put up for auction in America.'

'America? What about America?'

'We could achieve an advance of over a million dollars, with luck.'

'How much?'

'Call me back in ten minutes.' With that, Reggie Masters hung up.

M. René felt like begging for one thing at a time. He had just organized things in his mind, and now this had to confuse the issue. On his way into his den, he thought a million was absurd. Nobody gets that kind of advance. It must have been a slip of the tongue, or a partially clumsy effort to influence him. He opened the drawer of his writing desk where his abandoned manuscript was kept. It was empty. Had he moved it inadvertently? No, he was sure he had not. Mme Radibois? She was not sufficiently literary to care for more than articles of clothing. Then, in a flash, he remembered the young people showering after their tryst. She, grinning from ear to ear, giving her lover a thumbs-up sign. What does a thumbs-up sign mean normally, if not a demonstration of success, in this case, of theft? M. René was furious. So that is why she had tried to persuade him to pursue the line of least resistance, to sell himself, like a whore, a subject she knew all too much about.

He cursed them both, until he remembered that he had promised to call back whatever his name was within ten minutes with a decision which would be difficult to reverse. Still, he had changed his mind once. He could always change it again. What was urgent was to punish these young renegades, with their cheap thrills in the grass, and the more expensive, but unpaid for, thrills on their howling motorbike. It was a coldly decided M. René who called back, asking to speak to whoever it was he had spoken to ten minutes previously. He could tell from Mr Masters' voice that he was smiling.

'Well, now. Have you reached a decision?'

'My manuscript has been stolen.'

'Have you any idea by whom?'

'Oh yes. A young prostitute living with my nephew.'

'I don't think I caught that.'

'My nephew is living with a lady who does not confine her activities to the night. It is – too complicated a situation to explain on the telephone. They stole my work. Both of them. They are accomplices.'

'I see. Your nephew? Do you know when it was stolen?'

'Precisely. They came to my house asking to use my shower after – evidently, they were in urgent need of a shower, and I am not one to deny a nephew of mine a shower if he says he needs one. They took it in turns, and he went first. While he was showering, she engaged me in conversation, encouraging me to commercialize my experiences of a lifetime. Evidently when I demonstrated some reluctance to do so, it only encouraged the two of them to steal my manuscript in order to derive the advantages of such an idea themselves. After her shower she came out much refreshed, and gave my nephew a thumbs-up sign which I interpreted as an appreciation of hot water and its benefits. I only realize now that while she was out of the room, she entered my study and stole my manuscript.'

'You must be very disillusioned by your nephew's behaviour.'

'Oh, I was disillusioned by it long ago. This has only added fuel to my mistrust of him.'

'Listen, M. René, can you fax me a deposition, repeating precisely what you have just told me? I'll give you my fax number. I'm sure that will be enough to obtain an injunction. Newspapers are particularly unscrupulous these days, but they tend to fight shy of material they know to have been stolen, and which may easily become a pretext for litigation. We need this very urgently, as you can imagine, if we are to stop them getting away with it.'

M. René promised to deliver his testimonial. Although he had no fax machine himself, the shop where he bought his mobile phone had facilities. Before hanging up, he couldn't prevent himself from asking about that extravagant sum of money Mr Masters had mentioned for the advance. 'There must have been some mistake,' he suggested.

Mr Masters spoke in his most suggestive and mellifluous tones, with a confidentiality which made him practically inaudible at times. 'You have no idea, M. René, of the possibilities of a book these days if, I repeat if, it is handled with imagination, and what I like to call ingenuity. A book, you see, is not merely some writing contained in a couple of pieces of cardboard. No. No. Dear me, no. It is a potential newspaper serial, as I am sure you have already understood. It may be a CD record. It represents potential film, video, CD Rom rights. And there are foreign rights, with all they represent. New possibilities are discovered practically every day, but it needs vision to realize all this promise, and the kind of experience we believe we possess. What I like to call my team and my good self. I mentioned a figure of a million dollars for an American advance. It needs luck, but if there's an auction with more than one bidder, it's by no means out of the question. No, M. René, it was certainly no slip of the tongue. I'd go as far as to say we don't permit ourselves slips of the tongue, not where money's concerned. I'm sure you'll be satisfied with us, and when the time comes to look back on our mutual adventure, you will be congratulating both us for our efforts and yourself for your choice.'

M. René said, 'I hope so.' It was the first time he had been conscious of someone on the telephone whose smile was audible. It was not an element which made for trust.

'I must be the final arbiter of what is printed,' he warned.

'Within reason, within reason,' Mr Masters replied. 'There is a widely accepted formula in contracts, which reads – "Which must not be unreasonably withheld—."'

'Who is to decide what is unreasonable?'

There were peals of delighted laughter from the other end. At last something had managed to put a stop to the smiles. 'We must be the final arbiter, once we are risking our money and our time. Oh, incidentally, in the light of this injunction, once it is behind us, we will be sending you a new contract to sign, and whereas we reserve the right to use what we wish of Miss Whitlop's work, we intend to send out a more experienced ghost-writer in the shape of Gilbert Gordie. This will mean giving up twenty-five per cent of your royalties, but from our researches we're convinced that you will do better with Gordie than you would have done with Miss Whitlop. Gordie's a first class man, an ex-journalist, with a gossip column of his own in a leading tabloid, "Gordie's Goodies", you may have heard of it?'

'No,' said M. René reasonably. 'But tell me, does he still write it?'

After a moment, Mr Masters replied: 'No, not now.'

'Why not?'

'Personal reasons.'

'Once he is to take a quarter of my earnings, do I not deserve to know at least that?'

There was more laughter. 'You have a lawyer's mind.'

'No, sir. I have a concierge's mind. With a lawyer's mind, I would have failed in my profession.'

'Oh, he fell out with management.'

'What management?'

'You're a regular terrier, aren't you? Won't let go. The management of his paper.'

'Fell out? What does that imply?'

Mr Masters showed the first symptoms of his true character. 'D'you remember a stripper and rock singer called Sugar Cone?'

'No.'

Mr Masters stopped in disbelief. 'Are you serious?'

'Why should I have heard of him?'

'Her. Her. Gordie revealed that he was really a man.'

'So?'

'He wasn't. She was a woman all the time. And she, he, or it, sued the paper for twenty million dollars, claiming mental torture.'

'In America?'

'Where else?'

'And won?'

'Even more after their appeal was turned down by another judge. The paper and Gordie parted company. And we're delighted. It released a top ghost-writer from his contract. You'll see. You'll be delighted. He's in another league from the girl we sent you, although we're all grateful for the spade work she did.'

'First of all, stop my manuscript from being published. Then we'll see.'

A silence. The smile effectively vanished from Mr Masters' voice. It took on a conventionally sinister ring. 'M. René. Are you still there?'

'Is there any reason I should not be?'

'It doesn't work that way.'

'No?'

'No. We have been more than generous up to now. We have overlooked the time you have wasted, as well as the money you have thrown down the drain through your indecision. I refer to items like Miss Whitlop's salary, her board and lodging, to say nothing of the fact that you wouldn't have known about the impending publication in a notorious tabloid if we hadn't found out through our contacts and warned you. Now, of course, if you are willing to pay us our financial investment back, together with an estimate of the time you have cost an executive board and items such as postage and phone calls, and if you are willing to allow publication to go ahead without raising a finger in protest, I am sure we can be persuaded to be as generous as before, and not ask for more than, say, something in the region of 20,000 pounds in indemnity.'

'That is blackmail,' snapped M. René.

'I am not aware that services rendered can be called blackmail.'

'Why didn't you warn me before?'

'I did not think you to be so naive, sir. Have you ever got something for nothing, except on your birthday?'

'I expected – I don't know what I expected,' M. René admitted.

'We're not a charitable organization, sir, to keep our clients in pocket money. We are investors, sir, and on this occasion, we have invested in you.'

M. René was horrified, and lost for words. He had never really understood that the hours he had spent with the young lady implied a commitment of some sort. On the contrary, he imagined he had made a concession by devoting so much attention to a scheme which, in the end, displeased him. But he now realized in a flash how ridiculous it would be to claim that he had a case. He felt trapped, and worse, that it was his own fault. As a concierge, his assessment of human motives would never have allowed him to fall into such a trap. It was either age, or else the fact that he was no longer working for employers which had made such stupidity possible. It is hard to work for yourself if you're not used to it. Especially in retirement.

It was clearly expedient to play for time.

'You prevent the stuff from being published.'

'Send me the fax saying it has been stolen, sir.'

M. René hated the burgeoning of 'sirs' among the fellow's words. They sounded like a paean of victory, a seal on his humiliation.

'I will. And . . . oh, incidentally, what do you intend to call my masterpiece?'

'Ah . . . you're going to love this, sir. It was Gill Gordie's idea, and we all think it a selling title of genius. Are you ready, sir?' That awful smile was back in the voice again, cheeky, cocksure, and charging.

'Yes,' replied M. René.

'What the Concierge Saw.'

# XII

He called Urs Mildenegger on the telephone, early the next day.

'I trust I let enough time elapse before calling you.'

'Yes. This is not the United States or England. The reporters haven't got helicopters to hound you with, nor do they lie in wait for you. There is no hot news in Switzerland. All news is cold. And I'm grateful for it. My chief anxiety was explaining why you happened to be on the spot, so far from home, at eight o'clock in the morning. But no one ever asked. They are too obtuse. Good at leader writing, hopeless as newsgatherers.'

'How did you explain why you were on the spot, let alone me?'

'A last minute anonymous call. That's always useful, and untraceable.'

'Why would you be called, the day after retirement?'

'You can't expect Serbs to know that. They only have one way of retiring, by blowing each other up in booby-trapped cars.'

'Anyhow, I wanted to thank you for protecting the identity of my informant.'

'How could I do that? Even I don't know who it is.'

'You knew it was someone, and you steered the pack away. Thank you.'

'I told them you were on your way to the airport when you passed that way.'

'It's nowhere near the route from my house to the airport.'

The ex-Chief laughed incoherently. M. René began to wonder how much of all this was true.

'Are you drunk?' he asked, bluntly.

This occasioned more laughter, which resulted in painful coughing, and even a risk of throwing up.

M. René reflected how lucky he had been to pass into retirement without too great a physical or mental change. Of course, he had never accepted idleness as an alternative to work. He had mobilized his faculties in the pursuit of new activities, somewhat scatterbrained as it turned out, but always positive. The coughing and retching only increased his impatience. When he felt he could be heard again, he spoke with unaccustomed energy.

'I can see you, seated in the middle of all that wreckage in your flat, slowly sipping away at a bottle of the hard stuff. Are you dressed yet?'

'I'm in pyjamas,' yelled the ex-Chief, 'and a dressing gown with marks of tinned soup and toothpaste on it! Are you satisfied, you tight-lipped Calvinist spinster!'

He was trying hard to be offensive, that was obvious. M. René realized it was useless to show anger, or even irritation with a man in such a condition. He spoke quietly. 'I'm only thinking of your own good, Urs.'

'My good is drink!' he cried.

The doorbell rang.

M. René frowned. The shape just visible, moving through the frosted glass, seemed familiar.

'I'll call you later.'

'No use calling me later. I'll be blotto.'

'I'll call you later still.'

'I might not be here.'

'Adios, my friend.'

He hung up before the ex-Chief found any new outlets for his sense of the dramatic. The bell rang again, more impatiently. He opened the door. Immaculate in her insolence, it was Kuki, her oily hair cascading over her leather-clad shoulders. She looked unhappy, and vaguely dangerous. M. René's eyes narrowed as he controlled himself visibly.

'Well?' he asked.

'You win, you old bastard,' she whispered.

'I win?'

'They called. From London. They've issued an injunction, whatever that is. Now I won't be able to get Louis out of gaol.'

'Louis? Where is he?'

'They caught us, yesterday. He was being protected by someone in the police force. Yesterday, it all changed. They got us. They let me go, for the moment. I had to leave an address. I haven't an address. I left yours.'

'Are you mad? Come indoors.'

He shut the door behind her.

'Why did you steal my manuscript?'

'What a stupid question. To sell it, of course.'

M. René gave her an opulent thumbs-up sign. She laughed coldly. 'Right.' She returned the sign. 'You remember.'

'And why did you give the police my address?'

'I don't know any other.'

'And how did you expect to get Louis out of gaol?'

'I talked to the agency. If the bike is paid for in full, they're willing to overlook the past. Of course, they needed a reference. I gave your name.'

M. René looked grim. 'You are trying, one would say desperately, to provoke me. Why?'

'I am throwing myself on your mercy. I've nowhere to go. I'm desperate. I don't want to go back to the night club. I care for Louis.'

'And since I'm family, you also care for me. That much is evident.'

'You're old enough and experienced enough to look after yourself.'

He changed his tone, now that her impudence was becoming clear as the surprise of her arrival wore off.

'You say I win? I wonder. In order to earn that injunction I had to promise to go on with my autobiography.'

She brushed this aside. 'You do win. Thanks to me you're going to be stinking rich. Normally, you'd have to pay me ten per cent — fifteen even — for having forced you to go on with it. And what do I get out of it? Nothing but a hot shower.' It was evidently her intention to be hurtful. 'You're worrying about your fucking autobiography when your nephew, your flesh and blood, the only flesh and blood you have, is in prison, your name dishonoured, discredited.'

'We do not have the same name,' M. René said, and almost immediately regretted it. It sounded calculating, under the circumstances. He explained his remark. 'Louis is my sister's child.' It only made his remark sound worse.

'And what happens to me now?' she asked emotionally. 'That's much more to the point. Where do I sleep?'

'Your place in the grass is still available, but owing to circumstances, you will have to sleep alone.'

After a second of surprise, she swung at him with the back of her hand, catching him on the side of his chin. He reeled backwards. It was in moments like that that he felt his age. He slapped her face with far greater accuracy and economy. She winced, more in disbelief than in pain.

'Now, you'll have to take me,' she growled, and tackled him in a way which left no doubt about her ultimate intention. He protected himself as best he could by seizing her hair with some displeasure, and forcing her head backwards. She began to scream. He cursed her, wondering if she could be heard from outside. He relaxed his grip on her hair as a kind of absurd bargaining point, which did not stop her screams. While still dangerously upright, but locked in an ungainly posture, they seemed momentarily to be indulging in some new dance which had caught the public imagination. Then they lost their balance in the doorway to his study, falling against a delicate occasional table, and shattering its legs. It seemed only reasonable to him to ask for a truce in order to assess the damage, but the idea of arbitrary destruction only seemed to excite her further. She groped for his genitals with eyes glazed with desire. He found her hair again, and pulled with all his might. It was war without quarter, which only came to a momentary halt when physical exhaustion set in. As they lay, immobile

among the debris around the collapsed table, he glanced at a
photograph which had fallen, freed of its broken frame and
shattered glass. It was of his wife in a flowery summer dress,
holding a parasol, and smiling with determination. 'Who's
that?' asked Kuki, in a breathless voice.

'My wife. My late wife.'

'I don't have much opposition, do I?' She panted, quietly.
In spite of their parlous position, he was impelled to laugh.
She joined in.

He asked her in a calm and puzzled voice: 'What exactly
are you after?'

She hesitated. 'I want a father,' she said.

'And you want to start your new relationship with a
little incest?'

It was her turn to laugh, his turn to join in.

An air of deceptive serenity hung over them as they
lay, deadlocked, on the carpet. All he could hear was her
breathing, apart from his own, that is. And after a moment
the situation became almost normal, as though they had
fallen onto the grass haphazardly after a cycling trip in
the mountains, and now they were recovering from their
efforts in a quiet appreciation of nature. Of course, here
there was not much evidence of nature, just his heavy and
unadventurous furniture seen from a different angle. His
massive desk, with the drawer from which the manuscript
had been filched, still slightly ajar. Why had he never
noticed it before? The framed photography of royalty,
signed, Alfonso XIII of Spain, Marie of Romania, Geraldine
of Albania, all of them staring resolutely into the future, and
seeing nothing. Why did the only photograph to fall to the
ground and shatter have to be that of his wife? And also,
why did he have to wait for his seventieth birthday for this

sudden series of unprovoked contacts with the opposite sex? For decades, he had acted being old before his time, which, in a way, had been part of the job, only to be propelled into a series of confrontations which forced on him the impression of being young after his time; the virtual rape in his own bed, followed by the late springtime of true love, then the strange doubles entendres of Mme Radibois, and the almost religious ritual of the lost button and obsessive interest, worthy of Lady Macbeth, with the cleanliness of his sheets, and now this ridiculous wrestling match, in its aura of cheap perfume mellowed by the unpleasantly sour smell of leather and of sweat.

His mind wandered, and he admitted to himself that this carnal proximity was not without having its effect, a thought he chased away like a blasphemy, as though one could compare the uniqueness of Agnes with this spiritual chaos, even if the consequences were similar. He thought briefly of his nephew in the grass under similar circumstances, and it was enough almost to kill the comparison. Almost.

He seemed to be in Africa for some reason, he could not think why. And then as the heat and the drums grew in intensity in his mind, a great image of Mme Radibois appeared to him, large as the Cheshire cat on the ceiling (or was it sky?) above him. She seemed to eye the broken table and the scattered objets d'art with a bleak, admonishing appraisal. Her gaze switched joltingly, as though she were a badly made toy, onto the manhandled black business suit, and then the look fixed him with a saucy amusement. He willed her to fade away, and reveal Africa in all its mystery, with its powerful odours, and turbulent sense of rhythm. Suddenly he saw himself above the crowd, dressed in khaki pyjamas from which one button was missing, covered in military insignias, and with a jaunty jockey-cap on his head made of zebra skin. In one hand he held a javelin, in the other, a Marshal's baton, crafted in wood. But was it really him? Yes, for though his skin was undeniably darker, the cut of the pencil thin moustache, now barely visible over the mouth, gave him away. As the frenzy heightened, he raised his javelin to great popular acclaim, and threw it into the arena. However, he had no great experience in throwing things, and it dropped into the crowd, killing someone instantly. These days there are always casualties. There are just too many people. As the festivities began, he caught a glimpse of the victim being carried away for burial. Despite the blackness of her skin, she bore a striking resemblance to his wife. He moaned guiltily, and moved into the dancing crowd, only to wake when a not insensitive hand gripped him by the testicles. Age has its disadvantages. He had dropped off, relaxing his hold on her hair, and she had profited stealthily from this inattention. He spoke in a voice which displayed more authority than volume, for the simple reason that he recognized his vulnerability.

'Now stop this tomfoolery this minute, and help me to my feet.'

The tone took her by surprise, and she withdrew her hand.

He added: 'It is your father speaking.'

She rose to her feet, and extended a helping hand. It took more than that to get him to rise. First of all, he knelt on broken glass, cutting his trousers about the knees, and then needed a chair, which she quietly displaced for him. Once standing, he looked around him. 'Look at this mess. Don't you ever do that again.'

'I'm sorry, Father. Truly sorry.' She overplayed the contrition by behaving as though she were only ten years old.

He fell into the trap as clumsily as anyone without experience. 'If you ever do it again, I'll really become your father, and give you a thorough hiding.'

She began breathing harder again, and suggested: 'Do it now.'

'Not this time,' he replied, confused.

'D'you want me to break some more furniture? Is that it?'

'If you do—'

'Yes?'

Without waiting for his reply, she slipped off her panties, approached his ear while taking his hand, and whispered: 'Come and spank me in the shower!'

Quick as a flash, he found the answer, faced with this emergency.

'If you don't get dressed at once, and leave me alone, there'll be no financial assistance.' Once more, he could have kicked himself as soon as he had uttered the words. Once more he had been forced into a concession merely in order to protect his position. Even if giving a few francs to a vagrant girl bore fewer consequences than spending dreary hours with a ghost-writer, they both represented a certain kind of blackmail which had succeeded.

She took the hint, and climbed back into her panties.

'I said, get dressed.'

'That's all I had on.'

'That's all? Oh, well . . . it shows me I'm getting old.'

'Not as old as that,' she said, coquettishly, 'we could have had a really good time, you and I.'

'Aren't you forgetting something?'

'Dad,' she added, putting her finger in her mouth, and wagging her hips.

He was forced to smile, even if rather grimly. Reaching into his wallet, he counted out one thousand francs.

'This should keep you going for a day or two. It'll give me time to think how we go on from there,' he said.

'Thank you,' she said, in a colourless voice.

'You were hoping for more, I know,' he said, 'or at least for a more permanent arrangement, but it'll have to wait. The cleaning-woman will be coming very shortly, and I have to clear away this mess before she arrives.'

'Perhaps I can help you, Daddy, and at least earn a little of what you're giving me?'

'Later. Later. I must get rid of you before she comes.'

'Do I look like someone you have to be ashamed of?' she asked, with an unpleasant hint there could be a resumption of hostility.

'No, of course not,' he lied brazenly, 'but she has a very possessive disposition, which has only increased since my wife shook off this mortal coil.'

'Did what?'

'Died.'

'Get rid of her. That's what I'd do. There are plenty of people qualified to tidy up. I'd do it if you made it worth my while.'

'She is not here to tidy up,' M. René said acidly. 'I can do that. She's here to clean. And now, if you'll forgive me—'

'And how about Louis?' she asked, on her way to the door.

'I'll . . . think about that too.'

He half-opened the front door. She insisted on kissing

him. He shut the door again while it lasted, then opened
it wide, and every gesture, every infinitesimal movement,
encouraged her to get out, and stay out. He bolted the
door so that she could still hear it, and glanced at his
watch. In a quarter of an hour, Mme Radibois would
be there. There was no time to lose. He swept up the
debris as best he could, then, with considerable difficulty,
deposited it in the attic. He did not trust himself with what
was left of the table, however, and opened the door of the
holy of holies, his dead wife's mausoleum, with its freezing
draughts and smell of camphor and of death, pushed the
remains of the table in there to die, and locked the door
once again. There were only five minutes left. He took
off his shirt, tie, and suit, packed them into a shoulder
bag, put on new ones without bothering too much about
colour combinations, and left the house in a hurry, locking
the front door.

As he turned to leave, he saw Mme Radibois' hat
travelling along the top of the hedge leading to his garden
gate. He cursed his luck, ran nimbly to the back of the
house, and waited. He heard her footfall up the drive,
and even heard her singing discordantly as she fumbled
for her key. The 10.01 to Nyon, Rolle, Morges and
Lausanne rattled by. Both the train and Mme Radibois
were exactly on time, which was only to be expected. The
front door shut. He waited a moment, then walked back
to where he had come from, clinging to the house, and
then proceeded to the garden gate on the grass. Once in
the street, he considered his priorities. The first was to let
his suit be invisibly mended and the shirt be restored to a
pristine condition without the attention of Mme Radibois,
the second was to work for the liberation of his nephew,

which was the only way he could think of to get that awful girl, with her abrasive techniques for arousal, off his back, and third, and by far the most important, even if the least urgent, to begin plotting with the drunken ex-Police Chief for Agnes' early release, whether she wanted it or not.

It was in his interest to remain absent from his house until four o'clock. Normally, Mme Radibois left at three, but he thought he had better leave an extra hour to be sure a confrontation would be avoided. So he walked to a shop in the neighbourhood specializing in invisible mending. He kept the address in a little red book dating from his golden years as a concierge, when urgent repairs to clients' clothes, for a variety of reasons, was at times called for. The old man in the shop, who had been on the verge of retirement for years, examined the suit with the application of a watch maker.

'How on earth did you manage to do such extensive damage?' he asked.

'You never asked me questions in the old days,' M. René replied.

The tailor looked at him with baleful amusement over his glasses. 'They were never your suits in the old days,' he said.

'True, let's just say I had an accident. I knelt on broken glass.'

'And tore your suit in annoyance.'

'That'll do.'

'I'm not inquisitive,' the tailor went on with a sigh, 'it's just that it takes great strength to do this amount of damage to a well-made garment, and I must congratulate you, at your age . . . but perhaps you had help?'

'Why not imagine I did? Is it redeemable?'

'I'll do my best.'

'No man can do more,' M. René reassured him, leaving his telephone number. As he left the shop, he thought of how much easier it was to field the questions of a man than the uncomfortably possessive ones of Mme Radibois. Since the weather was fine, he walked a long way to the concessionaire of the motorcycles. He knew vaguely where it was, and it took him the best part of an hour, but since one of his aims was to kill time, it enabled him to think of his health, among other things.

The shop, when he eventually found it, was not of a kind to excite his interest, neither from the point of view of what it sold, nor from the type of men whose careers were devoted to selling it. There were motorcycles of all types, from brutal machines with artwork from comic strips, to innocent doe-eyed scooters. There were also life-size cutouts of two extremely dirty men, one of whom had recently won a Grand Prix, and the other a rally across the Sahara. A suave man wearing a vulgar stone on his ring-finger approached M. René.

'Can I be of any help?'

'How much are these?' asked M. René, waving a hand as though they were fruit.

'Which one did you have in mind?' enquired the salesman. He had a habit of shutting his eyes when he spoke, at the same time smiling indulgently.

'All of them. Any of them.'

'Over there, finished in opalescent green, with the Tarzan artwork, is the 250 c.c. Twin-Cylinder Super Mountain-Bike, a special series called the Matterhorn, which comes in at 28,000 Swiss Francs.'

'How much?' M. René paled.

'Including tax. Then, over there, in the blue spectra-sheen, a patented finish which has the effect of gold dust sprayed on the blue background, is the 500 c.c. SPL type, which is rather more expensive at 43,599 francs.'

'I don't believe it.'

'And finally, that friendly red machine with an outer space motif is the top of the line 750 c.c. Predator, coming in at 69,999 francs.'

'But, they're more expensive than cars!'

'In many cases, yes. They are also faster, and far more exclusive.'

'And the little ones?'

'Yes, Monsieur, have you a daughter?'

'No.'

'Is it for yourself?'

'No. I have a nephew.'

'A nephew?'

'I believe he bought a machine here.'

'Bought one here?' The man's eyes were open now.

'Yes. How shall I put it? He paid the first of forty-eight instalments, is that right?'

'A young fellow, dressed in leather?'

'Possibly.'

'It was seventy-two instalments, and the first was paid for by a cheque, which bounced.' He called out. 'Signor Del Santuario!'

A swarthy man appeared from an inner office, his hair billowing under a coat of brilliantine. 'Si!'

The assistant explained who M. René was, and all goodwill faded from the newcomer's smile, although, for the form, the smile itself remained in place.

'And now you come to settle your nephew's bill,' he said, in a heavy Neapolitan accent.

'Not necessarily,' replied M. René, striking a discordant note. He was in his element again, after all his more intimate adventures. He knew how to deal with men; the more evidently corrupt and unpleasant, the better.

'First of all, kindly inform me about the price of the machine my nephew has been testing.'

'Testing?'

'Yes, testing, to see if it met his requirements.'

'He has had it for nearly three months.'

'He is slow to make up his mind.'

Signor Del Santuario was furnished with some typed information by his assistant.

'He was in possession of the 850 c.c. SS Plus Exterminator Masterpiece, priced at 76,000 francs.' And he held up a warning finger. 'After reduction from 79,999.'

'My nephew, after mature consideration, has decided against taking it.'

'Your nephew?' cried Del Santuario. 'He's in prison, where he belongs.'

'All the more reason for not wanting your motorbicycle,' replied M. René.

Del Santuario became aggressive. 'He owes us 76,000 francs—'

His assistant whispered in his ear. He resumed his diatribe: '—with superficial damage and wear and tear, our bill comes to 87,313 francs. Until this is paid in full, he stays in prison.'

'D'accordo,' said M. René, in perfect Italian.

Del Santuario registered a sudden misgiving. 'You are Italian?' he asked, in Italian.

'What difference does it make?' M. René replied, moving his cupped hand, thumb touching the other four, in a traditional gesture of resignation to the obvious. 'I hear the boy enjoyed the protection of the police?'

'Who told you that?'

'I have my informants.'

Del Santuario became more cautious. 'Thank God, the Police Chief has changed.'

'I know,' said M. René, 'Mildenegger has retired, and given way to Beat Kribl.'

'And high time,' Del Santuario said. 'How do you know all this?'

'It is common knowledge.' M. René brushed the question away, in Italian, of course. And he went on: 'It is possible that Mildenegger declined to arrest the lad out of deference to me—'

'Why? Who are you?' demanded Del Santuario.

'But, corruption doesn't work that way. As often as not it has little to do with an exchange of money, but rather of favours. If Mildenegger, out of the goodness of his heart, decided to show his consideration for me by not cutting short my nephew's pleasure, what reciprocal oversights did he register for you?' He smiled. 'What these favours are, I can only guess at. Is there some irregularity about the import of your vehicles? Is money laundered, using your normal conduits as a trader? I have no idea, but it should not be too difficult to find out. And, no doubt, the new Chief, Kribl, will unravel the mystery before too long. After all, almost his first act was to arrest the boy. One brick has been removed from the structure. The other bricks will tumble before too long, as light is shed on them. And Kribl has none of the humanity –

should one call it understanding – which characterized Mildenegger.'

The motorcycle experts retired into a whispered huddle. Del Santuario returned to the fray.

'If we made you an offer . . .'

'You think I couldn't refuse?'

'60,000 francs. A write-off.'

'Refused.'

Del Santuario became violent. 'Be reasonable, whoever you are. We're not in this business for our pleasure. We have to survive.'

'You have the machine. You can sell it as shop-soiled, in mint condition, only one dissatisfied owner, whatever you like, and presumably recoup more than 60,000 francs.'

'It's that . . . such top of the line machines are hard to sell at the best of times.'

'I understand what you're saying. You mean it needs the occasional idiot like my nephew to fall into your trap.'

'Shall we say it needs a connoisseur?'

'Exactly, an idiot. Listen, do what you wish. If you wish to leave my nephew languishing in prison, it's all right by me. We are not as close-knit a family as you are, less sentimental, more realistic.'

'What do you mean?' snapped Del Santuario.

'We only talk about La Famiglia.' He dragged out the word to make it vibrate momentarily in the air. 'My nephew is a responsible adult. If he chooses to break the rules, that's his business. But at least in prison we don't find his body in a ditch, riddled with bullets. This should make it clear to you that I will not be bamboozled into paying a penny towards that hideous machine, which has caused me sufficient misery as it is, with its earsplitting racket, its

acrid fumes, and its vulgar appearance. Ciao, Signori. I will
hasten to lunch with both the present and the late Police
Chief to find out the state of play. If I find anything out,
I will not hesitate to let you know, so that you may react
accordingly. Tanti saluti!'

'But who are you?' yelled Del Santuario. A new idea
struck him. 'If we wish to make another suggestion, who
do we contact?'

'I am not open to other suggestions. Release my nephew,
and then we'll talk.'

'We have no authority to do that!'

M. René made a helpless gesture, suggesting that we're
all victims of the powers that be, and he was off.

He found a taxi, and although he had not phoned for an
appointment, he decided to visit Urs Mildenegger. He rang
the doorbell with some trepidation, and his anxiety grew
when there was no answer. He tried again, twice, and was
about to give up when he fancied he heard a noise. He stood
quite still. Then a hoarse, muffled voice called his name. He
answered at once. There was a long pause.

'You can't come in. I'm too embarrassed.'

'Embarrassed?' said M. René softly, through the door.
'You don't have to be embarrassed with me.'

'I've let go, old friend. Let go.'

'Don't be so stubborn in your misery. Open the door
this instant.'

To M. René's surprise, the voice began to sing. 'Open
the door, Richa-a-ard, and – let me in.'

'That's it, Richard, open the door.'

There was a rattling of chains, and then a noise of a body
falling against the door. Then silence.

'Urs!' More silence. 'Urs!'

'It's no good, I can't pick myself up.'

'Who will pick you up if you don't?'

'I'll just stay here, and die. That'll be . . . the best solution.'

'Listen, I can smell the stench of rotting vegetables from here. You don't want to add to the pong, do you? They'll break down the door, and think how embarrassing that'll be.'

'If I'm dead, I won't feel the embarrassment, will I?'

'Well, you'll have to hurry, because I intend to go for help this instant!'

He stopped talking for a moment, since an elderly lady passed by the door, searching for her keys.

'René! René!' called Urs, from the floor. 'Are you still there?'

'Yes, I'm still here,' replied M. René, smiling indulgently at the lady.

'If you go for help, I'll crawl into the kitchen and cut my veins.'

'That's a silly threat, unworthy of you. As it happens, I have some help already. Madame . . . ?' He asked for her name.

'Is that poor Monsieur Mildenegger?' she replied. 'He's taken his retirement awfully badly.'

'May one know your name, Madame?'

'Madame Poncin.'

'Madame Poncin is here, Urs. The longer this goes on, the more embarrassing this will become, so open the door.' He made the gesture for Mme Poncin to speak.

'What do you want me to say?' she asked.

'Just register your presence. Confirm what I am saying.'

She knocked at the door. 'M. Mildenegger, this is Madame Poncin, your neighbour.'

'Tell him to get up off the floor, and open the door,' hissed M. René.

'Please rise from the floor, and open the door. We are here to help,' she hooted in a small voice.

'I'm going to the kitchen to fetch a knife. I'm going to cut my veins,' he roared.

'Oh!' Mme Poncin whimpered, looked around miserably, and swooned. M. René was just in time to catch her. With Mme Poncin limp in his arms, he suddenly saw red.

'You blithering moron,' he shouted, 'you've now caused the good lady to faint with your amateur theatricals.'

He was interrupted by a sound he quickly identified as that of helpless laughter. It came, of course, from the floor, beyond the door. He judged that it was now safe to help Mme Poncin to her front door, to select a key, to open her front door, to lower her onto a chair in her hallway, to resist a ferocious assault from an elderly Pomeranian dog, to fetch her a glass of water, and to enquire if she was all right.

Without waiting for her reply, he made his way back to outside her flat, kicking his legs wildly as he went to keep the dog from finding a toothhold, eventually slamming the door to a cascade of hysterical barking. When he reached Urs' door, it was ajar, with Urs, dishevelled and bearded, looking shyly out. M. René pushed open the door with a disgusted cry, and led the way through a sea of newspapers into the drawing room. Things had not improved in the interior. The smell of decaying food from the kitchen was almost unbearable, since every window seemed to be tightly shut.

'This cannot be allowed to go on,' said M. René quite

simply, 'you'll have trouble with the sanitation people before long. Rats and mice, have you considered that?'

'They're company,' Urs replied. 'Better than nothing.'

'Ridiculous. Have you lost all dignity? Aren't you just a little ashamed of yourself?'

'No.' Urs spoke without the slightest sense of melodrama. 'I've reached the bottom. I no longer wish to live. Would it surprise you that I've made several attempts to commit suicide?'

'I am not surprised at all that you failed,' M. René said, with a touch of calculated cruelty. 'What did you do, lie below the level of the bathwater while pinching your nose between the thumb and the forefinger of your hand?'

'How did you know?' asked Urs, softly.

'It won't work. Your reflexes come to your rescue.'

'Have you tried it?'

'Never. It's common sense. What else did you do? Saw at your veins with a blunt knife?'

'No. With a fork. I tried with a fork.'

'Just to be different?'

'I thought, four small holes. It would take longer.'

'Which means you didn't really want to die.'

'I always hated knives. Even as a boy. I was frightened of them.'

M. René sat down on the arm of the sofa. 'You were frightened of everything, weren't you? However did you end up Chief of Police? And it wasn't just knives and guns, was it? You were frightened of marriage. You were frightened of friendship. And yet, I have no doubt you were a good policeman, despite – perhaps because of – these anomalies.'

'Thanks for saying that.' Urs' face brightened. 'It's true.

I was a damn good policeman. I had nothing else to think about, you understand. No distractions. No private life. No friends. A one-track mind, you might say.'

M. René looked him deep in the eye, leaning forward intensely. 'Well, one thing you'll have to get used to, shocking as it may seem to you, you have a friend now.'

'Who?'

'Me.'

Urs held out a hesitant hand, grey with dirt, with a tramp's fingernails. M. René took it without hesitation, and covered both hands with his other hand, in a gesture of protection and confirmation.

'A friend?' Urs asked in a small voice.

'Yes. It's a wonderful word in its simplicity, it implies so much which is unspoken. And do you know why we're friends?'

'No,' said Urs, frowning, eager to learn.

'Because we feel for the same woman. Usually that breaks a friendship. Not in this case. Why? Because neither of us have her.'

'That's true. Neither of us have her.'

'No, but we are for ever linked by our love, our respect for her. You see, in a sense you allowed yourself to be fascinated by her, and finally let her enter into your consciousness as a secret object of desire by the fact that she was unattainable. Not only did she escape from all the traps you set her, but, in your heart, you never really wished her to fall into them. Perhaps without realizing it, you always gave her an easy way out.'

Urs smiled bitterly, on the verge of a surrender to his emotions. 'Oh, I realized it, I knew what I was doing. But you are uncanny, dear friend. How could you have guessed all of this?'

'I was part of the whole story. Don't be upset, but the fact is that, for some reason, she selected me. I don't think I deserved it, but perhaps you were a little too much the policeman not to be identified as the enemy. Still, let me say this – if she had understood your quality of heart, she might even more easily have subjected you to the sudden orgy of love which was unleashed on me, by the purest chance.'

Urs bit his lips. 'You are just saying that to be kind.'

'It would be so if I had been the winner, but we are both losers.'

'Yes – but you were the winner for a moment. Tell me. What was it like? Say anything you wish, I can take it.'

'It was magical. And to tell you the truth, it still is.'

'There you are. Don't tell me that you are not the winner.'

'I have a memory, yes. A memory which I cannot really share with you. I can only describe it at moments, as a friend. But for the rest, it defies description. In that sense, I am the winner. Undeniably. But as a consummation of happiness? There we are both losers.'

Urs took this in, and suddenly shook his head in agreement.

'You were good enough to speak of my quality of heart. I'm surprised you noticed it. It's not something a Chief of Police is anxious to parade under normal circumstances. But I will tell you something which may amuse you. One method of suicide which you did not guess correctly – perhaps, if I'd given you time, you could have done. It is the window.'

'You thought of jumping out?'

'I stood on the ledge for a long moment, holding onto the roof behind my back with my fingers. Can you imagine what held me back?'

'I can only imagine what would have held me back. Cowardice.'

'No. No. It's a momentary decision. There's no turning back. It's relatively easy if you're that way inclined, which you're not. It's easier than the fork or the bathwater. No, I saw people walking peacefully on the pavement, children playing, and I thought to myself, what right have I to suddenly appear in their midst, splashing blood all over the place? Isn't there enough in life which is unpleasant and unpredictable without adding to it?'

'When did this happen?'

'Not long ago. I couldn't immediately answer your knock because I was busy climbing back through the window.'

'Oh my God.'

'Yes, quite recently.'

They looked hard at one another, smiled grimly, and nodded.

'This is the moment to change the subject,' said M. René, letting go of Urs' hand, and rising. 'We must decide how to tidy this place up.'

'Hopeless.'

'Nonsense. But before we make plans, there is something I have to tell you. It is not my intention to take the incarceration of Agnes for granted. I intend to do everything humanly possible to assure her release from prison.'

'Be reasonable. You will have great opposition. I would say, insuperable opposition. First, she has confessed to three murders. Secondly, she has no desire to be released.'

'Have you talked to her?'

'Yes.'

'And?'

'She will see no one. She didn't want to see me.'

'Is she – sane?'

'Don't ask me. I always wonder if nuns are sane. She's much like a nun. A permanent smile on her lips. Disconcerting, to my mind. Of course, something may have happened since. This was immediately after her confession. The last day of my duty.'

'Has the court appointed a lawyer to defend her?'

'Yes. A Maître Muresanescu.'

'Romanian?'

'Origin. A youngish fellow in his thirties. Never heard of him before.'

'And a psychiatrist?'

'Yes, the usual, Madame Szepainska. She's good. Professor Szepainska.'

'Polish. What happened to all the Swiss?'

'They're suffering a crisis of self-confidence.'

'Listen, I want you to organize a lunch, inviting both of these people.'

'At the Mouton Enragé?'

'Why not? So much started there. It's where our Odyssey began.'

'Yes, but I can't go to the lunch. Not in the state I'm in.'

M. René removed his jacket.

'I'll now teach you a little about friendship,' he said.

'What are you going to do?' enquired Urs, in some alarm.

'I'm going to run a bath, which you are going to take,

whether you like it or not. And no tricks below the surface of the water! And you're going to shave with this razor and cream I have brought. Meanwhile I'm going to do that mountain of washing up.'

'No, no, you can't do that. And incidentally, I don't know how ethical such a lunch would be at this juncture.'

'I've noticed that when people are well dressed and well spoken, things immediately become much more ethical. There are many things I can tell them about Agnes, and there are still things I intend to find out. I don't see how a meeting of the minds can be unethical at any juncture of a murder trial.'

The conversation from this point was carried out at the tops of their voices, the one in the kitchen, to the background of running water, the other in the bathroom, with more running water, curling steam linking the two open doors in the corridors.

'By the way, did you protect my idiot nephew on that ghastly motorbike of his?'

'Protect is going a bit far. We could have arrested him at any moment. He did nothing to make himself inconspicuous. I decided to give him a bit of rope once he was destined to hang himself in any case.'

'You knew he was my nephew?'

'Oh yes. We arrested him once before for fornicating in a bus shelter during a rainstorm. It was then we took down his particulars.'

'He was with that girl of his?'

'How did you know?'

'He could hardly have been caught fornicating alone.'

'No. No. Of course not, silly of me. There was no way out of it. When they began, the bus shelter was empty.

With the rain, it filled up, but they were so busy they didn't notice. And people complained. You know Geneva.'

'Did you tend to overlook his misdemeanours because he was my nephew?'

'With your instincts, I'm surprised you need to ask. No, it's merely, with your impeccable reputation, I didn't see why you should be embarrassed gratuitously.'

Here, the conversation became so sensitive that M. René wandered into the bathroom, drying a plate at the same time.

'Tell me,' he said, more intimately, 'did you overlook similar peccadilloes in Signor Del Santuario's behaviour as a compensation for your refusal to arrest Louis?'

Urs Mildenegger was basking in the warm water, his eyes shut. He had cut himself shaving, and a diminutive trickle of blood ran from his chin into the water, discolouring it locally.

'Another suicide attempt?' M. René asked.

'No, I cut myself shaving. I have lost the habit. In answer to your question, as I said, I let the boy run because I knew I could arrest him whenever I wanted to. With our friend Dante Del Santuario it was different. I surrendered to the old police temptation of hoping he might lead me to bigger things – to bigger crimes and bigger criminals. The motorcycle shop is merely a front. That much is obvious.'

'So there is no connection whatever between your attitude towards my nephew and that towards the motorcycle dealership?'

'None whatsoever.'

'I was wrong.'

'Wrong?'

'I went there.'

'To the shop?'

'Yes. I pretended to be your close friend and that of Kribl.'

'That oaf?'

'I spoke my most liquid Italian, my concierge's Italian, and suggested I had knowledge of the deals which had been made with Cosa Nostra.'

'With whom?'

'Cosa Nostra. The Mafia.'

'And how did he react?'

'Nervously, I would say.'

'No wonder. These people are all members of the Neapolitan Camorra and their great fear is to be invaded and swamped by the Sicilian Mafia.'

'Oh, my God. So I did the right thing without knowing it?'

'Mark you, these people have a guilty conscience, almost by definition. They practically lead you to their Achilles heel once you are on their wavelength. Will it surprise you to know that the motorcycles they sell, all of them belonging to an obscure Japanese make, highly thought of by the cognoscenti, are, none of them, new?'

'None of them? In other words, they had no right to try to sell my nephew the bike as though it was new?'

'Absolutely not. How much did they ask for it?'

'87,313 francs, including minor damage incurred.'

Urs laughed. 'It was without doubt involved in an accident during a rally or road race, and restored by their experts, working under cover of a sect, the Moon Babies, high up in the mountains of central Switzerland.'

'The Moon Babies?' M. René repeated, incredulous.

'They have a couple of small banks, Banco Della Sacra

Corona and the Banca Immaculata, both engaged mainly in money laundering, an import-export business dealing with Russia, Kazakhstan, and so on. And via Siberia, a direct contact with Japan as an outlet for the Motoyama Company, manufacturing motorcycles, beer, power stations, and harpsichords. Does all that sound rational? They also deal in prefabricated coffins whenever the demand for ancient keyboard instruments drops. In other words, Motoyama is a typical, pragmatic Japanese conglomerate, as honest and straightforward as such a commercial giant can be in the modern world. They probably export crashed motorcycles at relatively low prices, either whole or in fragments, and allow locals free rein with their fancies, and their prices. Factory teams often win races, which keeps the name Motoyama in the eye of the susceptible public. It's a modestly lucrative enterprise among many others. And the more modestly lucrative enterprises there are, the more lucrative the coordinated effort becomes. And now, if you will excuse me, René . . .'

Urs began to rise laboriously from the bath, and M. René, with respect for his privacy, returned to the kitchen. When the washing up was finished, M. René regarded the kitchen with a sense of achievement, shared by the damp-eyed Police Chief, retired. M. René called for a taxi. It was now just after four in the afternoon. Urs promised to organize the lunch when the new protagonists were free, and M. René engaged in an emotional leave-taking with a man he had called back from the brink of incoherency.

He reached his home to find, to his alarm, that Mme Radibois was still there, an hour and a half after her regular leaving time, usually respected so meticulously.

'Mme Radibois, you are working late today.'

'Not really,' replied Mme Radibois, with a sad smile. 'If I'm sure you will be late, I don't mind leaving. But normally, I prefer to wait until you are back. I don't like to leave the house empty.'

'I see.' M. René walked about the house for a moment.

'Anything new?' he called out from the bedroom. He preferred not to be in the same room as her when he asked the question.

'No.'

He wandered back in the hall.

'No phone calls?'

'One, from London, I think. I don't speak English, and they seem to speak nothing else.'

'I can imagine who they are. Nothing else?'

'Nothing else,' she echoed, with her superior smile.

'Nothing untoward,' M. René found himself insisting.

'Why should anything be untoward?' Mme Radibois shrugged with a little dismissive laugh. 'Good afternoon, M. René.' She gathered her things together, and left the house, but not before a last lingering look at her employer, imbued with a weight of insinuation.

'Good afternoon, Mme Radibois,' he said, and thought, thank God she doesn't come in tomorrow.

# XIII

THE NEXT morning, M. René was prepared for a day of joyous belligerency. He planned to revisit the Neapolitan motorcycle shop and drag out his revelations of their duplicity, and finally deliver Louis from the hounds of the law. Admittedly he had given Kuki a thousand francs, but whereas that would have been enough to tide the frugal Swiss over a moment of difficulty, he dreaded her reappearance from one day to the next with the excuse that she had run out of cash. But if he had been honest with himself, he would have admitted that whereas the night with Agnes was the spiritual experience of a lifetime, he thought far more frequently about the outrageous struggle with that cheap tart, an event as tantalizing as it was unresolved. The husky invitation to spank her in the shower echoed and reechoed in his mind. He both regretted that he had not accepted her invitation, and thanked his lucky stars that he had not.

Curiously enough, the carnal side to what amounted to his rape by Agnes faded into insignificance, and turned

the awakening of his dormant emotions into an almost
religious experience, perhaps also coloured by reports of
how it had affected her. 'I do not deserve such happiness.'
What was that if not a renunciation of earthly pleasures in
favour of self-denial on a higher plane, a plane, it must
be admitted, of selfishness, of pious self-indulgence? With
Kuki there were no such complications, and no such
spiritual preoccupations. She staggered from orgasm to
orgasm, always in search of new spices to save the favoured
dish from deadly monotony.

It was with such ideas in his head that he prepared to
leave on his errands. He stopped in his tracks when he
heard a key in the door. Who had a key? It could hardly
be Mme Radibois, who didn't come on even days of the
week. In any case, it was half an hour too early for her.
Had Kuki acquired a key by some underhand means of
her own? He braced himself for a surprise which was
almost bound to be rude. Silently Mme Radibois entered
his study. She wore a floppy white summer hat with a
garland of artificial daisies on the brim. She was all in
white, with a belt, a blouse, a long skirt, and shoes. She
resembled a tennis champion from the twenties who had
lobbed her way to many tedious victories. Now she sat on
the sofa without being invited to, and crossed her legs in
ostentatious relaxation. Then she did something else which
she had never done before, still in dead silence. She lit a
cigarette, and drew on it with voluptuous relish. M. René
recovered from his surprise by waving his hand in the air as
though dispersing offensive fumes.

'Mme Radibois, have you taken leave of your senses? You
know I can't tolerate cigarette smoke in my vicinity.'

'Like so many things, it may just be something you have

to get used to,' Mme Radibois retorted, and went on: 'True, your late wife did not smoke, nor did the late M Radibois. He always warned me against lung cancer, so that I had to go into the yard for a whiff. Yet it was he who was run over by a truck, so he was the first of us two to go. I think that is called the irony of fate, or something of the sort. Anyway, I feel I have reached the age to assert myself, and that my smoking, which I enjoy in small quantities, will in no way influence the driving habits of our long-distance truckers.'

M. René reverted to his old stiff image under such provocation.

'That is complete nonsense, if you don't mind my saying so. Just because the late M. Radibois, who I did not have the pleasure of knowing, was struck down by a truck, it does not follow that the same destiny is reserved for you, by osmosis. It may well be that you pass away in a hospital suffering from lung cancer, just because you failed to heed his warning. But all that fades to insignificance when I invoke the fact that you are an employed person, dependent on me for your survival. You know that I detest the odour of cigarette smoke. Is it really worth your while to antagonize me?'

Mme Radibois blew out an enormous cloud of curling blue smoke and laughed. This was another surprise. M. René had never heard her laugh. Then she stubbed the cigarette out.

'Of course not,' she said, and coughed slightly. 'I hardly ever do it. Perhaps two cigarettes a day. I was just testing you.'

'That is very good of you, I'm sure. But might one know why?'

'You have changed. First of all, there's a button literally

torn off your pyjama top. It took all my skill and a lot
of patience to save the garment from destruction. I don't
wish to know how it happened, but it showed that violence
had entered a life which up to then had been ordered and
without surprises. And that was only the first symptom. I
need hardly draw your attention to the state of the sheets
that night.'

'Mme Radibois,' snapped M. René stridently, 'I forbid
you to mention the incident ever again if you wish to remain
in my employment!'

'But that is not the end of it! The shattered table in the
locked room. How did you drag it in there, you poor dear?
You shouldn't be exerting yourself like that at your age.
You should ask for help. I would have done it for you had
you asked, whatever the reason for its destruction. Whether
it was the result of rage, or self-defence against aggression
is not my business, as you say. As someone enjoying the
benefits of your generosity, it would have been my duty to
do such menial tasks for you, no questions asked—'

'Not with words, perhaps, but with insinuations, with
sly looks, with innuendo.'

'Of course, I'm inquisitive. After all, I'm only human.
And then the broken frame of your life partner's photograph, the shattered glass, the sheer wicked power used to
destroy it.'

'It was in my wife's room. It was locked. How did
you get in?'

'The dear lady gave me a key – one of the last actions of
the dear soul. She had a premonition she was not long for
this world, and gave me the key in case of an emergency.
She thought you might be too occupied to realize she was in
trouble, and she begged me, if the worst happened, to look

after you in a manner she would have done if she were still capable of doing so. I swore I would.'

'Hence your inquisitiveness, as you call it, about that damned pyjama button, the sheets, the occasional table, and the grinning photograph?' He altered the tone of his voice to something darker, more unanswerable. 'Mme Radibois, my late wife is dead, irrevocably. It was a tragic occurrence, but, like nearly every tragedy, it purges the mind, and reveals advantages with the passage of time.'

'You can't be serious.'

'I am utterly serious. It has enabled me to find myself by making me realize how utterly I had been lost in habit, in routine. How little I had exercised my mind. To what extent I was inviting the visit of the Grim Reaper at any time.'

'The visit of whom?' Mme Radibois' eyebrows were knitted.

'Never mind. Suffice it to say that I have begun to live again since the death of . . . of my dear wife.'

There was a long pause while Mme Radibois drew another cigarette from her pocket. She looked up and met M. René's stony gaze. She decided against lighting it.

'I can hardly exaggerate my bitter disappointment at hearing you say that,' she said with difficulty. Evidently she was on the verge of tears, not an outburst, but the moist overflow of a troubled soul. M. René asked himself if this was really an act of devotion, mourning the absence of a trusted mentor, or was 'crony' the correct word? Why the surrender of the key? Did that indicate a greater complicity between the two women, comparing the sparse virtues and enormous inadequacies of both himself and the unknown M. Radibois? He had not even imagined the remotest contact between them. Was she snivelling and dabbing at her cheeks ostentatiously out of deference to the dead, or merely to disturb the living?

'Why should you take it upon yourself to express disappointment with my words?'

'Oh, don't worry. It's my silly fault. It's not the first time I have built my hopes on an illusion. I'll get over it.'

'Forgive me, but I am too discreet by nature to guess at your hopes, nor can I possibly imagine at the nature of the illusion.'

'Of course you can. You're not stupid.'

There was another long silence. And during it, in its growing tension, M. René had a brain wave. He kept it to himself for the moment. Mme Radibois half turned her back to him as she struggled to contain her tears. She spoke into the back of the sofa as though kneeling in a confessional.

'I watched your wife in her decline. She was unreasonable, quarrelsome, and selfish. And I watched you deal with the problem. Some would have described you as cold, because you preserved your necessary detachment from the sordid details of living with an invalid on her painful journey to the grave. I knew that behind that impassive appearance there beat a human heart of unusual sensibility. You repressed your need for human warmth, refusing to give back that which you were not given in the first place.'

'I was given companionship,' he said, rather foolishly, without wishing to be drawn into telling the truth to Mme Radibois, of all people.

'Companionship? What kind of companionship was that?' she blurted into her lace kerchief. 'That bitch never

spoke to you unless she wanted something. She was selfish
as they come. You were a martyr to her whims. At the end,
her senility had made your life impossible. Her whims no
longer reflected real desires, but the wildest fantasies. You
remember the day she wanted to take off for Honolulu?
She'd seen a report on the portable television you gave her,
and was seized with desire to ride a surfboard. "It must
be easy," she shouted, "once so many people do it." She
could hardly walk, and yet I found her on all fours trying
to pack a bag. "Where d'you think you're going?" I asked, as
I helped her back to bed. "Honolulu!" she screamed. I gave
her a sedative to make her forget her surfboard. Remember
that? And there are other memories.'

'All of them unpleasant, grating.'

'And how often during that time my spirit reached out
for you. I wanted to comfort you, to reassure you, to tell
you you were not alone . . .'

'I knew that, dear Mme Radibois. We never spoke about
it, but we both understood. We were like the staff of a
private mental hospital. We did our job, and there was no
need to talk.'

'There was every need to talk. We have both suffered, you
more than I, simply because I was spared Radibois' decline.
The truck killed him instantly. In the morning he ate his
breakfast noisily, using the filthy language which he really
enjoyed, because I so hated it, and in the afternoon he was
motionless in the morgue, waiting to be identified. A tyre
had crushed his skull. I can imagine what his last words
would have been had he had time to deliver them. There
too the end of a relationship came as a relief, even if I felt
safe from discovery in my black dress.' She resumed a more
pathetic cadence. 'And now, I suppose, with both of them

safely out of the way, I thought the road was open, for us, that is for you and me . . .'

He was at a loss. He repeated to himself the old French saw, '*Jamais deux sans trois*', and sighed deeply. She looked up at him with searching eyes, half smiling at the idiocy of human hopes when faced with the prosaic truth, and he noticed for the first time on her discoloured face the quantity of make-up she had used in an effort to make herself irresistible. The mascara had run down her cheeks, liberating her eyelashes from their bondage, and the rouge, too liberally applied, began to look like abrasions. None of this helped the dignity of her appeal.

He cleared his throat, a signal that his words would be weighty.

'Madame Radibois,' he said gravely, 'we are both too experienced not to know that life is never short of the unexpected — of surprises. It may be played like a game of chess, on condition we realize that the various pieces on the board possess lives of their own, and can always move as the spirit dictates, without taking into consideration the master plan we lay down for them.'

'I don't understand what you are saying,' she interrupted, a little annoyed, wiping black streaks over her face with the saturated lace handkerchief.

'You rashly thought it only took my wife's demise to free me for whatever use you envisaged for me.'

'Use? I envisaged?' she suddenly yelled, incoherently. 'I can't aim as high as love. That's for another class of people. I wasn't born to love, understand me? I never expected it. Companionship, that's about as far as my knowledge of human relationships goes. That's what I thought you needed more than anything, at your age.

Warmth. Friendship. Perhaps I thought you needed it because it was the one thing absent from my life. I took my wish for a reality. Why don't you say anything?'

'Why should I interrupt you when you are telling the truth? There's only one difference between us, separating wish from fact.'

'Yes?'

'I have experienced love.'

'Are you sure?' She hesitated, as though she really wanted nothing in the world less than an answer.

'Sure.'

'Long ago, in your youth?'

'Quite recently.'

'For the first time?'

'Yes.'

She let out a cry which sounded hardly human.

'I knew it! That button!'

The sobs became convulsive.

He went to her and lifted her gently off the sofa, and she fell quite naturally into his arms. He consoled her by patting her gently on the back. The more she tried to cling to him, the more he held her away from any undue physical contact with him. Apart from any obvious reasons for this, he was eager not to find traces of make-up on his suit.

'Madame.'

'Rose Marie,' she said miserably, provoking any meagre shred of comfort.

'Rose Marie. How strange. I never even knew your name. Listen, Rose Marie, you come here three times a week. I know your salary, obviously. What other work do you do?'

She shook her head negatively, utterly defeated, not daring to look up at him.

'No other work. My time was devoted to you, entirely. In case . . .'

'How can you live on that?'

A fresh surge of misery. 'I can't. I don't eat regularly.'

The brain wave was being set in motion. 'You should have told me.'

'I was too proud, too sure of my victory.'

'All is not lost.' He shook her slightly to make sure she was listening. 'Unfortunately I don't need help for more than three days. If truth were told, I don't really require that – but nevertheless, I am going to double your salary—'

She dared to look up at him.

'Moreover,' he went on, 'I have a client for your vacant days, for which I will pay. Is that clear? You will ask who it is? None other than the late Police Chief of the City of Geneva, M. Urs Mildenegger, who has just retired, and who is therefore less able to look after himself than ever.'

'Is that—?' She ventured, and hesitated.

'Yes?'

'Is that the gentleman I saw here not long ago? You were both standing exactly where we are standing now, blubbering like babies.'

M. René was embarrassed at the recollection.

'Quite possibly,' he said, and went on: 'There you have a real soul in distress. Just what you need at the moment. A target for all the human warmth bottled up inside you with nowhere to go. Have you followed me?'

She reverted to the Mme Radibois he knew, slightly furtive, not to say servile. She had rejoined her station in life with the obedience of someone who believes in that kind of thing.

'I don't know how to thank you,' she said.

'Don't go.' He walked into the bathroom, soaked two or three tissues in tepid water, and returned to her. Lifting her face, he wiped it gently.

'Not much make-up left, I'm afraid, but at least you look your usual self.'

'Do I deserve a kiss?' she asked in a small voice. 'For old times' sake?'

'Of course,' he replied, clearing his throat as he always did in moments of boldness, and holding her shoulders to make sure she was not tempted to take advantage of his gesture, he pecked her on the cheek. She closed her eyes in modest ecstasy.

'Come into my study for a moment. Sit down.'

Since she had never been invited to sit before, she remained standing.

He sat at his desk, took a piece of his notepaper, and penned a quick note to Urs Mildenegger.

'Dear Friend,' he wrote.

'This is to present Rose Marie Radibois, who will do for you three days a week (especially the washing up!). She is discreet and loyal, and continues in my employ for the rest of the week. The financial side has been looked after. Silence, monsieur! After all, is friendship just an empty word?

Your Friend

René

P. S. Organize that lunch! That is friendship too.'

He wrote the address on an envelope, enclosed the letter, and gave it to Mme Radibois.

'You can start today,' he said. 'Now!'

'I have to change first, I'm not dressed for work.'

'Of course, of course. I'll call you a taxi. Here is a hundred francs.'

'Don't be too kind to me. It'll merely rub in what I've lost.'

'No more tears, Rose Marie. Nobody can lose what they have never possessed.'

He called a taxi, and she stood patiently, waiting for it to arrive.

No words were exchanged during this small eternity, while M. René pretended to busy himself with matters lying on his desk.

When eventually Mme Radibois indicated that the taxi had arrived, he waved a hand in the air without turning round. 'See you tomorrow!'

'I don't know how to thank you.'

'Don't try. We kissed goodbye before.'

As she went on her gloomy way, he reflected that he was beginning to throw money around, money he had only been promised by a publisher who showed every sign of being unscrupulous, even on his behalf. He took off his jacket, fetched a clothes brush, and searched the garment for the merest trace of make-up. There was none. He had successfully held her at bay, and done a good deed into the bargain. He was in no mood to enjoy taunting the Neapolitans now. He remained at his desk, realized that Mme Radibois had exhausted him, and fell asleep.

# XIV

HE WAS woken by the telephone. It was Urs Mildenegger. There was such a noise that M. René could hardly hear.

'It is the vacuum cleaner. I am surprised it still works,' cried Urs. 'I've had it for four years, but I have never used it, never even read the instructions. It stayed in its box, the way it was delivered. Now, it's like the rebirth of something I'd given up, thanks to you.'

'Is she there?'

'As you can hear. Already there's not a dirty plate in the place. I hardly recognize it as home! I'm afraid I don't yet know the good lady well enough to telephone in front of her. I'm using the vacuum cleaner as a cover, deliberately. But I must say, she is of impeccable appearance, even if a touch melancholy. But that suits me. It doesn't do to break me into the world of equilibrium with a shock treatment. I'd never survive. Oh, incidentally, how about tomorrow?'

'What?'

'One o'clock, the lawyer and the psychiatrist? They've

both accepted, and seem eager to meet you, which I find surprising.'

'Where?'

'Le Mouton Enragé, where else?'

'A good idea. I'll be there. You're a friend.'

'Who isn't?'

There was a sudden silence.

'What has happened?' M. René asked, disconcerted by the stillness.

'She has stopped hoovering,' Urs said, sotto voce, and added: 'See you tomorrow.'

'Tomorrow.'

M. René replaced the receiver, and felt like congratulating himself for having engineered a good deed, which seemed to him of great ingenuity. How to mark the occasion? He summoned a taxi, and treated himself to a lunch far superior in quality to the Mouton Enragé he would be forced to endure the next day, at the Bijou du Léman, one of the sumptuous fin-de-siècle palaces dominating the lake. He even offered himself a half bottle of champagne, a beverage he did not take to with much enthusiasm, simply because it had become a symbol of celebration. Some people mutter silent prayers; M. René muttered a silent toast, to himself, the fortunate, the intelligent, the benevolent. His discreetly beaming face even caused a waiter to ask him if it was not his birthday. He had an immediate vision of a tiny cake with a harmless firework fizzing away on the icing, being brought in with a background of lowered shutters, followed by a sparse chorale of 'Happy Birthday to you' sung dutifully but unenthusiastically by other diners who had not come there for that. He hastily assured the waiter that it was not his birthday, asked for the bill, paid, and left. He then proceeded to the motorcycle shop, which had white paint on the windows, and notices of closure. There was a padlock on the door. A policeman, loitering in the neighbourhood, noticed M. René alight from his taxi and wandered up to him with the unhurried purposefulness typical of the breed.

'It is shut.'

'I can see that.'

'Were you wanting anyone in particular?'

'Absolutely not,' replied M. René.

'I am not sure if it will reopen.' The policeman was, like many of his fellows, scrupulous in his obedience to instructions, but unable to disguise the fact that he was the harbinger of secrets too heavy to be borne alone.

'You mean, it has been shut by the police?'

The policeman saw the red light.

'That is something I can neither confirm nor deny,' he said.

'It would not surprise me,' M. René told him, 'since I hear from an acquaintance in your service that the motorcycles for sale in here are all reconstituted wrecks.'

'Where did you hear that?' asked the policeman, amazed.

'Forget that I mentioned it,' said M. René, and walked away, leaving the policeman shading his eyes, and searching for a spot in the shop window which had not been entirely painted over.

The next day, he timed his departure for the lunch at the Mouton Enragé by the passing of the local train from Geneva – Nyon – Morges, calculated at 12.43. He was paying his taxi when another taxi arrived, disgorging Urs Mildenegger. They began to enter the restaurant, when Urs spotted a familiar car in the car park. Excusing himself for a moment, he walked down and spoke for a few minutes to the driver while M. René waited. As he walked back, Urs shook his head negatively, and drove a fist into the open palm of the other hand. It was clear that he was furious.

'Bastard!' he cried. 'That mean-minded super-cop Beat Kribl is in there, probably seated in the kitchen, and no doubt with a listening device under our table, waiting to record our conversation! I'm going to punch him in the face!'

Once more an inspiration seized M. René. He placed a restraining hand on Urs' arm. Urs stopped in his tracks, glancing at M. René questioningly.

'Don't throw away the opportunity,' said M. René under his breath, at the same time looking around to be sure they were not observed. And he went on: 'Who preceded you as Police Chief?'

'That blithering idiot, Gaspard Pupilleux.'

'And what was your first action on taking over?'

'Me? I tried to uncover all the mistakes he had made.'

'What is Kribl doing but the same to you?'

'So?' Urs was eager to find out what M. René was getting at.

'Ignore the fact he is using your methods to entrap you.'

'Ignore it?'

'Rise above it. Go into the kitchen, brimming over with your usual good nature, make him feel that he has fallen clumsily in a trap, and that you are overlooking his sordid strategy. Invite him to lunch with us.'

'Invite him—?'

'Why not? What have we to hide? We might even need his help at some moment. Do as I say, and you will automatically take the initiative in all future encounters. It will destroy his authority, can't you see that?'

'Would you ask him to lunch?'

'It will lose all its effect if it's me, or rather, if it's not you. Come on, be brave. You won't regret it.'

Slowly a grin broke over Urs' face, as though the logic of M. René's argument had reached him for the first time.

'I think you're right,' he said, and preceded M. René into the establishment.

He stopped in his tracks when he saw a half-empty cup of coffee on the table he had once occupied under similar circumstances. M. René and he exchanged amused looks. He felt the cup.

'Still warm! Stinks of emergency.' He went towards the kitchen, followed by M. René. M. Campella came out, and seemed eager to prevent them from going in.

'There is no one in there,' he said, his arms stretched out defensively.

'Then why do you wish to prevent us from going in? And why is Chief Kribl's car and driver in your car park?'

Campella lowered his arms, resigned.

Urs and M. René entered the kitchen.

Chief Kribl rose to his feet.

'Don't get up,' said Urs, generously.

'Excellent,' murmured M. René, under his breath.

'I was just—' began Kribl.

'I realize that,' said Urs. 'We were just wondering if you'd care to lunch with us. It's so uncomfortable eating alone, in the kitchen. And then, we thought our company might interest you, since you are following in my footsteps.'

'Well, since you—'

'Yes, yes, indeed. This is M. René, whom I'm sure I don't have to introduce. The King of Concierges.'

Chief Kribl was a loose-limbed fellow, not tall, but with occasional convulsive and uncoordinated gestures which spoke of difficulties with communication, probably of a nervous nature. For instance, he had a habit of nodding as though greeting a roomful of people, while his narrow shoulders moved as though he were swimming. His neck came forwards from his body as though the head might be capable of retraction, like that of a tortoise, while his eyes were invisible unless he made an effort to express surprise, when they revealed themselves to be large and black, but normally they were lost in swollen folds, a boxer on whom fortune had frowned, at the end of his career. A cluster of defiant hairs stood like an oasis at the highest point of his head, the rest being bald and shiny. Whiskers and a minute beard of such indeterminate colour and shape as to be almost invisible completed the outward appearance of the new supremo of the police of the Canton and Republic of Geneva.

His hesitation as to whether it would be more politic to refuse or accept this unexpected and embarrassing invitation was so protracted that Urs cut into it with a 'That's good, I'm glad that's settled then. Our other guests are Maître Muresanescu, of the Geneva Bar, and Professor Szepainska, the psychiatrist. We are here to discuss the case of Agnes S, the alleged murderess.'

'Self-confessed, don't you mean?' said Kribl, with a wild swing of an index finger at his own chest.

'If it were as simple as that, there would be nothing to discuss,' M. René suggested politely.

'That is not my information,' insisted Kribl, calling on a dozen imaginary witnesses.

'Where do they get them from?' M. René asked himself, but suggested they might go into the restaurant, since the kitchen was hardly the place for a protracted discussion. They proceeded to their table, Kribl nodding at the empty restaurant like a toy demonstrated on a pavement by a street trader.

'I don't care for this table,' declared M. René. Campella and Kribl exchanged looks of heavy-handed alarm.

'It's the one you had before,' said Campella.

'That enables me to speak with real feeling when I say that I don't care for it.'

'But we have laid it.'

'What happens when the restaurant is full? Do you keep clients away because the tables are not laid?'

'The truth is, I am a little understaffed.'

'We can carry our own cutlery to that table over there if need be.'

'No, no.' Campella looked at Kribl and shrugged his shoulders, agitated.

'Why are you consulting the Police Chief?' asked Urs, in all innocence. 'He only accepted our invitation a moment ago.'

Campella ignored the question, opened the kitchen door, and called 'Augusto!' An old waiter came out, walking with difficulty and evident signs of distress, and began laying the table selected by M. René. Apparently such an aura of poverty and pessimism hung over the Mouton Enragé that tables were never laid before people sat at them.

While this was going on under the mournful direction of Campella, who had only one employee to whom to give

instructions, Maître Muresanescu and Professor Szepainska
arrived together. He was a surprisingly young man, wearing
heavy-rimmed tortoiseshell glasses which underlined his
inherent earnestness. Because of his youth, the casual
observer could not help wondering if he really needed
those glasses, or if their importance were not, in the main,
a device to make him appear older. Professor Szepainska,
on the other hand, gave the impression of having nothing
to hide, perhaps because of the splendid dimensions of her
décolleté, which revealed acres of chest, and a cleavage very
low down on the body. Her hair was blonde, only very
discreetly assisted by artifice, and her expression one of
snub-nosed candour and openness. The introductions were
quickly effected, the seating somewhat arbitrary, since there
was only one lady present, and the choice of food decided.
Kribl made some fuss of sticking to the menu for reasons of
financial integrity. Urs did not know if this was the result of
an examination of his past expenses while Chief of Police,
but decided to counterattack nevertheless.

'Thank God I have retired, and no longer have to bother
with such considerations,' he said. 'I'll have the caviar, the
sour cream, and the trimmings.' It seemed to him that Kribl
grunted. Once they were waiting for their food, Urs called
the meeting to order, and asked Professor Szepainska to
open with a few insights into the case.

'It is an extremely complex one,' she began, 'and
especially difficult to explain to those whose duty it
will be to sit in judgement, by which I mean lawyers,
judges, what one might call the technicians of justice. It
obeys no rules in our daily lives, and is finely attached
to the unique experience of that indescribably brutal,
indiscriminate period of history, with its discovery of

crimes towards humanity, at least as far as it concerns those committed by whites on whites. Those committed by whites on those of other pigmentation have always existed, but have rarely warranted the headlines, or a total revision of our laws.'

'Are you serious?' growled Kribl. 'The law is the same for everybody, of whatever breed or colour. At least, it is here. Always has been.'

Professor Szepainska smiled, as though she was used to dealing with this argument.

'In the light of your statement, I feel justified in asking you if *you* are serious,' she said. 'Look at the facts. At the end of the war, the victorious Allies were embarrassed by the enormity of the Nazi crimes, and by their inability to sit in judgement on acts which, by their nature, defied all comparison with historical precedents. Thus the idea of crimes against humanity crystallized for the first time in the human mind, but before these monsters could be condemned specious links had to be forged between the legal systems of the United States, the United Kingdom, France, and Stalin's Soviet Union, four of the oddest goddesses ever to share a pair of scales and a blindfold. There has always been, in some minds, a feeling of unease that the rules of the game had to be invented retrospectively before culprits could be executed for crimes which had to be defined after they were committed.'

'What has all this to do with Switzerland?' asked Kribl, jerking his head up and down, seeking the approval of an imaginary audience.

'It has a great deal to do with Switzerland.' M. René took the initiative, since it had been his bright idea to invite Kribl to the lunch. 'Professor Szepainska is merely reminding us of the atmosphere prevalent at the time. Switzerland played a leading role in all this, as evidence the unfortunate contention about the fate of victims of the holocaust's funds invested in Swiss banks. Are you satisfied?'

Kribl nodded quietly, and suddenly leaped into unexpected life: 'I have my own opinion about that,' he cried.

M. René became the concierge again, dealing with an obstreperous client. 'I'm sure you do, but this lunch was not convened in order to hear it. We are in the presence of two experts who are defending a personal friend of mine in the courts, and since they have been good enough to respond positively to my invitation, I think the least we can do is to hear them out without interruption.'

Kribl seemed hurt. 'Experts,' he blurted. 'I am Chief of Police.'

'We all know who you are,' murmured Urs, as though humouring a fractious child.

Kribl looked at Urs as though to say: 'Why do you make me look like a fool?'

Urs countered with an expression which suggested: 'But, dear boy, you are doing all the dirty work yourself.'

Professor Szepainska was the soul of understanding, as befits a psychiatrist.

'May I go on?' she enquired.

Kribl nodded furiously.

Professor Szepainska elucidated them on the child Agnes' adventures and misfortunes in an eminently sympathetic way, while Kribl never stopped making notes, only raising his eyes when the handbag was mentioned.

'A handbag, at the age of five?' he asked.

'Exactly. It was a shabby enough article to start with, manufactured as a toy at a period in which the Reich was short of raw materials, and ersatz was the order of the day.'

'I have the original article,' said M. René.

'You have it? The actual handbag?'

'Yes. I refused to give it up to Monsieur Mildenegger, who was Chief of Police at the time.'

'He told me it would be a desecration to hand it over to the police,' Urs explained.

'Desecration?' asked Kribl, and began to nod, but with raised eyebrows.

'It is a strange word to choose,' remarked the professor, smiling as always, 'but no doubt we will find out why when you tell us what you know.'

M. René assented. Professor Szepainska continued. 'Evidently she enjoyed playing the lady from the tenderest age, and it was this particular fantasy of hers which caused such a present to be given to her. She never had any use for dolls. She never asked for one. She never had one. According to Frau Bruetschi, she used the stub of a pencil to simulate lipstick, the top of a biscuit tin made do for a mirror.'

'They are still inside,' M. René said.

'Really? But at the time,' Professor Szepainska went on, 'it was also given over to a more realistic purpose, one heavy with consequence. In the last hours left to them together, the mother wrote her guidelines for her daughter's education, the books she should read when old enough to understand them, Goethe, Schiller, Rilke, Heine, Karl Marx, Lenin, and much more important, the names of the three men responsible for their separation, Otzinger, Bompoz, and Zocco. "These are the men who killed your mother, and separated us, dear heart, for ever." She surrendered the document when she gave herself up. It is part of the record.'

Urs Mildenegger smiled fatalistically. 'I spent years suspecting that such a document existed, but could never find it. We conducted several searches of her rooms. They never revealed anything resembling it. But I would like to know, Professor, what interpretation do you put on it?'

Professor Szepainska became thoughtful. 'She remained a little girl until relatively late in life, still firmly locked into an unfulfilled relationship with her mother. Until she had killed off the last of her mother's torturers, she was still obeying instructions. She had no real life of her own, outside her filial duties. Then a slow awakening followed, but still her normal desires were dormant. Routine and efficiency were the criteria, although escaping detection was a minor excitement of a kind she had got used to while growing up as a member of a strange family in the heart of a strange land. And then, she told me, she became captivated by some initiative of yours, which began a new interest in life, up to the moment when the new interest switched from your activities to yourself. That part of the story, the part which led to the extraordinary act of surrendering voluntarily to the authorities after years of successful subterfuge, is far more nebulous. Would you enlighten us?'

M. René felt strengthened by the fact that these matters were at last being professionally aired and, for better or for worse, a concentrated effort was being made to cast a light into the dark places. He told his story from the strange feelings of arriving at the Biblical time limit of life span, the disconcerting feeling of living on borrowed time, and the sudden questioning of all past values, as though life's span was indeed over, and one were sitting in a last judgement on oneself.

Professor Szepainska was evidently pleased by M. René's revelations about himself, and the astonishing objectivity and coherence of his self-assessment. He spoke of his sudden doubts about the validity of a life helping some of the most sordid elements in it achieve their aims, rewarded with tips rather than by satisfaction. He spoke of his desire for revenge once there was no more obligation towards a hotel chain, and he was as conscious of his freedom as he would have been to an open window in winter. He then criticized with both wit and a sense of the absurd the utter inadequacy of his initial conspiracy, especially his ridiculous choice of fellow conspirators.

Urs Mildenegger rocked with laughter at all this, stopping every now and then to dry his eyes, watched with twitching vigilance by Kribl, who, as always, suspected that the police were being treated with disrespect.

M. René sketched the characters of his initial group whom he had managed to fire with his own sense of outrage, but who joined his movement more out of a sense of schoolboy truancy than true conviction. It was only, in fact, when Mr Butler recruited Agnes that an effective element entered their machinations. She fired them all, and obviously enjoyed their activities, which were for her merely a continuation of her way of life. 'Up to then, Urs Mildenegger woke me to the possibility of her being a murderess, but I didn't believe a word of it.'

'He suspected her?' Kribl broke in.

'Oh, I suspected her for a long time,' admitted Urs, suddenly rather sad. 'I was hoping against hope it was not true.'

'Hoping it was not true? As a police officer, I would have thought you would have hoped it was true!'

'As a human being, I hoped it was not true.'

'You can admit that?'

Urs smiled. 'You'll be amazed how much you can admit once you have retired. You wait and see.'

Kribl retreated into his unquiet shell. He had been made to feel inadequate.

'Please go on,' Professor Szepainska asked, quietly.

'Well, our initial lunch took place in this restaurant, at that table over there. Urs Mildenegger was not then an honoured guest, and friend, but . . . may I say it?'

'Of course, go ahead,' shot Mildenegger good humouredly – and then, as he saw M. René displaying some reticence, he spoke.

'I was playing the spy, eating in the kitchen, with the table rather clumsily bugged. I still possess the tapes, but you will be happy to know that they are practically indecipherable. I never have been, and never will be, a technician of any sort.'

Kribl brought his fist down on the table with enormous force. Since he had obviously hurt himself, there was a momentary silence.

Urs spoke with something like tenderness. 'What did you do that for? I was speaking about myself, not about you.'

'I know who you were talking about,' confirmed Kribl, nodding. 'You are wrong. That's why you chose another table. Well, I bet you won't find a bug at your original table.'

'A bet? How much?'

'I'm not a betting man. Ten francs.'

Urs Mildenegger rose. 'I apologize for this intermezzo,' he said. He crossed to the empty table, bent low while sitting on the upholstered bench which followed the wall, and found nothing under it. Puzzled, he stood up, and studied the lighting fixture. In a soft voice, he said: 'You owe me ten francs.'

Kribl smiled grimly. 'You've found it, you bastard.'

'Much better done than I could have done it. It shows that, unlike me, you are a technician.'

'I took a course in bugging at the police school.'

'I thought the practice was forbidden in Switzerland.'

'Everything's forbidden in Switzerland,' cried Kribl, 'if it isn't compulsory.' And even he was compelled to laugh at the absurdity of it all. It was laughter in which the others gratefully joined.

'Well, you can't really blame me,' he declared, threatening to grow serious again. 'I inherited not only your reports, but your marginal notes, and your doodles. Some of them make very interesting reading.'

'I'm sure they do,' said Urs soothingly, 'and I willingly bequeath them to you, now that they are of no further concern to me – but I would add a rider: what you are doing is absolutely normal. As I told M. René, just after I had spotted your car – our car – no, your car in the parking lot – my first days in office were spent deliberately discovering all that my predecessor had done wrong. I pursued this activity with a crusading zeal, until, after a week or two, I found myself doing what he had done.'

Kribl searched laboriously in his pockets, and crashed a ten franc note on the table as though playing a trump card.

'My debt,' he cried, with quite unnecessary force.

'Oh, forget it.'

'My debt,' he shouted.

Both M. René and Professor Szepainska urged Urs to accept it without further delay.

'Oh, well, if you insist . . .' muttered Urs.

'I do insist. I am a man of honour!'

'Thank you very much.'

'Thanks are unnecessary. I play by the rules.'

'And now, perhaps I may be allowed to proceed,' suggested M. René, 'before we lose the thread. Our first adventure in police work was a fiasco, although I believe we could have been successful with a little greater self-discipline.'

'And if the police didn't exist,' added Urs.

Kribl liked this, and nodded in friendly confirmation.

'I accept that. With Agnes aboard, everything changed. The others took fright because of the police involvement, but this only sharpened Agnes' resolve, and indeed playfulness. Despite the fact that my co-conspirators were consistently unavailable on the telephone, Agnes gave me a tip-off which actually bore fruit – a waiter of Dalmatian origin, in his case more Italian than Yugoslav, who was engaged during the lunch breaks at the Balkan conference which frittered on without reaching any conclusion until quite recently. He overheard a plot to kill a Bosnian leader by car bomb at a precise hour and a precise place. This was exactly as I had envisaged our work, not as a top-heavy organization trying to rival the police, but as eavesdroppers who can acquire information by the nature of their work. How Agnes knew this young man I don't know, but certainly his invaluable information was the result of her spadework. I passed on this information to Urs Mildenegger, who told me it was his last day in office, but that he would see to it that the new Chief of Police had access to it.'

'Which is precisely what I did,' remarked Urs. 'In fact, it was the last memorandum before quitting my post.'

'But in that memorandum, which I can produce, you said you lent no great credence to this information. That it came from a source which was unverifiable said Kvibl.'

'That is a fact, and I even turned up at the scene of the crime to watch the discomfiture of M. René. I hoped it would discourage him for good in his Quixotic pursuits. Tell me frankly, Kribl, how would you have reacted in my shoes?'

'The way I did react, by ignoring it. We react when the information is sure, not before. We suffer from sufficient false alarms as it is.'

'That's good to know,' said M. René. 'And what happens when a false alarm turns out to have been real?'

Kribl waved his arms around, apparently expressing fatalism in such cases, but his body language was more impenetrable than ever.

'I hope you take note of that,' said M. René, addressing Maître Muresanescu. 'Agnes, the accused, was instrumental in bringing a crime to the police's attention in which two men were killed, and in which there was much material damage. This crime could have been avoided.'

'Prove it,' said Kribl.

'That's the argument used by guilty parties in bad films.'

'I tell you one thing,' Kribl said, with renewed energy. 'If I had known that the information came from a woman standing trial for the murder of three officers, I would have paid even less attention to it than I did!'

'The fact remains,' added M. René, rather pointlessly.

'Please go on with your resumé, M. René,' asked Professor Szepainska, 'which will add more in casting light on this fascinating case history than will an inquest into police responsibility.'

'I beg your pardon. Of course. Well, during this period in which we were never sure if our phone calls were being overheard or not, she suggested that she would come to my home and cook me dinner, where we could discuss our future activities without risk of being overheard. It was during this dinner that she gave me the name and phone number of the Croatian waiter.'

'Is that all that occurred?'

'Far from it. The dinner was exceptional. The wines, the food, a cigar, which I don't smoke. She had thought of everything, including the fact that she had no intention of returning home to sleep.' He paused. 'It would seem that it would be hard for me to speak of such things, because it casts such a light on what my life must have been like before she broke into it as a thief, and left it, leaving behind a most terrible emptiness. Oddly enough, it is never as difficult to tell the truth as it is to lie.' He paused, as though collecting his thoughts.

Professor Szepainska spoke. 'You are among friends here.'

M. René smiled in recognition of her gesture. 'I know that. It is just that I belong to a generation which is not used to speak of such things. It needs courage to find a grain of poetry within oneself, without which it is impossible to do such rare moments justice. She certainly had a plan when she came to my house. I recognized it as soon as it began to unfold . . . and in retrospect, far from trying to defend myself, I became a willing victim of her strategy. I was hypnotized, and surrendered to the inevitable as some animals do when recognizing the superior force of a predator.'

He allowed himself a chuckle, and shook his head. 'There you are. I wanted to give the moment dignity and stature, and I talk about animals.' He sobered up, and made a fresh start. 'Let me say, once I have evoked nature, that I have always enjoyed the violence of thunder, snowstorms, the extremes, but always as a spectator, warmly dressed and comfortable. Never before have I felt part of a great natural process, in which one miraculously loses all fear of death. And it's only after the turmoil is over, and after a deep dreamless sleep has intervened, that one wakes up, and falls in love. I apologize to those more accustomed to the phenomena than I, and who obviously experienced them at a decent age, but it seemed all the more unique an event to me by coming so late in life. Well, after that, what can I say? With daylight we went to prose. Everything is easier to describe.

'She was still asleep when I woke up – at least, I thought she was. I tried to cook her a breakfast worthy of her dinner the night before. The eggs were getting cold. I went to wake her up. She had gone, without a word. Only the little handbag lay open, with a message inside. The words were written on a piece of wrapping paper, torn in haste. They read: "I do not deserve such happiness". This was the last time she spoke to me.' M. René's voice broke with emotion.

Professor Szepainska spoke soberly. 'Thank you, M. René, for your unique contribution to the understanding of this case. It is not usual for a person to see himself with such unsentimental clarity. May I ask, what was the writing material Agnes used?'

'Oh, lipstick.'

'How curious.'

'Why do you ask?'

'The instructions from her mother were also written on coarse paper, and in lipstick. They have become blurred with time, and are quite difficult to read.'

'My message was fresh, and its meaning was quite clear,' remarked M. René, his voice still quavering slightly.

Nobody spoke, but Urs Mildenegger suddenly rose and left the restaurant briefly, for a breath of fresh air.

THE MEAL itself was as mediocre as ever. Why this eating house had become practically a place of pilgrimage for them was clear to no one. While they were toying with their food, Maître Muresanescu gave a brief resumé of the legal picture. He said there was no escaping the fact that there had been three murders, all confessed to by the person he was defending. At the same time, the psychological facts behind these events were so bizarre that a case could be made, not for acquittal, but for circumstances which were more than attenuating.

'You tell me, Professor, that she is of danger to nobody now?'

'As I said, Maître, the chapter of revenge is closed. She was acting under instruction as an obedient child. There were no further instructions, therefore there can be no further homicides. Now, she is utterly docile. She dared, at one point, as M. René has described, to emerge from her nursery, and found the outside world too bewildering. Also, because of the excitement of all she had been missing, what she had done in killing three human beings suddenly came into focus, as though that were the price of being her age, an abrupt understanding of the truth. The difficulty in all this, Maître, is that prisons are intended for the violent, for the incurable. They were never intended for people like Agnes. Unfortunately, society does not have the imagination to conceive of an alternative place of therapy. And all this is complicated by the fact that Agnes is in quest of punishment, whatever punishment thick-skulled authorities believe fits the crime. She doesn't mope in her cell, waiting for the day of her release. She is utterly content as she is. She wants to live in captivity, if necessary to die in captivity. Oblivion is the sweetest thing on earth.'

'What a waste,' M. René said, spontaneously. 'Can I see her?'

'You think you can make a difference?' asked Professor Szepainska, with more than a hint of foreboding.

'I can but try.'

'Don't bank on success, even if it can be arranged. Can it be arranged?'

There was no reaction.

'I have seen her,' said Urs. 'I have no wish to renew the experience.'

'Chief?' Professor Szepainska asked Kribl.

After a moment, he began nodding, and rose. 'Of course. It's quite a story. The layman doesn't realize the fathomless depth of a person. We judge by very simple values.' He insisted on shaking hands with everyone present, nodding away, and showing rather touching magnanimity. 'Thanks for lunch. It made up in quantity what it lacked in quality.' He was more than pleased with his joke, and repeated it three times in case it had been misunderstood. With M. René's hand in his, he pumped away at his show of fraternity, saying: 'I'll make the necessary arrangements. It may take a while, since I have to square the prison authorities, and Max Aufdemdach is no pushover. Never has been. Incidentally, I let your nephew go three days ago.'

'Oh, thank you very much,' said M. René, without much enthusiasm.

'Well, there was no point holding him, once we arrested the Neapolitan connection.'

'All of them?' asked Urs.

'All of them,' confirmed Kribl.

'I bet there are others,' grumbled Urs.

'There are always others,' stated Kribl.

'That's true too . . .'

Kribl crossed to the door, turned, and waved. 'The company,' he called, confirming his words with his head. The others all waved back.

'I've never seen a man who more desperately wanted to be liked,' remarked Urs, 'with the possible exception of myself.'

'I'm glad we asked him. After a shaky start, it will pay handsome dividends.'

'Yes,' sighed Urs, 'your instinct was right. Like most of us he's just a silly, sentimental fellow entrenched behind an exterior of intractable stupidity, out of fear of being laughed at by those more sure of themselves than we.'

Professor Szepainska laughed. 'Don't be hard on yourselves. Always remember, the intellectually accomplished have a far greater canvas on which to demonstrate their stupidity than have the stupid. Also, they have far greater possibilities of attracting attention to their foolishness.'

Urs smiled. 'Obviously yours is the voice of experience,' he said.

Maître Muresanescu closed his briefcase with a click. 'I must get back to the office now. Thanks for lunch.'

None of them had taken much notice of him and, after his departure, they agreed he was either somewhat colourless, or else of extraordinary brilliance. His main physical feature seemed to be his glasses, which so distorted everything seen through them that he had to be extremely myopic, one hoped only physically. Professor Szepainska said that she had never met him before, but that he left a somewhat ambiguous impression.

'With you, on the other hand, I believe my Agnes to be in extremely good hands,' remarked M. René.

Professor Szepainska blushed involuntarily. 'It's one thing to understand. It's another to persuade the authorities,' she said.

'I know from experience that understanding is over half any battle. I rely on you to understand,' said M. René, crisply. 'I will do the persuading.'

'Well, there's not much we can do for the moment, until the commission decides upon a direction for the prosecution to pursue. It may seem an easy decision on the face of it, because it is clear cut, but there are many reasons for confession, many arguments for mercy.'

'Despite her determination to be guilty?' asked Urs.

'Perhaps because of it,' replied the professor. 'You know, the law is frequently as perverse as an individual, at least in practice.'

'Well, I intend to engage a private detective,' announced M. René.

'Whatever for?' enquired Urs.

'I want to know what the world has lost with the poisoning of those three individuals.'

'Whatever you discover, it will hardly influence the court one way or the other,' warned Professor Szepainska.

'Before it can influence a court, it must first convince me,' M. René said. 'Let us say that I am doing it entirely for my own satisfaction . . . for the time being.'

'It is an expensive way of satisfying one's curiosity, hiring detectives.'

'Perhaps,' admitted M. René, enigmatically.

They all went towards the door. Before they could reach it, Signor Campella appeared.

'I hope everything was to your satisfaction?' he asked. Nobody had the heart to answer.

# XV

AN ALMOST regular series of communications from the bank began to fall onto M. René's welcome mat from that time onwards. He only glanced at the contents because he could scarcely believe them, and the cinnamon-coloured envelopes with an angry-looking antelope logo became an instant source of superstition. Each of these communiqués announced the transfer into his account of sums larger than he had ever received in his life. They were advances for his book in England, in Australia, then in the United States and Canada, the result of the auction the publisher had talked about, as well as the British serial rights, and the rights for a television series on a privatized network. All this seemed unreal to him, since he had done no work on the autobiography except several tiring sessions with the young lady who had gone home after he had given up on it.

Now, with true Swiss thoroughness and sense of house-keeping, he opened several new accounts at other banks, amusing himself by restlessly transferring funds from one account to another, largely in order to mystify the banks themselves as to the extent of his total assets, but also in order to make sure the funds were really there. He was amazed that a life of virtual drudgery could have passed so meanly rewarded, and how the accumulation of half a century of ephemeral anecdotes should occasion such a flow of capital into his coffers. And what was even more astonishing was the fact that not a single one of his anecdotes had been made public, and that this sudden wealth was accumulating in anticipation of the tale he had to tell.

His superstition took the form of trying to read the contents of an envelope without opening it, by simply holding it up to the light. And then, when that proved impossible, of perversely not opening it at all until several days after its arrival, in the meanwhile trying to guess the sum of money which had come his way, and the nature of the sale effected. Needless to say he was always wrong, and invariably pleasantly surprised. In this new and disturbing atmosphere, he endlessly took stock of his changing situation, without for a moment coming to any conclusions about it. It was too unstable for that. At moments, he had the unpleasant sensation of being fattened, like a goose, for the quality of his liver.

This continued influx of unearned money worried him in one sense, while charming him in another. He was not the kind of man who would have been happy winning a lottery. He had an almost religious reserve about winning a fortune without giving more in return than the price of a ticket. And this rigid internal balance, a quality he had learned to admire in himself because others so admired it, was now beginning to vacillate. He had opened his heart before strangers who were destined to be on his side in the greatest struggle of his life, and now was the time to assess what they had said, the impressions they had formed of the task in hand. With the best will in the world, when he looked back on that thrilling night, so full of surprises, of discoveries, he had to admit to himself that it was beginning to fade with the passage of time. He could remember facts, but not emotions. Perhaps women were more gifted than men where the retention of precise impressions is concerned.

He could never have expressed himself by declaring that he did not deserve such happiness, whatever the circumstances. Now, he began to wonder what form his all-important meeting with Agnes would take. Should he dress formally or casually? He thought probably casually would be more appreciated, although for what he considered vital meetings he always felt more comfortable, more himself, if formally attired. But then, he reflected that he was no longer a concierge. Agnes had never known him as a concierge, and it was idiotic to evoke ghosts which had not been shared. To visit his wife in hospital, he would certainly have dressed as a widower, but only because she would never have taken a hint, other than to treat it as a mark of respect.

How had Agnes known him? He could hardly go in pyjamas, with a button ripped off. That would be in bad taste. Civilized people don't remind each other by day how they appear to each other at night. But, flowers. He'd have to take flowers. There's another silly tradition. What can those in prison do with them? Are vases allowed? Could suicide be attempted with a broken vase? Even if permitted, are flowers not a symbol of liberty, of open fields? Could their introduction into a cell not be construed as cruelty? He had never visited anyone in gaol. He had never felt the need to know the protocol. He already had a sinister premonition that his visit, whatever form it took, would never succeed in evoking that magic night, a night he knew to be magic, not because his memory of it was vivid, but because his memory told him it had been magic, as a fact.

At moments such as the waking hour, when the warmth of the bed encouraged a moment longer between the sheets, he found himself thinking of Kuki, not as an object of love, but as an unfulfilled promise. He remembered her scandalous proximity on the floor, as well as her assault on his person, a daring exploration into forbidden territory, with a wealth of squalid experience. Truth to tell, she had left a greater void than Agnes, but the void could hardly be described as aching, which that of Agnes was, at moments. Rather it was something he recognized as a missed opportunity. Its thrill was its baseness, and it owed its longevity to its never having been consummated, remaining a tantalizing, recurring regret. It was something he would admit only to himself. Most of the time, not even that. In the battle for the low ground of his mind, there was no contest. Agnes reigned over the high ground, of which he was not ashamed. But the mind wanders.

He had time to hire a detective, one Max Domani, to dig out the dirt about the surviving relatives of Agnes' victims. M. René had been warned at lunch about the doubtful value of such an initiative, but he made up his mind to keep busy, and with his rapidly growing wealth he felt he could afford such eccentricity. His successful career in hotels had taught him to identify and recognize the many voices used by money to make itself felt, sometimes blatant and vulgar,

sometimes dulcet, insinuating. He was certainly not one to
believe in the integrity of the legal system, or that lawyers
and even judges are beyond the reach of influence. Money is
perhaps less perceptible in the defence of the innocent than
it is in the defence of the guilty, but wherever it is found, it
has never learned the art of discretion. That is why it never
passes unnoticed.

Max Domani was hardly to be taken seriously. He
had served in the French Foreign Legion, and therefore
spoke with a thick German accent. His face was a map
of narrow squeaks, bullets and bottles having left their
marks on it, avoiding a nose which had been reduced
to a fleshy button by a series of fists. For some reason,
his appearance inspired confidence. It suggested, perhaps
erroneously, that he got things done. M. René willingly
left the business of tracing the existence and whereabouts
of the surviving relatives of the three victims of Agnes'
attentions to him.

Meanwhile he received the half expected visit of the
feared Gilbert Gordie, the ghost writer who was to take
a quarter of his royalties. He stayed at one of the best
hotels in town, and came to M. René's house by taxi,
refusing to let his collaborator do anything to make his
visit agreeable. Whatever else he might have been, Gilbert
Gordie was a professional. Everything was done with the
strictest economy. Even his smile was rationed.

He began his stay on M. René's verandah, reassuring the
latter: 'This shouldn't take more than a day or two.'

'How is that possible,' M. René asked, in alarm, 'when
it took the young lady two weeks of hard work to do about
twenty pages?'

'The young lady . . . Miss Whitlop . . . was lacking in

experience in this kind of creative writing. She is more by way of being an apprentice.'

The publisher had sent an apprentice to record his memories? For a moment, M. René flushed with indignation. Mr Gordie was at least sensitive enough to register protest. Perhaps he was used to it.

'Understand me,' he said, 'she is a talented girl, who will go a long way, but ghosting is a profession largely different from being a writer. Often a ghost has to be even more creative than a budding author for a variety of reasons – the incoherence of the subject in question, his or her reticence before real or imagined breaches of confidence, an inability to be as ruthless as need be in the description of the victims.'

'Ruthless? Victims?'

'Our first duty is towards the public. It is our duty to entertain them.'

'I thought that your first duty was towards the truth.'

Gilbert Gordie grinned. 'Has the truth ever let loose an avalanche of shekels? If it has, tell me about it.'

He saw from M. René's glum expression that the conversation was leading into a dead end. In any case, he was lost when it came to talk of integrity, the truth, ethical details. He cleared his decks of all traces of cynicism, and looked at M. René with all the simplicity of which he was capable.

'Listen, M. René, nobody in his right mind would want to betray you. After all, these are your memories and no one else's. I can only interpret what I believe to be your desires. In that case, may I ask you a few questions?'

'Of course. That's what you are here for. It merely surprised me that it would only take a day or two.'

'Truth to tell, the book is largely written. It merely needs clarification of a few questions I have.'

'Must I remind you the young lady only stayed long enough to cover a quarter of my career?'

'Good, but she made a mass of notes. A mass of notes,' he reemphasized. 'Now, let me ask you, is it true that Winston Churchill set fire to the hotel he was staying in by smoking a cigar in bed?'

M. René looked aghast. 'He probably made a hole in the sheet, but he certainly never set fire to the hotel, or even to the eiderdown.'

'But he did smoke in bed?'

'He had that reputation.'

'Which means – if he had dozed off – that he could have set fire to the room, and eventually to the hotel.'

'Every time I cross the road, I run the risk of being run over. Up to now, it hasn't happened.'

'How can you prove it? Simply because you are alive. Churchill isn't. Who's to prove he didn't burn down the hotel?'

'I am,' replied M. René, with acidity. 'As you say, I am still alive.'

'OK. I understand. The Duke and Duchess of Windsor?'

'What about them?'

'You knew them, of course.'

'I accepted tips from them. If that constitutes knowing them, yes, I knew them.'

'They must have known whom they were tipping. Which means that even if you cannot claim to have known them, they obviously knew you?'

M. René sighed. 'Very well, you win. I knew them.'

'Was there anything particularly scandalous about their relationship?'

'If there was, it was our duty to look the other way.'

'But then why write a book?'

'Why? I just thought it might interest people to know what the life of a concierge was like.'

'Not if you avert your gaze any time anything worthy of record occurs. It's a reckoning, this book. A vengeance. That's what you told Miss Whitlop. A settling of accounts. Come on, man, loosen up. The cash flow is assured. Now, by God, the words have got to flow. Or else . . .'

'Or else? Or else, what?'

'You'll have a mass of legal actions on your hands. You allowed Reg Masters to believe that you were in agreement. He managed to secure an injunction on the newspaper which had acquired your manuscript. That entailed some legal fees. Then we've sold the rights to the Yanks at an auction. There are many other lucrative deals in the works. If you walk out on us now, we'll sue you for all you've got, and more. You're getting your money. Now you've bloody well got to earn it. We don't ask for the impossible. Just a signature on the contract which I have with me, and the answers to a few questions. Then you can put your feet up, and listen to the shekels rolling into the piggy bank.'

M. René was exasperated by Mr Gordie. He failed to understand the vernacular. Why shekels? And what did that have to do with putting one's feet up? He started the conversation afresh, making sure by his tone of voice that he considered it a fresh beginning.

'Listen, Mr Goodwin, is it?'

'Gordie. Just call me Gill.'

'Later, perhaps. If all goes well. I always thought writing one's memoirs would be a joy, a relaxation in the autumn of life, an agreeable chore, something to occupy the mind—'

'Did you?' interrupted Gordie. 'The only snag being, you're not writing them. I am. And let me tell you, it's not an agreeable chore, it's a colossal fucking bore!'

M. René thought briefly of Kuki, but it was no time for her to occupy his mind.

'I've got you squeezed in between ghosting the confessions of Tom and Mirabelle Gazoolie, the perpetrators of the midwife murders in Hemel Hempstead, you may have read about them—'

'No.'

'They were hospital workers who killed thirty-two midwives, exclusively midwives, last summer, and buried their bodies in discarded fridges. Tom was a male nurse, his companion, Mirabelle, a chiropodist. None of the corpses had toes. Work that one out.'

'I can't. How did you? By interviewing them?'

'Shit, no. You're a luxury, René. There aren't many opportunities in my work to talk to the living, or at least, to those at liberty. Guesswork. Nous. What you don't know, make up. Or else? No shekels. Savvy?'

As before, the conversation was plunging into obscurity as far as M. René was concerned.

'You said you were squeezing me in between the murderers and who?'

'Ah, Guru Rajputi Shalimapur, the man who spirited away the life savings of thousands of poor families in Wisconsin to maintain his lifestyle. Eighty-six women were suing him for harassment at the time of his death in his burning Rolls-Royce. You know how it is in America. One embittered spinster has the idea, and eighty-five others catch on.'

'You have a lot of work to do. I must say, I am quite

flattered to find myself sandwiched between a toe fetishist and a lascivious guru.'

'Yes, but you're the luxury, René. The others give me freedom, know what I mean? One hundred per cent of the lolly flows my way. No need to share.'

'Lolly?'

'Shekels. Mazooma. The bread.'

'I see. It would be easier if I were dead.'

'Oh, yeah. Much. I wouldn't have to badger you about the contract, would I? And I wouldn't have to take care of your scruples, would I now? And I wouldn't have to give up seventy-five per cent of my salary to an old fart who can't look a gift horse in the mouth without blushing.'

Gordie eventually left with the tart reflection that that was enough for the first day. He was exhausted by having to explain everything. He wasn't used to it. He left the contract for signature. He expected it signed by the morning.

'May I offer you dinner?' asked M. René.

'Christ, no, not if it means conversation. Call me a taxi, will you? And what are your favourite fleshpots lakeside?'

M. René did not know of any, even by name, except the one in which Kuki was an intermittent hostess. 'The Bel Amour.'

'God help you if it's no good.'

'If it's no good, you only have to bump me off and keep all the shekels, Gill.'

# XVI

M. René spent a restless night, swimming in contractual obligations, way out of his depth. He sat in pyjamas, ironically the same red and white striped pair so miraculously rejuvenated by the hopeful hand of Mme Radibois, his half-glasses on his nose, a red pencil in his hand, grimly struggling with British legalese, which made no more sense than the staccato tissue of Mr Gordie's vernacular. In general, was he selling his soul to the devil in the classic, but far less lyrical, manner of Dr Faustus? Worse, had he already sold his soul, since shamefully he had already spent a little of his shower of affluence on luxuries like private detectives? He imagined M. Domani in cahoots with Gill Gordie, getting his reward for having made the first hole in his moral coffin. Then reason stepped in again with a face-saving balm. We live in modern times, after all. Why should we still be haunted by images from another age, spectres of superstition, laws of a jungle long brought to heel, with freeways running all over it, painfully bereft of mystery and dark places to fear?

He had made a little money out of spilling some beans. Do fifty years of listening to the woes and desires of the crème de la crème not warrant a little harmless jocularity at their cost? But then again, was the ribaldry really to be as harmless as if it had come from him? What would the odious Mr Gordie invent on his behalf? He shuddered to think, and also to reflect on an accident of life (what else could one call it?) that had played his destiny so negligently into the hands of unscrupulous merchants. That witless Kuki, that stupid bitch with the glorious body sheathed in leather, profits from his human generosity by stealing a manuscript from his own desk, and then sends it to a notorious tabloid in London, hoping to make a killing. And she nearly succeeds. Nearly? She did succeed, but not on her own behalf.

He realized, when he glimpsed the details of his sudden wealth, that whereas the injunction had been enforced, in fact it only delayed the inevitable, the same tabloid having acquired the right to publish an improved version of the original – improved by Gill Gordie. Far into the night he studied the contract, and had fallen asleep twice before he admitted to himself, in a loud, clear voice, that he had understood none of it. The temptation to sign and be done with it was ever-present, dictated by fatigue and even self-preservation. Perhaps he was old-fashioned, and the world had moved on, leaving him to fret about details which had been important once, but now had lost their value except as memorials to a past which was beyond retrieving.

The inflow of cash on an unprecedented scale was far

from disagreeable, and made even more flattering to the ego
by the information that a film deal was in negotiation, the
leading part being coveted by a distinguished Hollywood
comic actor who had risen to enviable eminence from
humble beginnings in the New York Yiddish theatre.
Although the star in question, Fitzroy Nudelman, was
burly and ungainly, and spoke with the unmistakable lilt
of Brooklyn, M. René could not but feel flattered that such
a prominent personality was eager to play the leading role in
his autobiography. *His* autobiography?

For one last time he studied his notes, the mass of question marks, the requests for elucidation in understandable
language, then screwed the papers into a ball and threw it
on the floor. Without allowing himself further thought, he
signed the contract, and felt immediately a huge sense of
relief, of liberation. At last the trickle of money into his
numerous bank accounts was really his. He would live
with the times, no longer attempting to swim against
the tide of events, but drifting with it to an unknown
but carefree destination. What was the point in insisting
on ancient values like truth, honesty, and the like, when
they are discredited today? Indolence is rewarded and there
are always those who are ready to do the drudgery for you
for a consideration.

The Gill Gordies of the world, Mr Twenty-five per cent,
seeking relief from the ardours of intellectual effort in the
fleshpots of Geneva, of all places. M. René laughed aloud,
then sobered up with a fresh reflection. And who was he
in all this? Mr Seventy-five per cent. Which only meant
that even slippery operators like Masters and Gordie had to
admit that the memoirs were his and no one else's. Without
him and what he had lived through, there would be no

need for a contract, no need for negotiations, no reason for Fitzroy Nudelman's eagerness to play the part of M. René! He prepared for bed, asking himself why he had had to shed so many scruples before signing that piece of paper.

The next morning, Gill Gordie arrived earlier than expected, and in a bad mood. He cheered up considerably when M. René showed him the signed contract. He patted it as though it were the hand of a dear friend, in need of reassurance. 'You won't regret this,' he said. 'From now on in, you'll be laughing all the way to the bank, as the saying goes. Bread on a scale no baker would ever dream of. Ever dream of,' he repeated for emphasis. Then his tone changed. 'I can probably get a plane this afternoon.'

'But, I thought—'

'Never research anything you've got the possibility of inventing. That's been my maxim all along. How d'you think I could have got such a lot of ghosting done without the odd flight of fancy? And so long as such flights are frequent, why bother to look at a gift horse, savvy?'

'A gift horse in the mouth,' M. René corrected. 'You got it right yesterday.'

Gill Gordie became suspicious.

'What are you trying to tell me?' he asked.

'A gift horse in the mouth is the usual phrase, deriving, I believe, from the Trojan War.'

'Which war?' asked Gordie, drawing out a notebook. 'I'll make a note of that. Local colour.'

M. René waited for Gordie to be ready.

'I don't know why you are making so much of this. It's not something I would usually say.'

'No?' Gordie was mildly disappointed. Then he regained his confidence. 'What would you usually say?'

'It depends on the circumstances,' replied M. René, a little on edge. He was beginning to be as eager for Gordie to leave as Gordie himself was eager to go.

'Under these circumstances,' Gordie insisted.

M. René allowed himself a rapid sigh. 'I don't see what this has to do with anything, but since you insist – a long time ago there was a war called the Trojan War—'

'That doesn't surprise me. Do you know, there are four hundred wars of some kind or other going on as we talk? I read that somewhere.'

'So did I,' M. René confirmed, 'the only difference being that this one took place in prehistory. It was fought between the Greeks and the Trojans. The Greeks won by a low trick.'

'That doesn't surprise me,' said Gordie, knowingly.

'They gave the Trojans the gift of an enormous horse.'

'How big?'

'Enough to contain a military company.'

Gordie whistled. 'Who'd want a horse that size? What can you do with it? It's too big for the mantelpiece. It'd take up most of the average suburban garden. If I were a Trojan, or whatever they were called, I'd smell a rat as soon as I saw it.'

'In that case, it is perhaps unfortunate that you were not a Trojan, since they looked the gift horse in the mouth, failed to see the Greek warriors sizing up the opposition through the gaps in the teeth, and allowed themselves to be overwhelmed.'

'Hence, looking a gift horse in the mouth?'

'I presume so.'

'But I thought it meant to be foolish not to accept a gift when it is offered.'

'It does.'

'In that case, it must be a Trojan saying, not a Greek one, dating from before they were taken in.'

'I really don't know. I'm not expert enough in philology to pass a judgement.'

'Expert in what?'

M. René allowed his exasperation to show. 'Look,' he said, 'all this because I corrected a phrase of yours which was incomplete in the form you used it. If we were speaking French instead of English, the question would never arise, since such a phrase does not exist in French.'

Mr Gordie smiled slyly. 'There's only one snag,' he retorted.

'Yes?'

'I don't speak French. Savvy?'

There was an ominous pause.

Mr Gordie became coy, almost ingratiating. 'You want to be rid of me, don't you?'

M. René replied with all the equanimity he could muster. 'Well, once you have made it clear to me that you can invent what lies in my mind and heart better than I can express it, there seems very little point in dragging out a relationship which has given me neither pleasure nor satisfaction.'

Gordie laughed. 'There's my lad. I've got a skin like a rhinoceros. You can't hurt my feelings, for the simple reason, I got no feelings. Could be because most of my clients are dead. I get used to dealing with people as though they don't exist. Perhaps they did exist once? I can never be sure.' He ended his reverie. 'I'll be glad to go too, not because of you. As you point out, I know you from copious notes rather than from yourself. I've got nothing against you personally. But this town is a dead loss.'

'Geneva?'

Gordie dug into his pockets, and threw down three brightly coloured packets on the table.

'What are they, cigarettes?' enquired M. René.

'Condoms. Contraceptives. French letters. That must have a French equivalent.'

'Yes, capotes anglaises.'

'Never without them. These days you can't be too careful. And they show what I think of this morgue of a city. Not one packet's even opened.'

'You can put them back into your pocket.'

Gordie smiled. 'Shocked you, have I?' And then continued, with surprising simplicity: 'I can't help being oversexed, can I? It helps my writing, that's what our Reg Masters says. He tells me there's a connection between my love life and my computer. Your prose has rhythm, that's the way he put it.'

'Shall I call you a taxi?'

It was while telephoning for a taxi that M. René resolved, in a trice, to carry his surrender to the inevitable to its logical conclusion. He would not even read the book when it was published. Why make oneself miserable? 'Take it easy' was the motto of the new society. Now M. René understood what it meant. Don't torture yourself with details. Reap the benefits without having anything to do with their acquisition. Let others fret, let others scrounge. There is such a thing as privilege. There always will be. It takes hardship and longevity to acquire it, but once you're over the summit, it's downhill all the way. It's the least the world can do for a man.

The taxi took a long time in coming. M. René confined himself to showing Mr Gordie where the bathroom was and

how the television worked, in case he wished to avail himself
of either. Then he went into the porch, and waited. At long
last the bell rang. He rose from his seat. Gordie's voice rang
out. 'I'll let myself out. Happy days.'

M. René let him go, but after hearing the door slam,
went out to make sure he had really gone. He returned
to the sitting room, unsure as to whether he was angry,
disgusted, or relieved. In his haste to gather his notes
together, Gordie had left one slender pack of condoms on
the table, and it lay there with the arrogance of a visiting
card, challenging him to a duel of opposing spirits. Was the
gesture deliberate? Was it planted as a gratuitous aftertaste
of a most distasteful, disillusioning visit? M. René came to
the conclusion it was exactly that, and was about to throw
it away when he remembered it was Mme Radibois' day,
and he shuddered to think of the shower of innuendos he
would suffer if she found it in the dustbin. He placed it
in a compartment of his desk, turned the key, and put
it in his waistcoat pocket. He had thrown his clothes on
because Gordie had arrived so obscenely early, probably
because of his unsuccessful safari into the fleshpots of
the city. M. René shuddered at the thought, while being
astonished at his own sudden serenity. What reason had
he to be abruptly unaffected by all that had occurred? Was
it, he wondered, because he had simply changed his mind?
He would never read his own memoirs. There is no need
to make oneself miserable. He had disowned them. The
situation was identical to that when he had sent the young
female packing.

The only difference being that a book would appear,
bearing his name, and purporting to be his recollections,
refined and selected for publication by Mr Gill Gordie.

Who cares? It had been a negotiation typical of the epoch of the all-important market. He begged its pardon; *global* market. He had been paid for his abandonment of truth and honour. And how true can memories be at the best of times? Better Gordie spun his lies with his uncanny commercial instinct than that he himself did it owing to lapses of memory and feelings of unrequited hostility towards some.

He sat at his desk for consolation, and examined closely the collection of tabs from his bank announcing credits. He had never done this methodically before, since he had had a feeling that the money was not really irrevocably his before the contract was signed. Now he did so, and was amazed at the extraordinary growth of his fortunes, from substantial sums for British, Australian and other serial rights to dribs and drabs from the eager tabloids of Pakistan, Bangladesh and Mauritius. It was while assessing his true financial position, and in the knowledge that other rights, more important ones, were still in the offing, that he heard the key in the door. It was Mme Radibois. He imagined her standing in a long queue waiting to see Fitzroy Nudelman in the part of M. René, and smiled. He felt as though a great boil of worry, of doubt, had been lanced, and suddenly life was rediscovered. Of course, there was still Agnes, his loyalty, his inspiration. Nothing all the Gordies of the world could do would have access to that. He frowned.

'Bonjour!' Mme Radibois hooted from somewhere next door in a high good humour.

That was unlike her usual mousey self, with her almost oriental deference. 'Bonjour, Madame Radibois.' M. René sounded his usual curt self. She appeared, grinning from ear to ear.

'Will you be shaving? I want to know. In that case, I will not begin with the bathroom.'

'How did you know I have not yet shaved?' he asked.

'Your shaving brush is dry.'

The woman was diabolical. If only she possessed the gift of letters, she'd outdo Agatha Christie and the entire battalion of ladies who feel at home with murder. Thank goodness the condoms were under lock and key.

'No,' he replied on an impulse. 'I will not be shaving today.'

'Not be shaving?' Mme Radibois could hardly believe her ears.

'No. I have decided to change my personality, and grow a beard.'

'You? A beard?'

'Any comment?'

'Who am I to comment? It's your face, after all.'

She left the room, with her laughter ringing round the house.

# XVII

As THE days succeeded one another without much change – Domani had not yet handed in his report, and the law was advancing at its usual snail's pace – M. René was seized with a ferocious desire to confirm his sudden wealth by spending, even recklessly. He visited a few larger houses and his eye had fallen on one in particular, not better situated than the others, but only a stone's throw from the prison. In the absence of contact, proximity was the next best thing. He had not, however, entirely lost his head. That would have been out of character. He only contemplated houses for rent, not for sale.

The new place was too large for a solitary widower, but it reeked of success, of what is called standing. It had a lawn too large to be looked after by other than a gardener, twice a week at least, culminating in an ornamental pool, guarded by two gleaming ceramic windhounds. It had a conservatory, with the odour of tropical plants, heated up to their native conditions. There was a two-car garage, and the kitchen, apart from equipment which had been ahead of its times in the Twenties, possessed a display indicating in which of the many rooms the bell had rung.

M. René never for a moment contemplated this virtual emporium as a place in which to pass the closing days of life, but rather as an impressive mansion for two lovers who valued each other's independence. He had no reason for such optimism, which, by some perversity of the spirit, only made his buoyancy more rampant. And who was there to impress with such opulence? The woman of his life, and no one else. He could imagine her gasp of disbelief. 'All this for me?'

'Ah, my love, you deserve the Palais des Nations if I could afford it, and if it were available.'

'Oh, my darling. I was a little in love with your old place, trains and all. After all, that's where our adventure all began. It was a kind of monument to our love.'

'And yet, my darling, it is a law of nature that nothing can remain static, everything must move forward, day and night, the seasons, the years . . .'

He imagined her putting a hand over his mouth, and, closing her eyes, murmuring: 'Don't talk about the years.'

'Forget the years,' he conceded gently. 'You have no objection to the weather?'

She shook her head, her eyes tight shut. 'Sometimes it rains.'

'Sometimes it is sunny. It's the weather in the heart which counts.' He smiled with a sense of achievement as he managed to recreate a relationship in the mind, not only of ideal moments, but with a pang of feminine perversity as well, a touch of fatalism, a penchant for the tragic.

It was something he could live with. No, it was something he desired to live with. It broke the monotony of male
self-sufficiency. Yes, he decided, she would be impressed
with his initiative in renting such an absurd stockbroker's
house, even if he recognized that she would be appalled
by the extravagance. But then, it would prove him to be
capable of such extravagance. It was a matter of choice, not
imposed by circumstances.

The light-heartedness which he had shown in signing
the contract became contagious. He signed a year's lease
on the house without treating the document as other than
one of a pile of letters to be answered. He consequently
caused most of his furniture to be transported. The little
there was, was entirely lost in the immensity of his new
surroundings. Curiously enough, Mme Radibois was not
unduly depressed by the exodus of his belongings to a new
house. He told her the place was too big for her to handle
alone, and that she would need some assistance, possibly
even a live-in. She told him, with a new-found detachment,
that all decisions were his alone, in which she had no right
to interfere. She also dropped more than a hint that she
was thinking of retiring, and had been worried as to how
to break the news to him.

'Retire? Can you afford to retire?' he had asked. 'You
told me only a little while ago you could hardly make ends
meet by working only three days a week. Admittedly you
now work six, but you haven't done this for long enough
to build up any reserves.'

'I may find a way,' she had replied, enigmatically. He
reminded her that he had not sold the house near the
railway tracks, but merely rented the new place. All could
still change if the new place proved unsatisfactory. She

retorted that she was still inclined to retire. He bowed to the inevitable, taking care not to register too great a surprise. It is always a mistake to take anyone for granted.

On his last day in the old house, with merely a few sticks of furniture remaining, most of it from the kitchen, he fancied he heard something clatter on the drive. He listened carefully, then went to the door, and looked through the peep-hole before daring to open it. There was an object on the drive, difficult to identify. He opened the door cautiously. It was a rusty bicycle. 'Well, that can't be Louis,' he said out loud. He often spoke aloud these days, for company.

'Is there anyone there?' he called out.

There was no answer. Not wishing to go out, he shut the door again and walked to the back of the house, to the verandah. He cautiously opened one slatted blind, and saw a sombre figure standing in reverie over his Venusberg of old.

'My God, it is Louis after all!' He opened a window. 'Louis?'

Slowly the figure turned. Even in the sombre light of dawn, M. René saw that the rich mane of russet locks had gone, and the malodorous leather habit was now replaced by an ill-fitting dark suit. As a concession to his age group, he wore no tie, although his shirt was buttoned to the neck.

He waved feebly.

'Come in, come in. Come round to the front!'

As Louis prepared to follow instructions, M. René hurried to open the front door.

'Coffee?'

'OK.'

'I'm afraid you'll have to have it in a tooth mug. All the rest has gone.'

'What is all this? Where's the furniture?' asked Louis, as he entered the house.

'I'm moving.'

'You? Moving? What's come over you?' And he started to laugh with genuine amusement.

'What are you laughing at? Oh – that. I've decided to grow a beard. What's so amusing about that?'

'You? With a beard? It's the last thing anyone would have imagined.'

'What about you without the hanging gardens all the way to the small of your back? Is that not as strange?'

'I suppose so. But you always cultivated such impeccable style, not a hair out of place and all that. I would never have visualized you with stubble, and the hair beginning to turn into curls round the back.'

'Well, now that you've got over the shock, perhaps you'll allow me to get over mine. You, on a humble bicycle?'

'I'm working.' He seemed almost ashamed of it.

'Working? At what?' M. René had misgivings.

'I've returned to the Ecole Hôtelière, if you must know. In my spare time, I work as a waiter—' and added, with heavy-handed irony, 'thereby following in a great family tradition.'

'But where do you live?'

'I'm sharing a room with a fellow called Fiorino, says he knows you.'

'Fiorino,' echoed M. René, pretending to have some difficulty placing him. 'Yes, yes, I know the young fellow . . . .vaguely.'

'He wants to know why you never acted on the information he gave you.'

'Oh, does he? Well, you can tell him – in confidence, of course – that I transmitted his urgent message, and it was the police who failed to act on it.'

'They did? I would have thought – if you can prove it of course – that you'd have a very good case against the police.'

'It . . . it doesn't work that way . . .'

'Why not? It ought to. There were murders, weren't there? Well?'

M. René sighed. He wondered briefly how deeply they all were involved in compromises without even knowing it. For instance, to tell Louis now that he had enjoyed police protection during his sinister joy-rides would smack of favouritism and invite protest. He shook his head.

'It just doesn't work that way, that's all. I can't tell you more . . .'

Since only silence greeted his explanation, he was compelled to add: 'Blame the police and they will always come up with a logical reason for not having done what they ought to have done. They are a closed shop. Attack them, and they will immediately overlook all their internecine quarrels and remind you that they have a monopoly over law and order, the dispensation of justice, and that blows below the belt to enforce confessions not perceived by the general public are "merely imponderables of the métier".'

'How odd to hear you speak like that – you, who I always took to be a beacon of the establishment.'

M. René spoke quietly. 'We all live and learn – at any age. My experience of life is not yet over. I am altering my opinion by the hour. You too, I gather. There's a rusting

2

bicycle on my drive instead of that gleaming monster. What happened?'

'You know perfectly well.'

'I don't. You come here, and don't ring the bell. You walk straight to the back of the house, and I catch you standing over that memorable patch of high grass as though meditating by a tombstone.'

Louis swallowed hard. He looked as though he were about to break down.

'That's what I was doing,' he said, unsteadily, in a tiny voice. 'Meditating . . . by a tombstone.'

'Good God, surely it's not as tragic as all that?' And then, appalled: 'Is Kuki dead?'

And he remembered: she never came back for more money.

'As good as dead. She's in Phnom Penh.'

'Phnom Penh!' M. René spluttered. 'Nobody in their right mind goes to Phnom Penh these days!'

'She sent me a postcard. She's tested HIV positive.'

'What!'

It was like a rapier thrust through M. René's favourite and most secret erotic fantasy. He shut his eyes to absorb the news. Then he opened them with a sense of emergency.

'And you?'

'Me? Oh, I don't think so,' Louis replied bleakly. 'She must have contracted it out there.'

'But you're not sure?'

'One can never be sure about such things.'

'It's one's duty. Think of future partners.'

'I can't afford to at the moment.'

'Listen. Any expense. Any. You've got to be sure.'

And with a sudden surge of emotion, he clapped his hands over Louis' hands, resting on a kneecap, and said, with a rare intensity: 'You're all I've got. Jesus Christ. You are family. The totality. All of it. Like a son. I want you so desperately to be happy.'

'OK, OK, I'll have the tests, so long as you foot the bill.'

'Anything, I tell you, anything. Nothing in the world is as important as health. Hey, I've got something for you.' M. René rose, and went to the writing desk, one of the last pieces of furniture waiting to be transported. He opened a drawer with his key, and withdrew the garish packet of condoms. Reentering the kitchen, he threw it down on the table.

'What are these? Condoms?' asked Louis, amazed. 'This is really a day of surprises. The last gift I'd ever expect from you is a pack of condoms.'

'A business associate left them here by mistake.'

'By mistake? To shock you, more likely.'

'That too is a distinct possibility.'

'Well, thanks anyway. I've no prospects at the moment, but it's always better to be on the safe side.'

'Always better. Was Kuki . . . I mean, you seem so upset . . . did it look like . . . the real thing?'

'I don't know,' Louis answered reasonably. 'At times, yes. But there was no holding that girl. She was all over the place. She exhausted me, and even that wasn't enough for her. If it had gone on, I don't know how long I could have lasted. And I know I wouldn't have been sufficient, and that's a terrible feeling.'

M. René nodded.

Louis went on: 'It's funny to hear you talk about the real

thing. Once again, you're the last person I'd have imagined using such a phrase.'

'Why?'

'Was my aunt the real thing?'

'No.' M. René smiled. 'Louis, we have so much to talk about now that you have returned, like the Prodigal, to share your grief and your perplexities. I will make all the necessary arrangements with the clinic, and we will share what I believe will be the good news. All the same, poor Kuki. She is responsible for so much that has happened to me. I neither know whether to bless her nor to curse her.'

'I'm sorry about your manuscript.'

'It's being published, you know.'

'Go on? Was that Kuki's doing?'

'She was at its origin, but only indirectly responsible for what has happened since. Why d'you think I'm moving house?'

'I can't imagine.'

'I can afford to, that's why. There may be a film of the book. Guess who's playing my part?'

'I give up.'

'Fitzroy Nudelman.'

'Fitz—' And Louis relapsed into peals of laughter, enough to gladden any heart.

M. René laughed a little out of sympathy. 'What's so outrageous?' he asked. There was a pause.

'At all events, I'm happy you got rid of that horrible motorbicycle,' M. René said. 'At least, like this, you are able to take in a little of the beautiful nature which surrounds you.'

'Don't you believe it. I spend all my time avoiding being killed by the traffic.'

'You don't mean to say a bicycle is more dangerous than a motorbike?'

'Every time. On a motorbike, you create the chaos. On a bike, you're its victim.'

'Hm. That's worthy of reflection. At any rate—' he looked Louis deep in the eye, 'welcome home.'

'You say that at the moment of leaving.'

'You're always welcome to my new home. You can always stay the night.'

'Thanks. Where is it?'

'Villa Salambbo. Impasse de la Fraternité, 6.'

'Near the prison?'

'Exactly.'

'Well, well, well.'

How much did he know? Never mind. They were both alone, for the moment. He seemed very affected by the awful fate attendant on that bundle of perversity, that impetuous wildcat. She was just the type of person destined for such a mournful finish. The roulette wheel had gathered speed until it was invisible, life was a breathless, unstable flash of sunlight. It was begging for a sudden end. The poor boy had suffered his first rude shock, which had destroyed his irresponsibility. He had taken refuge in convention. Adventure had given over to menial disciplines, like waiting at table. Life had slowed to a crawl. He was beginning to understand. Even his acne seemed to have cleared up a little.

'Well, I'd better be off. I'm on duty in a quarter of an hour.' Louis rose.

'How was the coffee?'

'Fine. It had a lingering aftertaste of toothpaste.'

'I don't believe you. It's only because I told you it was the tooth mug.'

'Perhaps. I'm very impressionable, as you know.'

They looked at one another. Impulsively they embraced. Then Louis playfully punched his uncle. M. René nodded in acknowledgement of the gesture. 'Impasse de la Fraternité, 6,' he said.

Louis gave him the thumb-up sign. Without such a sign it wouldn't be Louis.

As M. René stood in the porch to wave, all he heard was the friendly crunch of gravel, and the squeak of a rusty chain.

# XVIII

A SOMBRE note was struck a few days later with the arrival at the Villa Salambbo of a small envelope, edged in black, forwarded by the post office from his old address by the railway tracks. M. René sat on his bed, eating his breakfast which was awkwardly perched on an occasional table by the Filipino house boy, Ramón, whom he had engaged to look after the mansion. Without admitting it to himself, M. René was a victim of that customary western prejudice which believes that Orientals are capable of longer hours than Europeans, and for less pay. Ramón was a somewhat furtive individual, his salient feature acquired throughout a life of constant refusals and endlessly accepted disappointments. To refer to him as a boy of any sort was a distinct error, since he was sixty if he was a day, and spoke no known language. Hermetically sealed in his total ignorance of what was going on, he preserved a kind of imperious detachment. Whenever M. René asked for coffee, Ramón brought a hot face flannel. Whenever he asked for the breakfast to be cleared, Ramón began hoovering. Their relationship was consequently one of equals, which eliminated the merest hint of enslavement. However, the absence of dialogue was a distinct relief after Mme Radibois. A mutual acceptance reigned in the house.

It was only after breakfast, and while Ramón was following a vacuum cleaner into every nook and cranny of the room, while singing a mournful folk song from his part of the world, that M. René risked opening the envelope with the black rim. The card inside was from Arnold Butler, and regretted the passing of Lambert Horatio Wales Butler, former Valet of Leading Hotels in his seventy-eighth year. The funeral service was foreseen for the next Friday, followed by cremation at the Municipal Crematorium. Requiescat in pace. M. René put down the card without any clear emotion.

They had known each other too long and too little. All the same, there was an awful finality about such news, to which the old are exposed as no other age group. That tearful eye was now dry as a bone, the hand's tremolo was still. There would be no more noisy inhalations as the nasal drip gathered into a torrent. A sad passing, a link with Agnes. The link with Agnes.

On the day of the funeral, M. René rose early. He ate an egg by fetching it from the kitchen, and showing it to Ramón. He expected it boiled, but it arrived as an omelette some time later, flavoured with spices too violent for M. René's stomach. This was an aspect of luxury with which he had not reckoned. He was not yet reconciled to sharing his domicile with another person. Agnes had been the only welcome intrusion into his blissful solitude. Ramón was something different. He possessed a snore which even the exorbitant dimensions of the villa were incapable of drowning. On the contrary, the vast open spaces of the hallway and central staircase acted like a cathedral to the litany of snores, which reverberated in the gothic cavities of the roof like the diapason of an organ with every stop adjusted to cause the maximum effect. M. René was quite glad to get out of his home, even to go to a funeral.

The congregation was already gathering, and he noticed many familiar faces. Was it his imagination, or did M. Arrigo and M. Alonso greet him with a certain reserve? It was no doubt the result of their guilt about their cowardice before the police admonitions. He bowed to them, his head held high. He immediately discerned Arnold, the Member of Parliament, a balding replica of his father, less choleric in colour, and less liquid too, but the same mannerisms were there, hands clinging to one another for comfort, and a feeling that breath was, in some way, rationed. Arnold was receiving the condolences of M. Gailhac, the Chief of the Ecole Hôtelière, a man, to judge from his body language, over-endowed with conventional consolations. M. René made his way through the crowd.

'You must be Arnold?'

'Yes. Yes indeed. Arnold Butler.'

'My sincerest condolences. M. René.'

'Ah, M. René! Good of you to come.'

'You've taken a brief rest from your parliamentary duties owing to this sad event?'

'What duties?'

'Your late father told me you were a Member of Parliament.'

'Dad said that?' Arnold smirked. 'No, I once stood as an Independent Conservative, and lost my deposit. Well,

simply because there are no such things as Independent
Conservatives.'

'Your father said you got in for Labour.'

'Labour? Dad would have slaughtered me had I done
that. He wouldn't have a socialist in the house.'

Why had Mr Butler lied? M. René wondered about this
as he made his way back to his pew. The appearance of an
Anglican clergyman brought a little order to the crowd.
After one or two banal hymns, heavy-handedly picked for
the occasion, with their copious references to eternal life,
angels, and all the celestial baggage attendant on the dear
departed, the clergyman extolled the virtues of Mr Butler,
with a special emphasis on duty and service, attributes sadly
lacking in the youth of today.

This morose paean to servility gave M. René considerable
pause to reflect. No doubt, Mr Butler had possessed, well
entrenched behind his sewing kit and shoe polish, a spirit as
doggedly vagrant as his own. After three score and ten years
of incarceration in an image of pious rectitude, he was as
bursting at the seams as had been M. René himself. He was
the first to agree to that original mad initiative. He had even
recruited Agnes, the only true activist among them. But, in
order to make this possible, he had to justify his recklessness
to himself. What more convincing than the invention of
a son in full revolt, which can happen to the best of us.
And what better disguise is there for revolt in the parent?
M. René felt a sudden bond between himself and the pine
coffin, all ready to glide silently into the flames. They could
have had an illuminating discussion in the light of what he
had discovered. But it was, as usual, too late. Ashes to ashes,
dust to dust, to borrow a phrase from the reverend. Soon,
it was over, with the clergyman shaking hands at the door,

accepting compliments on his uncanny ability to capture in words the very essence of a man he had never known, and Arnold, who could only confirm the accuracy of the holy man's assessment. Once in the open air again, M. Arrigo made a beeline for M. René.

'Ah, M. Arrigo! Are we on speaking terms?'

'You tell me, M. René.'

'As far as I am concerned, yes. I might have deplored your timorous nature at a certain moment, but all that is old hat now.'

'It is not every day that a self-respecting head waiter has to justify his actions before the Chief of Police, especially if he has done nothing illegal.'

'It is when he has done nothing illegal, I presume, that a self-respecting head waiter feels especially vulnerable.'

M. Arrigo ignored the allusion.

'Listen,' he said, 'we must talk.'

'Oh?'

'But not here. Away from the crowd.'

They wandered in silence to the neighbouring church-yard, which was deserted at that time of the morning. M. Arrigo sat on a particularly imposing tomb, and invited M. René to do likewise.

'Well? What's it about?'

'You have written a book.'

'Correction. I have written nothing. If you see the cover one day, you will see that, "As told to Gilbert Gordie" is written there.'

'It makes no difference. All who know you will believe that you are the author, and will be deeply shocked by its contents.'

'How do you know?'

'Your publisher sent an advance copy to the International Brotherhood of Concierges and Hall Porters, hoping for a favourable testimonial.'

'What? They must be out of their minds.'

'You have read the book, of course.'

'No, and I have no intention of doing so.'

'It is deeply offensive.'

'That does not surprise me.'

'Winston Churchill is depicted as a self-indulgent moron, who once burned a hotel to cinders out of sheer negligence. The British taxpayer had to foot the bill out of secret funds.'

'That's enough. I don't want to hear more.'

'Damn it, it's your responsibility, man! The Duke of Windsor liked to pretend he was a small boy, and the Duchess was his nanny. I won't elucidate further.'

'Thank you. What d'you want me to do about it? It's a fact now. There's no road back.'

M. René was so curt and economical in his reactions that M. Arrigo was bereft of words. He was reduced to pulling an object out of his pocket. It was the projected cover for the book, with a yellow line showing where the publishers hoped to place the testimonial. It was so outrageous that M. René was forced to look at it, despite his determination to remain inhumanly removed from reality. The cover showed him bent forward with his expression twisted into a cheeky wink. Over the open eye, there was superimposed a vibrant crimson keyhole. Behind his back, there was a montage, with a badly drawn Churchill, cigar in mouth, his nightgown on fire, and one or two scantily clad females caught in the blaze. Above this paroxysm of vulgarity was the title, 'What the Concierge Saw', and his name, followed by 'As told to Gilbert Gordie'. And there was a band, 'Soon to be a Major Motion Picture Starring Fitzroy Nudelman'. Had the deal then been concluded, or was this once again what is known as 'hype', wishful thinking disguised as fact? To M. René's own surpise, this was the only question arising from his revelation. All the rest was almost normal in view of his assessment of Gill Gordie's ethical standards. All that was really unusual was the speed at which Gordie had worked, and the velocity at which the presses had rolled.

M. Arrigo broke the silence. 'That someone should take advantage of commercial opportunity is only human,' he said. 'I forget if it was M. Alonso or I who asked you if your motivation in founding an ill-fated movement was money, and you confessed yourself to be deeply shocked. Both Alonso and I in our subsequent conversation agreed that it had been a perfectly normal question to have asked, and considered your reaction to have been puritanical and hypocritical.'

'You were probably correct in your assessment.'

M. Arrigo was momentarily speechless, but seized his chance.

'It was probably those very qualities which made you an ideal candidate for the Permanent Presidency of the International Brotherhood.'

'Probably.'

'Today it is less apparent.'

M. René looked sharply at M. Arrigo. 'Have you something specific in mind?'

'There is a storm brewing.'

'A storm?'

'M. Gaetano has read the book.'

'M. Gaetano?'

'From cover to cover. He is beside himself. He has declared that he refuses to serve on the same committee with its perpetrator. M. Wolfgang has read it also. He feels you should be put on trial as a traitor to the high traditions of the profession.'

'Does he know there is no such crime?'

'It's wishful thinking.'

'And M. Armand?'

'—is reading it at this moment. I tell you, once he has finished, there's bound to be a meeting of the full committee, with a logical consequence.'

'Which is, my expulsion from the Presidency?'

'Inevitably.'

'What do you want me to do?'

'Resign, before they have a chance to fire you.'

M. René laughed. 'Is that all? Don't worry. You have my resignation. Or rather, you'll have it in the morning. It's something I should have done long ago. For some time now, I've no longer been proud of my past. But . . .' he hesitated, '. . . why is it you telling me all this? You're a Maître d'Hotel, not a Hotel Porter at all.'

'For some time now they've felt the financial pinch, like everyone else. They've let others into the organization, and reduced the fees to accommodate other categories, such as Maîtres d'Hotel, Chefs, Pastrycooks, Sauciers and Housekeepers. It's no longer as exclusive as it was, and has lost much of its character.'

M. René smiled. 'It just shows what a sinecure my Presidency was. I knew nothing of all this. I was not even consulted. I'm resigning from nothing at all.'

'Whatever you do, don't give them that impression.'

'Surely a man resigning has the right to give whatever impression he wishes?'

'Don't give them ammunition.'

'To hell with them.'

Just then a well-dressed elderly lady appeared, laden with flowers. She said not a word, but just stood there, appearing to be mildly outraged that they had chosen that tombstone to sit on when there were so many others available.

Instantly they both rose, brushing the dust and traces of moss from the seats of their pants. They moved off in silence, with a nod of acknowledgement in the lady's direction. The lady promptly laid the flowers where they had sat, and knelt in silent prayer.

M. René managed a wry smile. 'Life is full of surprises,' he said quietly.

'Some pleasant, some not so pleasant,' M. Arrigo whispered. 'For God's sake take that ridiculous beard off. You make a lousy Bohemian, d'you know that?'

On reaching home, M. René wrote his letter of resignation. 'Messieurs,' it read, 'chers confrères. For a long time now I have felt that my Permanent Presidency of the International Brotherhood of Concierges and Hall Porters was a high honour which I no longer deserve, not because of any external factor, but because I no longer felt as proud of my achievements as once I did. Mark you, I was always conscious of my shortcomings. My contacts with the merchants of flesh were never as profound as those of dear M. Gaetano, who had instant sex at his fingertips, catering with superb authority for every perversion known to a refined clientele. My ability to cover up the aberrations of guests was nothing compared to the expertise of M. Wolfgang, who would have been in his element directing French farce in the theatre, because he succeeded in something even more difficult, which is directing French farce in five star hotels. As for M. Armand—'

After re-reading the letter thus far, he tore it up, without mentioning in-house rumours of M. Armand's legendary dishonesty as far as sharing tips was concerned.

He began again on a clean sheet of paper.

'Messieurs, chers collègues, I hereby resign from the Permanent Presidency of the International Brotherhood of Concierges and Hall Porters, since the post no longer conforms with my ambitions or expectations. My best wishes to my successor. Yours, with a distinct sense of liberation from a reputation I at no time deserved, René.' He asked Ramón for postage stamps. Ramón brought a split of champagne, which was at least as apposite. M. René toasted his liberation.

# XIX

Bits of what seemed to be good news followed each other in rapid succession. First of all, the news from the clinic, clearing Louis from any infection. Now the boy could make a fresh start in his new perception of existence without that hopeless feeling of being tarnished, indulging in a race with unknown researchers for the cure which had to be forthcoming one day. Secondly, Max Domani's full report arrived, which M. René immediately photostatted, with a copy to Maître Muresanescu and a second one to Professor Szepainska. It was extremely complete, and compiled with an intellectual finesse surprising in one of Domani's unscrupulous appearance. The third piece of news was perhaps the most surprising, although extremely flattering to M. René's achievements as a Samaritan. It was an invitation to the wedding reception of Urs Mildenegger, ex-Police Chief of Geneva, and Mme Rose Marie Widow Radibois, née Couche. It was to take place in their apartment after a very private ceremony at a register office.

When the day came, M. René called a taxi himself, since Ramón could not be relied on for a task of such intricacy. He took along his present, a superb set of French cutlery, a complete service for twelve people, costing the earth. Already, from well outside the flat, he could hear the ferocious gabble of a cocktail party, as well as the strident barking of Mme Poncin's dog, locked in her flat. The Mildenegger apartment was so full of well-wishers the front door had been left open, and several guests were sipping champagne on the landing, leaning against the wire surrounding the lift shaft. M. René tried to force his way into the apartment, one of those giving way to him, muttering: 'You'll be lucky . . .'

Once inside, he quickly found Urs Mildenegger, beaming from ear to ear, impeccable in a dark blue lounge suit. M. René fancied he recognized Mme Radibois' hand in his appearance, a total transformation from the drink-sodden scarecrow he had been.

Mildenegger came forward as best he could, both arms extended, muttering a tearful, 'There he is, the architect of my happiness'. M. René had to give over the present before being able to fulfil his part in the choreography of greeting. 'My God, you shouldn't have! What a royal gift to an old friend!'

'Where is Rose Marie?'

'Try to lure her out of the kitchen! She insisted on doing all the catering herself. Wouldn't hear of outside help. Think of the expense, she'd say. Quite unnecessary. She's a fabulous acquisition. I bless the day you sent her to me – in more ways than one.' His gratitude seemed almost excessive.

'That's friendship,' M. René shrugged.

'You never said a truer word,' agreed Mildenegger, and began pumping M. René's hands in both of his.

They made their way through the throng towards the kitchen, stopping on the way in the bedroom, in which Beat Kribl had taken refuge.

'Ah, M. René!' cried Kribl, nodding furiously. 'I want you to meet my wife, Ruth.'

In a wheelchair sat a woman who must have been attractive before being struck down by a cruel illness which rendered her wholly paraplegic. She recognized that she was being presented to someone, but a co-ordinated response was beyond her. One hand flailed around, until Kribl took it very gently, and steadied it for M. René to shake. The tenderness, which was evidently habitual, was quite remarkable. M. René tried to make a little conversation, but it sounded just as awkward as it was. Kribl came to the rescue by reverting to his usual robust manner. 'What's this? A beard? Trying to change your personality, are you? It's too late.' He pointed a finger as he ranted: 'We know you! You're on our files as you were.' And he nodded away furiously in confirmation of this fact. 'With me, it's different. I've always had a beard, but not so large as you'd notice it. I get away with it both ways.' When he finished laughing outrageously at his own joke, he bent down and muttered into his wife's ear: 'Don't worry, my darling, we're going now.'

The wife made some wild gestures suggesting that she was enjoying herself, but her husband admonished her secretly. 'We don't want you overtired, do we? You're not used to going out yet. Come home, and listen to the CD. Lovely music?'

The wife nodded with the over-enthusiasm of a child

promised a sweet. She even tried to say something which sounded like music.

'If you will forgive us, dear friend,' said Kribl, taking charge of the wheelchair. 'It's not every day we go out together. It's only because this is a very special occasion, with very special friends.' There was more pumping of hands, more sincerities exchanged, and then Urs and M. René went out to carve a way through the crowd, in the direction of the lift. While awaiting the lift, Kribl spoke again to M. René.

'Incidentally, the case of Agnes Schandenbach comes up next Tuesday. I'm hoping for a decision not to prosecute, but one can never be sure. Not in a democracy. In a democracy, one can be sure of nothing, not even the interpretation of the law, nor a correct assessment of danger. Perhaps now you can understand some of our difficulties.' M. René nodded. 'I'll arrange your meeting as soon as I can afterwards.'

The lift arrived. While Urs held open the doors, Kribl manoeuvred the wheelchair into the conveyance. 'One final word,' said Kribl, helping to hold the door ajar with his foot. 'Nobody seems to have had the courage to tell you, but Agnes spends all her time in prison with a nun. Catholic. Not my tradition. Not my cup of holy water. I've got to tell you honestly, I preferred her as a communist.'

He let the door go, and he and his wife disappeared out of sight.

'A nun?' M. René was thunderstruck. 'It's hard to believe.'

'Yes. People faced with a life in prison do strange things,' said Urs. 'A beard? You don't have to be locked up to take people by surprise. D'you know, my mind was on so many other things, I never noticed.'

'It's not important. Why should you?'

'Let me look at you. Frankly, it does nothing for you. That's not the M. René I know and cherish. Especially the curls at the back. They look like neglect.'

'That's what they are, neglect.'

'Come on, you haven't seen Rose Marie yet, and she hasn't seen your present.'

M. René restrained Urs for a moment longer. 'I say, did you know Kribl's wife was an invalid?'

'Did I know? I didn't even know he had a wife.'

'It's disconcerting how little we know each other. How it would have altered our opinion of him had we been aware of that concern, that tenderness in him.'

'It's you, the miracle-man. It was you had that extraordinary foresight to drag him out of his hiding place in the kitchen, and invite him to lunch with us.'

'You think that played a part—?'

'I'm sure of it. Before that, he hid his misfortune, and made her life a misery into the bargain. It was because you gave him confidence, and gave him voluntarily a responsibility he always had to insist on having before, that you opened his eyes to the meaning of friendship – as you did mine.'

'Well, it's a nice thought,' said M. René, as Urs' arm gripped his shoulder in a crushing demonstration of what men can be for one another.

'Come on.'

'A nun,' echoed M. René.

'Oh, it may only be a passing phase.'

'That's not what Kribl seemed to think.'

Urs adopted the same tenderness towards his friend as Kribl had shown towards his wife. 'I think, perhaps, we should refer to him as Beat from now on.'

'Beat.'

'Yes. Come on.'

The crowd had thinned a little, but only imperceptibly. They fought their way through to the kitchen. On the way, M. René saw, and greeted, both Maître Muresanescu and Professor Szepainska.

Maître Muresanescu merely nodded formally as he clutched an empty champagne glass, while M. René risked calling out to the professor, 'Tuesday?'

She held up crossed fingers.

'What's this about a nun?'

'Oh, that's a long story.'

'No one told me.'

The pressure of people took him out of range of her voice. 'Look who I have here,' cried Urs to his wife, who was at the sink, dressed in the same white outfit, and the floppy hat with the daisies, in which she had attempted to seduce M. René. He was momentarily embarrassed by the fact, as though a shameful incident from the past had been exposed in all its nakedness.

'And look at the gift he has brought us!'

'Oh my God, what an extravagance!' she cried, her hands wringing wet. 'What are we going to do with it?'

'It's by far the best present we've received!'

By her gesture, Rose Marie told her husband to shut up. People's generosity was tempered by their wealth. It's the thought which counts.

By tradition, M. René was forced to kiss her on the cheek, while avoiding her dripping red hands.

'I wish you all the happiness in the world,' he said, 'which you certainly deserve.'

'Yes, I think we do,' replied Rose Marie. She had certainly not lost her gift for enigmatic nuance.

'Well, I'll leave you to it,' chuckled Urs. 'I saw a lot of empty glasses *en passant*.' M. René desperately did not wish to find himself alone with his erstwhile domestic. There were two other guests in the kitchen drying plates, but they seemed fully immersed in an independent conversation.

'Well?' she asked. 'And who's looking after you now?'

'I have a Filipino house boy.'

'Oh my God, they're everywhere,' she grumbled, as the water poured into the sink, forming a whirlpool round the edges. 'I wonder the Confederation let them in. They're incompetent, lazy, dishonest, and they don't speak any known language.'

'How can you generalize like that? It's most unfair. Ramón speaks passable French, he's industrious, scrupulously honest, and trustworthy.'

'Then you're lucky, that's all I can say. So you've found a good replacement for me?'

'Nobody could ever replace you, Mme Radibois. I beg your pardon. Mme Mildenegger. I've got to get used to it.'

'You know,' she suddenly said, withdrawing her hands from the water, and looking directly at him with her grey eyes under their halo of daisies, 'you're a fool. You could have had all of this. The champagne. The excitement. All that is to follow—' and she returned to the sink as though it were a refuge from the bitterness of reality. M. René looked round furtively to make sure no one had overheard this scandalous remark. The other couple were so involved in their conversation they appeared to

have been drying the same couple of plates ever since he
had looked at them first. Through the half open door, he
saw Urs pouring champagne while laughing uproariously at
something or other.

'Anyway. There's no use crying over spilled milk, as the
saying goes. You've made your bed, you've got to lie in
it. Mind you keep a space for the jailbird — if she ever
gets out.'

'How dare you say that!' M. René didn't care who
overheard him. There were some allusions a decent man
just could not put up with.

'I can say what I like now. I'm no longer a menial. I'm
respectable. I'm the wife of a retired Chief of Police.'

'Does being respectable entail losing all sense of decorum?
That's new to me.'

'I can tell you what I think, on equal terms, without
impertinence, without having to light a cigarette in your
presence, without having to sit in one of your armchairs.'

M. René lowered his voice to a savage whisper.

'All you can't do is to treat my pyjamas or sheets as
though they were parts of your birthright, or spy up in
the attic, or into locked rooms with a key of your own.'

The words had obviously stung, since her head bent
lower over the washing up, and her next words were flecked
with tears.

Christ, thought M. René, and looked around again,
for fear Urs might choose this moment to resume his
bonhomie. He was nowhere in sight, but his laughter
resounded through the crowded living room. The other
couple were still drying the plates.

'Your beard makes you look weak . . . and your long hair
. . . it's not you . . . not the you I looked up to and . . . and

admired. Yes, I admired you!' she suddenly almost shouted. Then she remembered who and where she was, turned off the tap, took a cloth, wiped her hands and also her eyes, and declared that part of her endless chores nearly at an end.

'She spends her time with a nun, eh? That's a trap if ever I saw one. All that talk of paradise as if they owned the place. But, of course, it has to exist before they can own it. And where's the proof of that? I know. Radibois was a Catholic. God, I never thought I'd mention his name today of all days, but there you are, it never rains but it pours. He never missed a Mass on a Sunday, unless it was force majeure, a long-distance trucking job for instance, but when he was in Geneva we'd often get into an argument when he got home from church, invariably about faith. He'd cheerfully give me a black eye or knock me down a flight of stairs to make some religious point. Called me his india-rubber wife, because I always bounced back for more. Funny I should think of that today.'

Urs looked in just then. 'Remembering old times? That's right,' he grinned.

'She was just telling me of her happiness. Brought a tear to her eye,' smiled M. René. 'I really ought to go. Set an example. Where are you spending your honeymoon?'

'Locarno. It gives the feeling of being abroad, without being.'

'The 7.15, changing at Sion?'

'All the way through to Domodossola. Through Italy.'

'Oh, through Italy. No strikes?'

'Not that I know of.'

'Don't leave it too late.'

'We won't. We have a taxi coming. Our bags are already packed.'

M. René pushed his way to the door, followed by Urs.
'How can we ever thank you for your gift?'

'Invite me to dinner with nine other people,' M.
René quipped. Both Maître Muresanescu and Professor
Szepainska seemed to have left. M. René decided to use
the staircase in order to avoid any other possible delays,
so glad was he to have escaped from the kitchen and
its embarrassments. There was no immediate means of
conveyance, no line of taxis waiting, so he was forced to
walk. He fancied it did him good. A nun, he reflected.
In his ignorance of anything more explicit than the nun's
existence, he imagined the worst, which was normal. A
hideous harridan with skin like medieval parchment and
a rash from insanitary living, unblinking eyes like those of
a predator, enlarged to unnatural size by rimless lenses, and
an odour of disinfectant mingling unhealthily with crushed
petals . . .

M. René stopped himself. He was being as unfair as Rose
Marie. Did an elevation from one rung on the social ladder
to another automatically make of a simple-minded person a
bigot? Does the very fact of being able to air views with the
authority of conviction lead a person who previously held
scruples about expressing themselves at all, to be reckless
and unjust?

Rose Marie might have disagreed, owing to her personal
experiences, but there are undeniably fine, upright, and
compassionate Catholics. Or rather, there are fine, upright,
and compassionate people whose Catholicism was not
allowed to stand in the way of a free expression of those
qualities. But even that was a lopsided way of looking at
the question. There are simply those people who never
allow their religion to stand in the way of their human

qualities. That's better. Now we're getting somewhere. Try again, one final time. There are those with a high moral purpose whose religion is merely incidental to their attitude. Immediately religion becomes a motivating force instead of a mere adjunct to instincts all men are born with, it occupies too great a place in the psyche for a balanced outlook.

M. René reflected with some amusement that His Holiness the Pope and M. Radibois were both victims of this imbalance, the Pope's attitude being tempered by an acute political sense and an immense culture, to say nothing of a sense of humour, whereas M. Radibois' political sense had been his fists, his culture his rows with his wife, and his humour strictly at her expense. Now, of course, he was being unfair to M. Radibois, a man he had never known, but only seen through his wife's eyes, which were of proven unreliability. It occurred to him that, to be fair, he had never known the Pope either.

No, it would be better to assume, until proof to the contrary was forthcoming, that the nun in question was a rational person with Agnes' good at heart, unwilling to equate love with carnality. But, of course, the vital question was the effect of these particular pressures on Agnes' equilibrium. M. René was frankly more than scared by Beat Kribl's bold statement that he had liked her better as a communist. Now, in the whole of nature, there could hardly be a more instinctive or quarrelsome opponent of communism than Beat Kribl. For him to have made such a sweeping statement could only mean the glorification of personal guilt had made considerable inroads into Agnes' vulnerable spirit. There would no doubt have to be a showdown, a battle even before things fell back into place.

With so much to think about, to mull over and mull
again, it was early evening before M. René once again
turned into the drive of his stately home. A rusty bicycle
lay on the drive like the dead fire of an Indian smoke
signal. Lying on the steps was Louis. Ramón had evidently
refused to let him in. In the half light, M. René saw the
thumbs-up sign.

'It's OK. I'm clear.'

'I know. They told me. Ramón'll fetch us some champagne to celebrate. Have you brought your things to stay
the night?'

'I don't need any things. Ramón? He threatened me with
a knife. Would've called the police, but doesn't know how.
I tried to show him.'

'Good man. That gives me confidence in him. He doesn't
know you yet.'

M. René opened the door with a key. Ramón cowered
in the darkness.

'Ramón, my nephew, mi nipote. Hijo de mi hermana.'

It was no good. M. René was reduced to hugging Louis.

'Ramón, el Champan. La cava.' M. René mimed the
explosive opening of a bottle, froth overflowing, and the
first heavenly sip.

Ramón must have understood something from all that,
because he hurried away to return quickly with a copy of
the Yellow Pages. It was as good a way to initiate an evening
of revelry as any.

# XX

LOUIS GREW ever closer to M. René. He was now of an age and of a behaviour to understand a great deal more than he had when he was discovering the extremes of ecstasy with Kuki, and with his motorbike. Ironically, the same was true of René, for reasons of a retarded awakening. The idea of virtually stealing an astronomically priced vehicle by making one of seventy-two down-payments would never have entered M. René's head when he had been Louis' age. The concept of paternal disappointment was far too deeply ingrained in his whole being, which, linked to the spartan discomfort of his upbringing, was enough to discourage the vaguest thought of disobedience. Of course, Louis had never had a real father, M. René's sister's seducer being hardly worthy of that name. Everything about his childhood and youth had been haphazard and wayward. And by the time he was of an age to try his wings, existence had changed entirely for those on life's threshold. Subjects which had been taboo, or wrapped in salacious rumour, were now aired in public, and sung about in the impoverished thumping beat which goes for music, a tribal evocation of the sexual act by thousands of shrieking teenagers. Unisex is the garment of the ritual, electric guitars and microphones the symbols of the secular high priests, bandeaus, trousers as tight-fitting as the corsets of yore, tinselled sleeves like those which once adorned the tea gowns of dowagers, the order of the endless night.

Its appeal was lost on M. René. And yet, he was astonished how thoroughly Louis had survived the witchcraft, owing to the shock of Kuki's pathetic *cri-de-coeur* from the other end of the earth. Every phase of life is, thankfully, impermanent, open to change, ephemeral.

On Sunday, Louis' day off, they spent the day in the garden. Based on a theory M. René had developed, which was that adolescents become adults if they are treated as such, he confessed, in the smallest detail, his surrender to the inevitable when Agnes had invaded the privacy of his bed. His motives were not entirely altruistic. Just as the erotic power exercised by memories of Kuki had been entirely destroyed by news of her misfortune, so he hoped that, in telling the story of his love to a willing ear, he might rekindle the dormant embers of reality. There was a danger, he foresaw, that his unique emotion at the time might need refreshing in order not to become an abstraction, like religion. What he needed was the feeling of a vibrant human animal in his arms for all time, or at least for the time still at his disposal. Was he asking for the impossible, unheard of in human history?

The almost reverent silence in which Louis listened to his narrative showed him that the young man was infinitely flattered by being taken in to such unprecedented confidence, and at the end he merely murmured: 'Listen, I'll accept your invitation to stay here just as long as she's still in . . . where she is. The moment she comes out, I won't take anything for granted. You'll want your privacy.'

'I hope so. Thanks for your understanding, Louis. I feel I've not only got a son, but a friend.'

'Should be the same thing, shouldn't it?'

M. René broke into laughter: 'But even when she's back home, Ramón will probably need all the help he can get.'

'What are you going to do about him?'

'I haven't any idea. For the time being, he's very entertaining—'

'Yes, but faced with a professional housekeeper?'

M. René sighed. 'He's one of the many bridges we'll have to cross when we come to them.'

On Tuesday, Louis worked during the day. M. René had not been summoned to the meeting. Maître Muresanescu pointed out on the telephone that it was a purely legal occasion in which any emotional appeal would not only be out of place but actually have a negative effect on the decision. Max Domani's evidence was different, because it was factual, conducted by a source which had not known those involved previously. Maître Muresanescu was grateful for it.

Now, seated once again in the garden, but warmly dressed, M. René pored over his copy of the document Domani had provided, and imagined it was being evoked at roughly the same time in committee. It made interesting reading. First of all, the detective had managed to find Colonel Otzinger's widow, a very old Italian lady, full of character and a natural asperity, living incognito in a pension in Montreux. She called herself by her mother's

maiden name and an invented Christian name, Silvia
Veracini. Her motive? She had left Otzinger some time
before his death, and was frightened of his finding her. Now
that he was dead, she only continued with the subterfuge
because she was known by it. It was a matter of convenience.
'At my age, you can't keep changing your identity,' she had
remarked wrily. 'You have to think of other people.'

But why had she been so eager to escape from her
husband?

'He became a dangerous man.'

'Dangerous?'

'Ah, si. He wasn't always dangerous. When he seduced
me, he was extremely beguiling, even if a little on the burly
side. He danced divinely. And even if, as a well brought up
Italian, I had a little misgiving about the lure of uniforms,
I thought to myself, a Swiss officer will never be able to
do anyone any harm. How wrong I was! It all began with
Mussolini, whom he venerated, and the first time he struck
me in anger was when I dared tell him what my dear father
had said about the so-called Duce. *E un stronzo*. Mild language for a liberal, I assure you. But when it really became
intolerable was when the Germans took all Mussolini's ideas
and made them at once efficient and inhuman. Otzinger
kept a loaded service revolver hanging in its holster behind
the bedroom door, threatening to use it on me or anyone
else who dared utter a word of criticism of the Führer.
The Swiss allowed their military personnel to take their
weapons home with them in case of a sudden emergency.
It was a piece of extraordinary optimism which worked on
the whole, even if a superficial knowledge of human nature
proclaimed it to be unrealistic to a point of arrogance.
The authorities saw Swiss colonels as being, by definition,

reliable, calm, and deadly dull. I sometimes thought, when Otzinger had a bad day – was throwing furniture about, or posturing on the balcony – what would the other Swiss colonels say if I brought this erratic behaviour to their attention? First of all, with a ghost of a smile, they would register that the complaint had emanated from a woman, and come to the conclusion that it was therefore unbelievable.'

'What made you finally make a break?'

'A black day. I said I found it scandalous that refugees should be sent back to Germany to suffer degradation or even death in camps, and I felt embarrassed to be living in a country at peace, and ostensibly neutral, which lent itself to such practices. Well, I thought Otzinger had gone mad. He struck me a blow in the face while gripping his gun, knocking out several teeth, and shouting obscenities at the top of his voice.'

'Did he calm down when he recognized that he had gone too far?'

'No. He spat out: "Let that be a lesson to you, you Italian bitch", and left for his daily butchery. That was enough. I packed my bags while he was out, closed my bank account, of which he knew nothing, and sat huddled in obscure *pensions* from that day onward, the level of jam marked on the jamjar, and instructions not to be disturbed. I never saw him again.'

'Would you have gone back to him had he found you, and pleaded with you?'

'No. Italians can be just as unforgiving as the Germans, or the Swiss for that matter, if their sense of humanity is desecrated.'

'One final question. What was your reaction on hearing of his death?'

'Relief.'

'Will that reaction change if I tell you that the old verdict of suicide may be altered to murder?'

'I'd congratulate the murderer on his courage and sense of responsibility, although, on second thoughts, I'd be more inclined to think that, if there was indeed murder, the benefactor is more likely to have been a woman.'

'Why do you say that?'

'I have my reasons. Or rather, I have my instincts.'

'And you refer to the murderer as a benefactor?'

'Without apology, a benefactor. Not least, because he or she put Otzinger out of his misery. Under investigation for what he regarded as devotion to duty, deprived of his playthings, the conscripts, brimful of alcohol to make the act of breathing bearable, he had no way out but death. That's why I continue to believe it was suicide.'

'But, if it had been suicide, would he not have used his service revolver?'

'You don't understand. The service revolver was for other people. Not for himself.'

This was powerful and coherent stuff, and M. René reflected, as he absorbed the contents of the document, that Domani had even managed to attribute to the old lady an attractively buoyant and witty character, quite unsuited to her brutal husband. There seemed to be comment inherent in her insistence on calling her late husband Otzinger, a name with a cutting edge, as though a Christian name would be far too intimate and normal under such circumstances.

The case of Lieutenant Bompoz was far more difficult and obscure. Domani had found no living relatives, merely two men, one of whom had served with him under

Otzinger, a certain Corporal Brettschnyder, and the other who had been in an orphanage with him, a solicitor's clerk, by name Klage. Klage described Bompoz as a wild and lonely boy with an aptitude for making friends with wild animals, and an inclination to play unfunny and dangerous tricks on his colleagues.

'An orphanage?'

'Yes, we were both in the same position. No parents, no traceable relatives. He adapted himself better than I did. I was a bit of a cry-baby, I'm afraid. Felt my solitude. He didn't seem to care. Was always in trouble for his pranks. Sticking compasses into other boys, or putting dog shit among their sheets. We all admired him, in a way, while living in fear of him.'

Corporal Brettschnyder was more explicit about the mature man, although much of his information about the man tallied with Klage's description of the boy.

'I left the army about the time Bompoz was suspended as a result of the investigation into Colonel Otzinger's activities. He was desperate not to lose the few friends he felt he had made in the army. He wrote me several long letters which I couldn't make head or tail of. Full of self-justification, righteous indignation, all that. I had just got a job as a shoe salesman, and had got married, and I had no great wish to renew an acquaintance which gave me no pleasure, and which I feared I would have to justify to those closest to me. Quite apart from which, there were dangers attached to such friendship.'

'Dangers? That's the second time I have heard the word in the course of my investigations. What was the danger in this case? Was he a homosexual?'

'I never asked myself the question. You may be right. I don't know. All I do know is I never saw him anywhere near a woman. The only thing that seemed capable of awakening an emotional response in him was a dog.'

'A dog?'

'Yes, he had this, what do they call them, Rottweiler, is it? A dog with a head seemingly too large for its body, and a mean look. He never stopped training this damn thing, but the training never seemed to be complete. It would bark at a signal, foam at the mouth at another, go berserk at a third. Friendship would have entailed visiting him, taking the wife along, being social. I wasn't prepared to take the risk. I can be friendly with a person, but not to a dog with which I feel no affinity, and which is only awaiting instructions as to how it should treat me. And I was right to have such scruples. You remember the end of the story?'

'No.'

'Oh, you must have done at the time. You've forgotten, that's all. The dog got its signals mixed, or else Bompoz was too trusting. At all events, it allowed itself to be irritated by a three-year-old toddler, and mauled it to death. The dog was condemned to die by the Cantonal authorities. Bompoz locked himself into his woodshed with the dog, threatening to blow the head off any intruder. The gendarmes pleaded with Bompoz through the wall, to no avail. Eventually they broke a window, and lobbed a tear-gas canister into the shed. Bompoz at once kicked open the door, giving the dog an order to attack. This time, the dog obeyed the order, and savaged a gendarme, before being shot by his colleague. The next day, Bompoz was discovered, dead, full of weed killer or whatever he had at his disposal, wrapped in the blanket of his dead companion. No, I was never really a friend of his.'

The third alleged victim was a case at once more straightforward, and more mystifying. Captain Zocco had died leaving all his family behind in their farmhouse not far from Magadino, in Ticino. His sister Giuseppina, his mother Renata, his father Tiburzio, all willingly responded to Domani's questions around the dining room table. 'Tell me about Captain Zocco, in your own words.'

Mama was given precedence by the others.

Wiping away a tear which was either there or very close to emerging, she said: '*E bè*, he was a good boy, too good, killed by the army.'

'No, no, it wasn't that,' grumbled the father, a man of fearsome age. 'It takes men to interpret the thoughts of men. Those were terrible times, among the worst the human race has ever passed through. The tranquillity of Switzerland was rudely shattered, and it has not recovered to this day. To look at this lovely landscape, with its peaceful houses and reassuring churches, you'd never guess at the storms beneath the surface. Let it never be said that we were neutral in any way. We were not! We were too small for neutrality! The object of too much jealousy, too indispensable to all sides for any attitude so independent, so one-sided.'

'You're not going to say our son was too sensitive to survive?'

'No. He was closer to you by temperament than he was to me, but there's nothing wrong with that. I managed to accept military service as a necessary evil, which brings out the best or the worst in men. He could not see that, seeing only the worst. It was that which drove him so readily into the arms of Mother Church.'

'Did I understand rightly?' It was Domani in the type-
script. 'Mother Church?'

'Allow me to speak,' said Giuseppina, the angular, white-
haired daughter. 'I knew him perhaps better than Papa or
Mama, only because there was only one year between us.
We grew up together. He was, it is true, unusually sensitive
for a boy, just as I was unusually tough for a girl. Such
things happen, in families. He was horrified by his duties in
the army. He always had scruples about killing, in general.
He was a vegetarian. He refused to use insect repellent spray.
He destroyed barbed wire wherever he found it, and I've
seen him destroy mousetraps.'

'Should have been a Buddhist,' Domani allowed himself to suggest. Mother and daughter both shrieked with
delight.

'What did we call him, Mama, but Il Buddhista!'

'Yes,' admonished his mother, 'but only by way of teasing
him in a good-natured way. He was a good Catholic, you
understand.'

'Of course,' said Giuseppina, appalled at her mother's
archness. 'In fact, what he was asked to do in the army
under that Colonel Otzinger passed all expectations of
military service. It was literally, as he described it, often
crying with rage, grading living people like laundry, putting their clothes into categories, while being ordered to
overlook the fact that there were people wearing them.
The grading seemed to him totally arbitrary, as though
undertaken by whim, by caprice. Some were sent back in
as covert a way as possible, avoiding the scrutiny of the Red
Cross. Others were retained as ostentatiously as possible,
at least temporarily. My brother used to wake up at night
screaming, when he came home on leave. It was the inability

to sleep which really got to him, just as his crises got through to us. In that sense, Mama was right. It was the army which snuffed out his life. He was no longer normal when he went through the motions of preparing for the priesthood.'

'Did you feel he had a vocation?'

'He may have developed one in a panic. I doubt if he was born with one.'

Mama pushed a lace handkerchief against her mouth and shook her head negatively.

The daughter shrugged her shoulders as if there was no more to add. Only the old man seemed to be sulking.

'Signor Zocco, have you anything to add?'

The father laboriously lit a black cigar, shaped like knotted rope, to comfort himself and sharpen his vision.

'No,' he said, not without a hint of irony. 'The women have said nothing that I would not have said had I been allowed to finish. Except one thing. I never speculate about what you call vocation. I have nothing against priests, mark you, but I prefer them if they don't come from my family.' Here the women glanced at each other with a recognition of what they knew would follow. 'I always believe it such a waste for a man to be a priest. I'm a farmer. I have the same reaction with a barren animal, or a maimed bird. It's a waste, and a desecration of nature. For a man to voluntarily agree to become a eunuch is also a desecration of nature, an obedience to an absurd, self-flagellating law from the years of darkness, a vile defiling of human nature, vile because voluntary. I know the women disagree with me. When the boy opted for holy orders, they were both a-flutter, expressing a delight I could only find obscene. "What a waste", I could only repeat to myself.' And he shook with silent laughter, neither of the women risking an interruption. 'As I said before,' he said, 'I'm a farmer, and like all farmers I believe there's safety in numbers. We had eleven children in all, three of them died in infancy. That leaves eight in all, bravo Mama, but it's still fewer than my parents and less than Renata's parents had. A certain decadence has set in. So naturally, there's a sadness for those who fall by the wayside, but we can't allow it to last forever, just as there is grief for livestock who don't live up to expectations, or land which proves to be less arable than we had hoped. Mark you, I'm not equating children with livestock or soil, it's just that we take a longer view than most about all things. So Davide is dead.' It was the first time Captain Zocco had been accorded a name. 'We have shed our tears, and he is only a hundred metres away, resting in the churchyard if we wish to remember him. But Augusto is still alive, until recently running a supermarket. Married with only four children. Cosimo once played football with no great distinction for Locarno. He is unmarried, with roughly six children. Alfieri is in Leipzig, Germany, owner of a restaurant, "Da Alfieri". He works too hard to make ends meet. Married to a Polish woman. No children that we know. And the girls are all married, with the exception of Giuseppina, with children of their own, but that's not our family, of course, as far as the name is concerned.' Old Zocco puffed contentedly on his awful pacifier, and uttered a resumé.

'It's unfair to blame the army for Davide's death. A man makes of the army what he wants to make of it. I accepted it as a necessary evil. Davide regarded it as evil, but unnecessary. As a result, I could never have taken my own life. I don't have to tell you why. What a waste.'

'What would you have done?'

Old Zocco considered his reply, and became very still.

'Faced with a monster like Otzinger?'

'Yes.'

'I'd probably have broken his neck, taking care to make it look like an accident. I was very strong in my time.'

'But wouldn't you have considered that a waste?'

'Not for a moment. That would have been my vocation – and a pleasure.'

Mama shook her head negatively while Giuseppina sought to console her, looking mischievously reprimanding at her father, who gazed into the distance, clouding the issue in pungent smoke.

M. René lowered the report. There seemed nothing in it to confirm a suspicion of murder. The case of Lieutenant Bompoz seemed actually to rule out such a suspicion, so directly was the death concerned with the fate of the dog, and the circumstances of its killing. In the case of Captain Zocco, the family appeared to be resigned to the loss of one of its members inclined to hysteria under stress. As for Colonel Otzinger, Maître Muresanescu had pointed out on the telephone that the case was on the cusp of the Statute of Limitations, having occurred so long ago that legal opinions could challenge its validity as an affair still requiring solution under law.

Suddenly Ramón came running into the garden, carrying M. René's mobile phone.

'Yes?'

It was Beat Kribl. 'A piece of cake,' he said. 'What I so feared turned out to be a pushover. She's exonerated from all blame in the matter. Your detective's spadework produced a very good impression. It was certainly not the extravagance it appeared to us all at the lunch. Mark you, it was helped materially by a close examination of the original autopsies, which stated unequivocally that the quantity of arsenic was in no case sufficient to cause death by itself, but only in conjunction with other agents, such as weed killer, rat poison, or alcohol taken in exceptional quantities. The committee was struck by the strange coincidence that three officers of the same unit should be struck down in a somewhat similar manner, but the pervasive influence of Colonel Otzinger's madness was taken to be sufficient, under the extraordinary weight of the resistance to Nazi influence at the time, to justify such a coincidence. Our Polish lady made an extremely convincing impression in explaining away the unsolicited confessions of murder, and our Romanian friend was boring enough and sluggish enough to create a picture of unadulterated incorruptibility in those who count. There. The mixture was just right, and it worked on the three old fogeys who make up the committee. Now there is nothing against your visit to the prison at, say, eleven o'clock in the morning.'

'But what happens to her now? Physically, I mean?'

'She can't stay in prison, that's for sure. Whether she goes meekly to a convent or comes gratefully into your arms is up to you.' And he feigned jocular irritation. 'The police department has done what it can for you. You can't expect them to do everything.'

M. René smiled. 'Of course not. My regards to Ruth.'

There was a momentary pause. 'I'll tell her.'

# XXI

KRIBL'S CASUAL optimism was contagious. M. René slept
well and woke early, as he had planned. He decided a
neglected look was liable to play on her heartstrings, but
in no way wished to give the impression of being in any
way out of control, which would be counterproductive.
He dressed well, but casually. No tie, white shirt, pleated
trousers. It was ten-thirty by the time he had drunk
his coffee and begun walking slowly to the prison. He
reached there at five minutes before eleven, and declared
his identity through a grille, mentioning the appointment made by Beat Kribl. He was shown to a waiting
room full of microphones and barriers, through which
people could see each other but not touch each other, a
kind of bank for delinquents. As in a bank, the accounts
were numbered rather than named. After five minutes,
he was fetched by a female staff member and led in
silence down whitewashed corridors, in which their footfall
resounded eerily, and through gates which reverberated

with a metallic clank of horrible finality as they closed behind them.

Then, at last, a civilized room, not a cell, in which the object of his desire was sitting on a humble wooden chair, near the attendant nun. For a split second the pose they had adopted resembled one of the innumerable Annunciations by Italian Renaissance painters. Agnes, head cowled, at the receiving end of the good news; the Archangel with a little dribble emanating from its sexless mouth, which contained the good news itself, spelled out painstakingly in Italian.

Agnes rose to greet him, her arms outstretched in supplication rather than in welcome, and then spoiled the magic of the moment by dissolving into floods of helpless giggles. M. René immediately judged his appearance to be at the base of her reaction. Others had given him plenty of warning, but since the change for him had been gradual and not sudden, he was continually surprised by its violence. Now he tried to enter into the spirit of the moment, but managed it only half-heartedly, and somewhat grudgingly. The same went for the nun, who had never seen him before, and therefore had no yardstick to judge his appearance by. Her glasses did glint, as M. René had foreseen, but they were gold rimmed, not of the sinister rimless variety, and she herself was tubby and in no way medieval. Every time Agnes tried to control herself, a renewed outburst followed, until the laughter became physically painful. M. René could do little but just stand there, with the unpleasant sensation that the more perplexed he became, the more hilarious he looked.

'It can't be as amusing as all that,' he protested, and only added fuel to the flames.

He sought consolation in the fact that she was still

capable of such torrential outbursts, and had not slipped into silent contemplation.

'All right. You win,' he said, with sudden determination. 'You've made your point. The beard comes off this afternoon.'

She stumbled over her contrition.

'I'm sorry. So very sorry. I didn't mean to hurt your feelings. It's *your* face—' And another flurry of laughter briefly took over. '—It's yours to do what you like with.'

'No. It isn't. I don't live for myself any more. And it's certainly not a fellow looking like this into whose bed you crawled—'

She seemed highly embarrassed by the reference. Even the nun seemed ill at ease.

'I say, is it possible to have a conversation with Agnes alone? I have nothing against you personally,' he said to the nun, 'but do you have to sit there all the time?'

'It's that Agnes made me promise not to leave her alone with you,' replied the nun reasonably. 'I'm merely obeying instructions.'

M. René spoke with icy detachment, repeating the phrase slowly as though he had difficulty understanding it.

'She made you promise not to leave her alone with me?'

The nun nodded.

'You have only to ask her.'

M. René looked at Agnes in silent outrage. She flinched, and then beseeched him. 'Don't look at me like that, with such . . . such hostility.'

'What do you expect? What have I done to deserve this?'

Agnes could find no words.

'I don't deserve such happiness, you wrote.'

'Yes. Yes. I did. I did.'

M. René suddenly shouted: 'Do I deserve such unhappiness? Have you thought of that? My God!'

He began pacing nervously as his agitation grew slowly beyond his control. 'I have come here to fetch you away. I have bought a new house, worthy of you. My whole life changed when you broke into it, like a thief. I fell in love. Damn it, can't you understand that? For the first time in my life. At my age. *There's* really something to laugh at if you want to laugh. I talk to you all day long. I need you. I can't live without you. I don't want to live without you. I won't live without you!'

Attracted by the shouting, a dour Swiss official opened the door with a key.

'Need any help?'

The nun sketched a negative reply with her head. The official observed that the outburst had a domestic rather than a criminal character. He was used to both. He shut the door again, locking it noisily.

M. René recovered his composure, but not his reason. He did not want to recover it yet, there was too much on his heart. And the nun hardly helped by being so rational and silent.

'Did you hear that?' he cried with passion, but without volume. 'Need any help? Why don't you continue the travesty by crying out that you do need help? This uncouth bearded intruder is playing havoc with my privacy, with my muttered prayers. Take him away to where he belongs, to the dustbin, to the incinerator, to wherever you dump undesirables in this place!'

Agnes made mute efforts to interrupt, but M. René's

heart was too heavy. He refused to interrupt his flow just yet.

'"But what was his crime?" the man may ask. As though he cared. Oh, God sir, I invited myself to dinner at his place, which is a perfectly normal thing for a well-brought up woman to do, especially after the age of consent. I even made dinner, with champagne, Burgundy, caviar, a Havana cigar, which admittedly he didn't smoke. All I left out of my catering equipment was a pair of pyjamas, or a nightdress. I did remember a toothbrush, however. I was able to tell him, without blushing, that I always sleep in my birthday suit. He may have been surprised, but he raised no visible objection. So I took the hint. Once I had brushed my teeth thoroughly, and he gave every sign of being asleep, I allowed myself the final prank, which was to force my way under his sheets, and we shared the rarest distractions all night—'

Here, Agnes broke in. It was now his turn to wilt under the onslaught of bitter recrimination.

'Don't try to damage my memories by your horrible parody of what went on. Those moments were sacred for me, and still are.'

'Sacred!' he spat out. 'You laughed at me because I'd grown a beard, a superficial change, which can be eradicated by a shave in ten minutes. You have changed too, beyond all recognition, and the change in you doesn't make me laugh at all. It makes me weep. And to suddenly protest that moments which are sacred to me are equally sacred to you is really too much to bear.'

'Let me explain,' she implored, her hands joined to find strength, and emphasis. Evidently she found neither, which left her speechless.

'Perhaps I may say a word,' said the nun quietly. 'My side

of the story, if you will. I belong to an order of nuns which makes it one of its duties to visit prisons. I found Agnes here in the deepest perplexity, and she told me her troubles, not essentially because I am a Catholic, but perhaps more importantly because I am a woman. There are priests of all denominations who visit prisons. She did not confide in any of them, but came to me. I believe this fact tells its own story. And, let me add, it is not unusual. That is the reason why we go out of our way to visit prisons at all. Now, to clarify another point. I have no desire, and no need, to know what went on between you. I recognize the fact that it is none of my business. I even recognize that it is beyond my experience, for obvious reasons, and I therefore have no contribution to make.' (The confounded woman could even allow herself a pinch of humour on occasion. M. René regarded her with growing misgiving.) 'Now, there is one point in all this distressing affair which is my business, however, and which I cannot neglect at any cost, and that is that our friend Agnes still considers herself guilty of three crapulous murders, and is in need of expiation. Against that I can do nothing. If tomorrow, or now, she admits that she made a colossal error, that her memory was confused by the prevailing stress, or that her interests are better served by finding another solution to her feelings of guilt, I shall regret it, because she is a remarkable person, as I think you know, but I shall be the first to pack my bags and leave her to her own devices.' This was enough to sober up M. René.

'Well, I must thank you for your wonderful clear and generous comment on all of this, but I am in duty bound to ask you one relevant question.'

'Yes?'

'Does the fact that a committee has exonerated her from

all blame, to the extent that the idea of a murder trial is irrevocably discarded, go for nothing?'

'M. René. A person is the best judge of whether he or she is guilty or not. Not a committee.'

'Not necessarily,' M. René retorted doggedly. 'There are frequent incidents in the annals of crime of those who confessed to crimes they didn't commit. It is so comforting, so final, for a poor soul to allow a feeling of general guilt to go to his head. Dostoievsky, in *Crime and Punishment*, has one such confession, which the Police Chief is forced to reject—'

'Why do you think I leave the door open? Why do you think I suggest she may well change her mind? I am aware of the vagaries of the human spirit, and of its frequent lack of coherence, but you only have to hear Agnes—'

'I murdered them,' Agnes broke in, with the intensity of a prayer which has half-lost its meaning through too frequent repetition. 'I prepared the poisons. I murdered them, each in turn.'

'It may interest you to know that I hired a private detective to find out the backgrounds of your victims. His findings deeply impressed the committee.'

'You did what?' Agnes asked, her brow furrowed, incomprehending.

'I hired a detective. He located and interviewed the widow of Colonel Otzinger, who lives in a *pension* above Montreux. Otzinger sent your mother to her death, remember. She confirmed the fact that he was a brute and, eventually, a madman, from whom she had to escape when he knocked several of her teeth out in a rage. The detective asked her what her reaction was on hearing of his death. Relief, she answered. To the further question of would her reaction be different if his death turned out to be murder, she replied that she would congratulate the murderer for his or her courage and sense of responsibility.'

'The fact remains,' Agnes said, sticking to the point.

'And where did you commit the crime?'

'At the hotel in which I worked, and at which he was, by chance, a guest.'

'By chance? Which proves it was not premeditated. And it happened too long ago for there to be a conviction.'

'I don't understand what you're saying . . .'

'In the case of Lieutenant Bompoz, it was proved that you could not have been the culprit. His dog was condemned to death for killing a small child.'

'His dog?'

'His only friend, a ferocious Rottweiler dog. Bompoz barricaded himself into his woodshed with his dog until forced out by the gendarmes, who shot the dog and left him to take his own life immediately afterwards. There was no time for you to plan a murder after the dog was dead, and before the dog was dead there would have been no place for you in the woodshed. As a result it is useless to confess to this crime.'

'But I planned it. I know I did.'

'You may have done, but you had no means of carrying it out. As for the case of Captain Zocco, his old father, the farmer, quarrelled with the mother's allegation that the army had killed their boy, by asserting that the army has to be treated by every man of military age as a necessary evil, and react to it according to his temperament. Speaking for himself, he said his temperament would not have permitted him to take his own life as his son had done, but would rather have led him to break Otzinger's neck, while making it look like an accident.'

'The fact remains, I planned their death in every detail.'

'You may have done, but you had no opportunity to carry it out, in any one of the cases. Where did you go to murder Zocco?'

Agnes hesitated. She seemed to be consulting her memory.

'Bellinzona,' she replied.

'Magadino,' said M. René in triumph. 'Does a murderer, who planned a murder in the greatest detail, forget where it happened? Can that strike anybody as reasonable?'

At this vital juncture of his cross-examination, the key was once again heard in the keyhole, and the door swung open to reveal the same uniformed official. 'Time's up,' he barked.

'What are you talking about?' M. René cried. 'The committee yesterday decided unanimously that Fräulein Schandenbach had no case to answer. She's free as a bird. You can't restrict the time she spends with visitors.'

'Until I receive orders to the contrary, time's up. Out, out, out.'

'I never heard of such a thing. And they call this a democracy?'

'Let me clarify one point,' said the official. 'My mandate is not how long a prisoner stays with a visitor, because the prisoner only has to return to her cell in any case. My mandate is to impose the law in the matter of how long a visitor is allowed to stay here, because he has a home to go to outside the administration of the prison's system. Is that clear? And now, as I said before, Out!'

It was the nun who broke in, with the greatest possible

calm. 'May I ask for another five minutes, Monsieur l'Officier, on compassionate grounds?'

'Compassionate?' asked the official, suspicious only because it was not a word in current use in his vocabulary.

'And religious,' suggested the nun.

'Ah, religious. That's different,' he recognized. 'I'll have to register the fact that you asked for an extra five minutes in case of an enquiry.'

'You do that. We all expect you to do your duty.'

'I'll be back in five minutes from . . .' And he studied his watch. 'Now!'

The key grumbled once more in the lock.

M. René went straight on, in order not to waste a moment. 'Everyone is convinced of your innocence. Even Professor Szepainska, who must know you even better than this lady by now.'

'Oh, that one.' Agnes exchanged a look with the nun.

'Now what does that mean? Does the fact that I agree with her count as a black mark against me?'

'Although being Polish, and very conscious of Catholicism, her chosen discipline in life is distinctly secular. Scientific rather than spiritual,' said the nun.

'Up to now, sister or whatever you are, I have been impressed not only by your impartiality but by your openness. The way you pleaded for another five minutes spoke highly for your understanding of matters not necessarily within your grasp. Consequently I find your assessment of Professor Szepainska grimly doctrinaire and ungenerous.'

The nun smiled. 'I have nothing against Madame Szepainska personally,' she said, 'but I am as full of prejudice as everyone else, even though I try hard not to be. I admit that my viewpoint is avowedly Christian, and the more the focus narrows, the more Catholic it becomes. Madame Szepainska is undoubtedly a good woman, and certainly an intelligent one, but she has chosen different yardsticks from ours.'

'From ours? From you and Agnes? I suppose you know that Agnes spent most of her life as a communist?'

'You had no need to tell me that. It is they whom we welcome more than any in the bosom of the Church.'

'It was a fine idealistic philosophy before it was betrayed by the venality of man. But there is really nothing surprising in this. It has happened to all faiths from the beginning of time.'

'We like to hope there are some exceptions,' smiled the nun. 'And finally God is only what each one of us imagines Him to be. It's one God, one Allah, one Vishnu, one Buddha. The message lies in our hearts, awaiting identification, as in a lost property office.'

'I cannot agree, but this is perhaps not the place for such a discussion. The five minutes are almost up, and I don't trust myself to plead for another five more on the grounds of philosophy.'

M. René felt guilty at losing so much valuable time in argument, and looked at Agnes. She seemed to take little interest in the conversation, her eyes screwed up with effort, her gaze directed at nothing at all. Was she, in fact, mad? Had she, as they say, taken leave of her senses? In her seeming helplessness, he felt a great surge of love for the first and only time of his visit. It was not lost, merely hidden.

'Awake, ye dreamers from your slumbers,' he began to sing. The Internationale, as a lullaby. Slowly a smile of wonderful sweetness broke out over Agnes' face, and M. René fancied he saw her as a baby, a picture of docility while the man-made tempest broke all around her. Her smile continued as the tempest shattered the dream in the form of the Swiss official.

'Time's up,' he called. 'This time, it's final.'

M. René gave the nun the transcript of Max Domani's findings. 'For what it's worth,' he said, and gazed at Agnes' upturned face, its eyes shut, its mouth half open. He was tempted to kiss her, but that could be interpreted as a finality he was not yet willing to entertain. 'Goodbye,' he said quietly.

There was no response.

'Goodbye,' he said to the nun, 'and thanks.'

The nun nodded with an omniscient smile which would grow in aggravation in the memory.

Before returning home, M. René went to a reputable barber in a large hotel. He had his beard removed, and his hair cut, and graded with a razor. He indulged in a manicure and a pedicure at the same time. He did not really care for these additional luxuries, apart from the fact it was becoming slowly more and more difficult to reach his toenails, but he indulged in them for the same underlying reasons which motivated his other minor extravagances, and that was the fact that he could afford them.

He returned home by cab with a sense of sharpness which had been absent from his behaviour since the passage of Gill Gordie. Ramón was not in the house. M. René thought little of it until he noticed that there was no food in the ice-box, that the servant's quarters were bare, and that his cellular telephone, transistor radio and some petty cash were missing. He reacted with a little irritation at the thought that Mme Mildenegger, the vindictive Rose Marie, at present enjoying a complete break from housework in

Locarno, might have had a point about the import of Asiatic help. He wanted he needed a couple to look after a house of such dimensions. There were always masses of advertisements in the papers. He decided to telephone Beat Kribl. For this, he now had to rely on his normal telephone.

'Well, how did you find her?' Beat enquired.

'Disturbing. I asked myself at the end if she was entirely sane.'

'Ah. I have asked myself the same question, but I didn't want to alarm you unduly.'

'I mean, to some remarks she had a perfectly rational reaction. Like when I sang the Internationale as a lullaby. Her mother had done that, you understand, when she was a baby.'

'What did she say?'

'Nothing. She just had an expression of such indescribable sweetness on her face . . .'

'And that's a perfectly rational reaction? Well, I suppose so. You know her better than I do.'

'Some cretin came in and put an end to the magic by declaring that time was up.'

'Well yes, that's our problem, you see. Now that no charges will be brought, we can't keep her in prison. The taxpayer can't be expected to pay for an innocent person's keep.'

'You have to be guilty to get free board and lodging.'

'Exactly. This is the same in every self-respecting country. There's nothing exclusively Swiss about this.'

'So what do we do?'

'You still want to marry her?'

'More than ever.'

'You must be mad.'

'If that makes two of us, that's called compatibility, isn't it?'

'You know best.'

'Yes. Beat, may I ask you an extremely personal question, not really made to be asked on the telephone?'

'Of course.'

'Was Ruth always the way . . . she is today?'

'No. She was lively and bubbling over. The Badminton Champion of Switzerland.'

'Would you have married her if you had known what would happen to her?'

'Of course. I was in love with her at the time. I'm in love with her today.'

'In love? Literally? Or has it taken on a deeper hue?'

'Such as?'

'Such as . . . a religion? Does not such love, or, rather, love on such a level, for a person to all intents and purposes, inaccessible, take on the dimension of a religion?'

'I see what you mean.' Beat hesitated as he sought to organize his thoughts. 'Yes. Yes. A religion.'

'I mean, the objects of our devotion are both, in some ways, out of reach. Does that not make of our continued faith in something incapable of proving its own tangible existence, a kind of religion?'

'It's a bit complicated for me, I'm only a simple police-man, but I think I get the hang of it. Religion, that's what it is all right, much more so than what goes on in church. Which brings me to, what are we going to do with Agnes? She can't stay in prison. And she has nowhere to go when she leaves.'

'Of course she does!'

'I know, I know, but we've first got to square the nun. She's awaiting permission from the mother convent to allow Agnes to shelter there while preparing for her holy orders.'

'She may never pass her exams.'

'Or else, of course, she may.'

'Where is the mother house?'

'In Vézelay.'

'Where?'

'In France.'

'Oh God.'

'Exactly. Outside my competence. Listen, I'll try and see them again today, and find out if they'll see you again tomorrow. Any message you wish me to deliver?'

'Apart from the fact that I'm lovesick, I've taken my beard off.'

'Ah. At last a positive step in the right direction. Before you go, René, let me ask you a final question, as seemingly indiscreet as the one you asked me.'

'Yes—'

'You say you're lovesick. You insist you want to marry her. Are you quite sure about this?'

There was a moment.

'Why do you ask?'

'Because you spoke of religion. Is that not something one never questions, something one adheres to because one was born with it? Something beyond question, beyond contention?'

'Yes. What are you getting at?'

'You asked me if I would still have married Ruth had I known what was going to happen. I answered yes, because I had no choice. To say no at this juncture would have been churlish in the extreme. There was only one answer I could

possibly give you. It's that that has made a religion of what
was originally a physical and mental attraction. You still
have a choice, and for that reason I want to give you a
piece of advice, from my experience.'

'Yes?'

'If you were to ask me if Agnes will ever return to
normality, to joie-de-vivre, I would tell you personally that
I don't think so. Will you ever marry her? I daresay, no. I'm
not saying this because I am a pessimist, but simply because,
by always expecting the worst, you are never embittered,
and every surprise is a happy one.'

'Thank you, Beat. In my heart, there are times, many
times, when I share your misgivings. But why must one face
such important facts on the telephone?'

'Why did the Catholics invent the confessional? What is
that but a phone box?'

M. René went out briefly to buy a newspaper, and to
think of an uncertain future. He knew that if, by some
extraordinary chance, Agnes changed her mind about her
culpability, he would welcome her with open arms, and
trumpet his triumph to the skies. In his heart, he agreed
with Beat, however. Guilt was such a relief after the
uncertainties of doubt, and the need to keep secrets even
from oneself. Agnes had found serenity of a kind after
confessing to crimes she could not possibly have committed.
If he were to remain alone, he would be obliged to take
refuge in his own kind of madness.

As chance would have it, he was aided in this by the
newspaper. On the front page, what should he see but
a huge photograph of Fitzroy Nudelman, a black wig
with the brilliance of a patent leather shoe on his head,
and a pencil-thin moustache on his upper lip, rehearsing

for his latest role of M. René in the forthcoming film of the best-seller 'What the Concierge Saw', a literary work below the dignity of every self-respecting critic, but widely purchased, perhaps for that reason. M. René put a call through to London to enquire about his royalties. Reg Masters reassured him that the money had not yet come in, but that it would soon be under way.

After he had replaced the receiver, Masters had occasion to remark to Gill Gordie, 'You caught him just in time. He's beginning to understand.' Gordie's reaction was succint and unprintable.

As the late afternoon began to slip into early evening, M. René realized slowly that Louis was not going to come by after work. Perhaps he thought that Agnes would be released at the very moment of the committee's decision, or his non-appearance was due to his excess of consideration for a close relative's private life, or else, M. René recognized with a snort, the young fellow might have found a use for Gill Gordie's unintentional gift. After all, youth is impulsive, and given to expressions of delight after being cleared of killer diseases. It doesn't do for a proxy parent to go on being as possessive of every waking moment of their sibling's time as is a natural parent.

However, Ramón's defection posed its own problems. Later he would treat himself to an early dinner at 'La Perle du Lac', one of the best gastronomic addresses in town. He would leave a note on the door in case Louis turned up after all. For the moment, he wandered into the garden, and reflected on the glorious impermanence of nature. He was suddenly cheered by his searching question to Beat, and his consequent definition of the kind of love forced on both of them as a religion. He felt calm and strong in the face of whatever quirks nature still had to offer.

He glanced at his watch. 'Hello, the 17.00 Lausanne, Morges, Rolle, Nyon, Versoix, Geneva should have passed by now,' and then he suddenly realized he was no longer in his old property, but was separated from the railway track by miles.

Not only calm and strong, but senile, he grumbled to himself. And he went indoors, not only because he felt a chill in the air, but because he sensed a strong desire, before dining in a public place, to trim his moustache, as had been his habit in the past. Admittedly, he had had it done professionally only some four hours before, but in this unpredictable life you never know what the next moment will hold. He trimmed a single hair which he fancied had a mind of its own, and reflected that at such prices the barber was extremely slapdash not to have noticed it. At last, he was beginning to reason as someone who had been born to wealth.